I0625112
ALL FALL
DOWN

ABERDEENSHIRE LIBRARIES
ABS 2035986

ORCHARD BOOKS
338 Euston Road, London NW1 3BH
Orchard Books Australia
Level 17/207 Kent Street, Sydney, NSW 2000

This edition published in 2015 by Orchard Books

ISBN 978 1 40833 437 9

A CIP catalogue record for this book is available
from the British Library.

1 3 5 7 9 8 6 4 2

Printed and bound in Great Britain by CPI Group (UK) Ltd, Croydon, CR0 4YY

Typeset in Berthold Baskerville by Avon DataSet Ltd, Bidford-on-Avon, Warwickshire

The paper and board used in this book are made from wood from responsible sources.

Orchard Books is an imprint of Hachette Children's Group and published
by The Watts Publishing Group Limited,
an Hachette UK company.

Ally Carter

ALSO BY

Ally Carter

GALLAGHER GIRLS

BOOK 1: I'D TELL YOU I LOVE YOU, BUT THEN I'D HAVE TO KILL YOU

BOOK 2: CROSS MY HEART AND HOPE TO SPY

BOOK 3: DON'T JUDGE A GIRL BY HER COVER

BOOK 4: ONLY THE GOOD SPY YOUNG

BOOK 5: OUT OF SIGHT, OUT OF TIME

BOOK 6: UNITED WE SPY

★

HEIST SOCIETY

BOOK 1: HEIST SOCIETY

BOOK 2: UNCOMMON CRIMINALS

BOOK 3: PERFECT SCOUNDRELS

★

EMBASSY ROW

BOOK 1: ALL FALL DOWN

For Kristin Nelson,
Literary agent extraordinaire

"When I was twelve I broke my leg jumping off the wall between Canada and Germany," I say, but the woman across from me doesn't even blink. I don't ask whether or not she has ever heard the story. I'm pretty sure she probably has, but I keep talking anyway.

"My brother said that the fall would probably kill me. But it just broke my right femur in three places. I totally showed him."

"I see," the woman says, stony-faced, and I go on.

"I fractured my left forearm when I was ten, and dislocated my right shoulder five months later. Have you ever been to Fort Benning?" I ask, but I don't really wait for an answer. "Well, you might think that big tree outside the Officer's Club is climbable. Trust me – it isn't. OK. Where was I? Oh, fourteen was the year of the concussion. There were two of them. We were stationed in San Diego then. I didn't break my ankle until we moved to Alabama."

I take a deep breath. "And that brings me to now. Now I'm here."

"And you're not bleeding," the woman says. "What an excellent start."

"So in answer to your question, Mrs Chancellor—"

"Oh, it's Ms Chancellor, Grace. I'm not married."

"Sorry. *Ms* Chancellor. I don't mean to get into trouble. Trouble just sort of finds me."

Behind her dark-rimmed glasses, I can see a glint in Ms Chancellor's brown eyes. Her mouth ticks up in something that isn't quite a smirk but definitely isn't a smile. I can tell she doesn't believe me – but I also know that she would like to. Everyone wants me to be different than advertised. Grace: the new-and-improved edition.

What Ms Chancellor can't possibly realize is how nobody wants that more than me.

"Well, let's hope trouble doesn't have your change-of-address card," she says. "Your grandfather would like this to be a fresh start for you, Grace. A new city. A new home. We would like this to be a chance for you to get away from your issues."

She could have tried to be nice about it. To be...you know...*diplomatic.* That is the purpose of this place, after all. But I guess diplomacy doesn't always extend to teenage girls with my sort of reputation.

"Is that all?" Ms Chancellor smiles a little. It's almost like she's daring me to top myself.

"Well, I did watch my mother die right in front of my eyes when I was thirteen. But you already knew about that, didn't you, *Ms* Chancellor?"

She recoils as I say this. People always do. To tell you the truth, that's kind of why I do it. I mean, it's not like avoiding the topic of the fire will bring my mother back. It won't make me un-see what I saw. And, besides, I know Ms Chancellor really wants to ask me about it – to see if I'm as crazy as advertised. This is her chance. If she's crazy enough to take it.

But she's not.

Instead, she stands and starts toward the door.

"Well, Grace, why don't I take you to your room?" she asks, but I can almost hear what she's thinking – the undercurrent of questions and doubts. My life is a never-ending conversation of the things that people do not say.

Ms Chancellor smiles. "I bet you'd like to get settled in."

When I follow her out into the long hall, I can't help but glance at the double doors of the neighboring office. They're big and heavy – stately – with the US seal in the center and two flags flanking them. They look so official and so strong, but the most important thing about these doors is that they are tightly closed. Even to me.

"Is he here?" I ask.

I haven't seen him in three years.

"No, Grace. Your grandfather is a busy man. But he's asked me to make sure you're settled in." She gives me a wave that's a little too eager, a smile that's a little too bright. "Come on. I'll give you the tour."

"I've been here before," I say, following her toward the stairs.

"Of course, but *I've* never had the privilege of showing you around."

"I lived here every summer until my mom died. I know the way around."

"Of course you do, but you and I have never really gotten to know each other. I would like for us to be friends, Grace." Ms Chancellor stops on the highest step, her hand on the railing. The light from a big round window catches the highlights in her auburn hair. It's pretty. She's pretty. I bet she was a real looker in her twenties, but she's only a few years younger than my grandfather, which makes her at least sixty now. Her auburn hair, I realize, probably comes out of a bottle.

"Chocolate?" She pulls two blue-wrapped sweets out of the pocket of her tailored jacket, offers one to me, and keeps one for herself.

"I'm sixteen," I tell her.

"So?"

"So I'm not a little kid. You don't have to bribe me with candy."

"Good. Then I get to eat yours." She unwraps one piece and pops it into her mouth.

Every year the Swiss ambassador gives a huge box of chocolates to my grandfather for Christmas, and I know from experience that the candy Ms Chancellor is offering me is smooth and sweet and unlike anything else on earth, so I take my piece and unwrap it, hold it in my hand for a second before taking a bite. A thin layer of chocolate covers my fingers when I'm finished.

"Here," she says, handing me a handkerchief.

I rub my hands on my jeans.

Ms Chancellor eyes this, sees it as proof that the ambassador's granddaughter is just as wild and untamed as advertised.

I start down the stairs and summon my most regal tone as I glance back over my shoulder. "I feel we're off to an *excellent* start."

The embassy looks smaller than I remembered. I know buildings are supposed to shrink as you age, but I hadn't been expecting this. When we reach the stairs, my hand feels too big on the railing. I wonder what Ms Chancellor would do if I were to hop onto the banister and slide down to the black-and-white-checkered floor like I used to do when Jamie told me not to.

"There are fifty-five Americans employed by the embassy," Ms Chancellor says, slipping back into tour-guide mode as if I'm just another visiting dignitary. I can't really blame her – I'm a big job, after all, a responsibility she isn't exactly trained for.

"A few live on the embassy grounds. But most reside in the city. We are the face of the United States here in Adria. We do important work for an important cause. And now, Grace, you're one of us!"

"I know," I tell her, but she just talks on like it's all news to me. Like I didn't spend every summer of my life here up until three years ago.

"Some of the people who work here have children about your age," Ms Chancellor is saying. "I suspect you are going to make some great friends here, Grace."

"Yay."

If Ms Chancellor hears my sarcasm, she ignores it.

"We also have about forty Adrian citizens who work with us. Not for us. Never *for us.*" She adds the last part a little under her breath.

When we reach the end of the hall, I see a big round window with a cozy seat nestled into the alcove beneath it. Heavy velvet draperies hang on either side, ready to block the world away. Light ripples through the wavy glass, and I feel myself stop and stare.

In the distance, I can hear a woman counting.

"*Twenty-seven. Twenty-eight. Twenty-nine.*"

A child laughs.

There are footsteps on the stairs.

"*Ready or not, here I come!" the woman yells, and the laughter grows louder.*

"*Gracie!" The woman's voice echoes through the hall. "Gracie, where are you?"*

"Grace?" The voice is louder – closer. It cuts through the fog that fills my mind. "Grace," Ms Chancellor says, and I shudder as I remember where I am. *When* I am.

"Grace," she tries again. "Did you hear me?"

"Yeah," I say, shaking my head. "They work with us. Never *for* us. I've got it."

She eyes me, not sure if she should be worried or

annoyed. "What I was saying *after* that is that security is our top priority here. Adria is a very friendly post, but we live in a dangerous world. That's why security protocols are not optional. We do not prop open doors. We do not give out access codes. And we never, ever jump off of walls."

She removes her glasses and stares at me with eyes the same chestnut color as her hair, and I know she's not messing around.

"While you are in this building, you are on American soil. This is your country. This is your home. But step outside these walls and you are a visitor in Adria – a visitor with a very important job. Grace, I need to know that you understand me."

"Sure," I say, because I have heard this all before. I have done this all before. I have ignored this all before.

"We must respect our host country and we *must respect our neighbors.*" She lowers her voice again and grows more serious. More intent. This is a woman who means business as she warns me, "Sometimes the walls that stand between us and our neighbors are all that stand between our country and war."

"I understand. Don't worry. I am not going to cause any trouble."

And at that moment I mean it. I really, really do. Ms Chancellor must see it in my eyes, because she reaches out. But as soon as her fingers touch my shoulder, I feel a shock and jerk away. I'm almost certain I smell smoke.

"Grace?" Ms Chancellor's voice is too soft – too

distant. “Grace, do you know why your grandfather asked you to come live with him?”

“Because my dad’s unit is being deployed to the Middle East and war zones aren’t as kid-friendly as they used to be?”

“No. You’re here because your grandfather has worked in Adria for nearly half a century. He married a woman from here. He raised his family here. This was your mother’s home, Grace. It is *your* home. And your grandfather wants you to know it and love it as he does. He has always wanted you here.”

“OK.” I do not ask how – if Grandpa loves me so much – it’s possible that I haven’t laid eyes on him since before my mother died.

Ms Chancellor smiles at me. She thinks we’ve just bonded. I don’t have the heart to tell her she’s wrong.

I’m here because there’s no place else for me to go.

Ms Chancellor thinks the room at the end of the hall is mine.

I am so paralyzed by her mistake I don't even know how to tell her that she's wrong. So I just stand perfectly still, watching the lights flicker and buzz when she flips them on. It's like the room is having trouble waking up from its long slumber. It hasn't been used in years, after all.

Three years.

The electrical outlets all look funny and, in the attached bathroom, there is one spout for hot water and another one for cold. These are the things that remind me where I am – how far I have traveled. This isn't just another relocation from one army base to another. This time I am deep in enemy territory, and I am on my own.

Ms Chancellor opens the window and lets the cool breeze fill the room. It smells like the sea.

"Now, I know we've arranged for the majority of your

things to be shipped over, but— Oh, good, someone brought your luggage up." She motions to the big rolling suitcase and duffle bag that sit beside the bed. "You should have plenty of time to unpack before dinner. Would you like some help?"

She stops and watches me for a moment. Eventually, though, the silence is too much and she blurts, "So? What do you think?" She smiles too brightly; I feel like there's too much riding on whatever answer I'm being asked to give. "Do you like it?"

Someone has put fresh flowers on the desk, and I reach out to touch them. I eye the white lace curtains and the big queen bed with the twirly, twisty frame and soft-pink canopy. It is every little girl's dream room. Too bad I'm not a little girl.

Too bad I'm not my mo—

"I think there's been some kind of mistake," I say too quickly. "I'm always in the yellow room." I point in the direction of the smaller bedroom three doors down. "That's my room."

"Well, your grandfather and I thought that you'd be more comfortable in this room. Since you'll be staying with us longer this time. It's larger, see? And, of course, it has its own bathroom, and—"

"This is my mom's room," I say. As if she doesn't know. As if it isn't obvious.

The signs are everywhere, from the ballerina-topped jewelry box on the dresser to the stuffed animals in the window seat. Every summer of my childhood, my mother made a pilgrimage back to a room that never changed. She grew up, but it did not. When I was a kid, I thought it felt like a time machine. Now it feels like a shrine.

"We can redecorate," Ms Chancellor tells me. "Of course, you should pick out your own things. We have a lovely selection of furniture in the attic. Do you like antiques?" she asks, then realizes how silly it sounds. "Of course you don't like antiques. Well, maybe we can ship some of your furniture over from the States if you'd prefer."

"That's OK," I tell her. "I don't have a home there either." For a second, she looks at me like I'm the saddest little orphan in the world, so I point at myself and say, "Army brat," as if living on ten bases in fifteen years has left me impervious to change. As if what happened is just something else I can move away from and forget.

"Oh." She nods. "Well, how about we go look around the attic, just in case? Or you can move to the yellow room if you think that would be better."

As she talks, I pull aside the lacy curtain and stare out the window. Mom's old room is at the back of the embassy, right beside the ancient wall that runs around the city's edge. From my place on the third story, I have a bird's-eye view of the Russian flag that waves atop the next building over. On the other side, I can see Germany and a smidge of Canada – dozens of embassies all stacked together like dominoes in a ring around the city. Suddenly I am overwhelmingly afraid that I'm going to knock them all down. It's just a matter of time.

That's why, even with the window open, I'm finding it

hard to breathe. Ms Chancellor is saying something about dinner plans and a midnight curfew. She doesn't notice that the walls are closing in. Her wrists don't itch so badly she wants to scratch them until they bleed. When she opens the closet and pushes aside a red sundress, she doesn't hear the voice in the bathroom, calling, *"Gracie, honey, can you zip me?"*

I close my eyes and take a step back, but Ms Chancellor doesn't notice. She's not looking closely enough.

"Grace?" Ms Chancellor says. "What do you think?"

I think I have to get out of here. I need to run. To breathe.

"It's..." I start, struggling for breath.

"Grace, are you OK?"

I've got to get her out of here, I think as I turn to the window and notice the tree that stretches up to the sky, its big branches easily within my reach. "It's perfect."

When Ms Chancellor leaves, I know I'm supposed to unpack and settle in. But I can't touch my things. There is already a hairbrush in the drawer in the bathroom. An old raincoat and umbrella hang from a hook on the back of the door. The dresser drawers are empty, but the shelves are full of books. My mother's books. Nancy Drew and Agatha Christie. She always loved a good mystery.

And the one thing I know for certain is that I don't want to be here. Not in this room. Not in this embassy. Not in the city of Valancia or the country of Adria.

I. Don't. Want. To. Be. Here.

The cry is in my throat, rising up, but I don't dare let it out. Instead, I open the window wider. I've already thrown one leg over the sill and am reaching for the nearest tree branch when I hear a small voice say, "Where are you going?"

I freeze.

It's always quiet here. I'd forgotten that about Embassy Row. You would think that so much diplomacy would make some kind of noise – a hum at least. But all I hear are birds, the wind in the tree. Maybe a little bit of traffic in the distance, but for the most part it is silent. I stand perfectly still, waiting for the voice to come again.

"Hello! Hello!"

Then I see her, sitting on the edge of the wall, back straight, one skinny arm waving in my direction. She can't be older than twelve. She has pale skin and white-blond hair. It's like looking at a ghost.

"Where are you going?" the girl asks again. Her accent is northern European – German, perhaps.

"Nowhere," I say.

"You look like you're going somewhere!" she yells.

I climb back into my mother's room and rush out the door.

I'm not going to have a panic attack. I'm not going to let it come and sweep over me. I'm not going to give anyone a reason to call my father or the doctors, to count my pills or make me talk. I solemnly swear that I will never talk again if I can help it. So I run faster. The stairs come two at a time, swirling, spiraling. Taking me away from the room with the canopy bed, from the hairbrush and the mysteries, from the problems I can't solve.

But as soon as I reach the landing I can see the bottom of the stairs and the boy who is already standing there, waiting.

I freeze, stunned.

He is not supposed to be here.

When he says, "Well, if it isn't Grace the Ace," I know it is too late to run. Wherever I might hide, he'd find me. He was always able to find me.

"Isn't that what your brother always calls you?" the boy asks, but doesn't wait for an answer. "Anyway, welcome back."

He smiles like it's the easiest thing in the world. Like he's exactly where he's supposed to be. But he's not. His accent alone is enough to tell me that he is on the wrong side of the wall.

He's not supposed to be here.

For a second, I almost wish Ms Chancellor was still with me. I feel too small again, the embassy too big. It's like I'm ten and about to be in trouble. Locked in a closet, then scolded for following the boys and told to go back to my room. I feel the sudden urge to jump off the wall or out the window, just to prove I can.

"So when did you get in?" the boy asks.

"I'm sorry," I say, forcing myself to walk closer to the blue eyes that are staring back at me, too big, too intense. It's a gaze that might burn if I let it, so I decide not to let it.

Not even a little bit. I cock my head and eye him. "Have we met?" I ask.

The boy laughs. "Nice try, Grace. So how's Jamie?"

"Perfect. As usual. If you actually knew my brother, you'd know that."

"Oh, but I *do* know your brother," the boy says, his accent stronger. "In fact, I know *you*." The boy doesn't wink, but he gives me the kind of smile that goes with one.

"Oh, gee, I'm sorry I don't remember," I say as I reach the main floor and turn to start down the hall. "I guess you didn't make much of an impression."

"Sure I did. Of course, the last time we saw each other they were scraping what was left of you off of the German courtyard, so I can see how your memory might be impaired."

"Canadian," I say. "I was in the Canadian courtyard. I've never fallen into Germany."

I start to push past him, but the boy moves to block my path.

"How long are we going to play this game, Gracie?"

"I'm sure I don't know what you mean."

"Then allow me to introduce myself," he says, playing along as he gives me a low bow. "Alexei Volkov, at your service. I live next door." He nods out the window toward the Russian embassy.

Because that's the thing about Embassy Row. The boy next door is probably Russian.

He is *not supposed to be here.*

"Then shouldn't you be getting home?" I ask. "I'd hate

for us to have an international incident. It's only my first day back."

"Actually, that's why I'm here. You see, I'm the guy your brother put in charge of you."

At this, I have to laugh. "Oh, he did, did he?"

"Yes. I am to – and I quote – 'keep Grace from killing herself or anyone else.' Especially me. He was most emphatic about that last part."

"I don't need a babysitter."

"That is not what I hear." Alexei crosses his arms and leans against the wall, blocking my way. But there's something in his eyes as he looks at me. "You grew up, Gracie."

"People do that. Even little sisters."

"You will always be Jamie's little sister."

"So he likes to remind me. But that doesn't make me your problem."

"I guess this is where we must…what is it you Americans say? Agree to disagree."

Alexei has lived on Embassy Row since he was three. He's attended the English-speaking international school since he was five. His English is as good as mine, but he likes to play this game. They all do. I don't play any game that I can't win.

"How have you been, Gracie?" he asks. His voice is too soft now. Too sincere. And I hate the sound of it. It makes me wonder: *what does he know? What has Jamie told him?*

For better or worse, I lower my head and say, "Alive."

"Good," Alexei says. Then a darkness crosses his face, and I can feel the words coming even before he tilts his head and says, "I was very sorry to hear about your mother. She was always very kind to me."

"I..."

The doors to the formal living room are open, and when I stare through them *I see blankets draped over chair backs. Somebody has built a fort.*

"Jamie!" a little blond girl calls. "Alexei!"

But the boys are nowhere to be seen.

A woman sweeps into the room, takes the little girl in her arms. "Gracie, what's the matter?"

"They left me." The little girl's voice quivers, full of tears she won't let fall. "Jamie and Alexei left me!"

"Oh, Gracie." The woman holds her tighter. "That's why I'm here. I will never leave you."

"Never leave me," I whisper.

"Grace?" Alexei's voice comes to me. But it's deeper than it used to be. He and Jamie will never build a fort again. "Grace, did you say something?"

"I...I have to go."

"Grace—"

"I have to go now!" I shout because he is too close. The past is too close. The emotions I keep bottled up inside of me are pushing to the surface. And, most of all, I am tired. I'm so, so tired. And if I have to stay inside this building one moment longer I might not make it. I might just crumble into ash and blow away.

There's a small courtyard behind the embassy. It's

filled with rose bushes transplanted from the White House and secluded benches – a few meandering paths that criss-cross the grounds.

As I reach for the door, Alexei says, "Grace, you can't go that way."

I spin, throw my arms out wide, and shout, "Watch me!"

Then I back into the door, pushing as hard as I can. But I'm bigger than I used to be. Stronger. And the doors open too easily against my weight. The stairs are slick and I lose my balance as soon as I'm through the door. I can feel myself slipping, falling.

A hand grabs me from behind, but it is the exact wrong sensation at the exact wrong time. I feel like a rope has been fraying inside of me, slowly unraveling until…

Snap.

I turn and lash out. A cry rises up in my throat, primitive and raw, and then I'm pushing and lunging. Falling. As I land in the rose bushes, I can feel the thorns of a rose bush tearing into my skin, clinging to my clothes. But I can't stop. I have to get away, so I push to my hands and knees and try to crawl through the dirt, but my head is spinning. I see stars.

But…no. Not stars. The bright lights flash with quick clicks, rapid-fire. I brush my hair out of my eyes and look up at the international press corps that stands around me, cameras raised, capturing my every move. There must be at least fifty people in the courtyard. From the edge of the crowd I see Alexei's father looking on, horrified.

"That's why," Alexei says so softly I barely hear him.

Only then do I realize I am not alone on the ground. The Russian ambassador spits and gags beside me. Blood runs from his nose and he brings a hand to his mouth as if he has been hit.

Because he *has* been hit.

I look down at my own hands. They're shaking. And on my knuckles there's a faint smudge of blood.

"Hello, Grace, darling."

Instantly, I recognize the deep Southern drawl that even after decades in Adria he still hasn't lost. I squint up through the sun. Vaguely, I make out a dark suit, a red tie, and white hair – a smile I haven't seen in years.

I wipe the mud from my face and steal one last glance at the obviously upset Russian.

Then I turn back to the man offering me his hand and say, "Hi, Grandpa."

I can hear the shouting, but I can't make out the words. Maybe it's because the doors to the ambassador's office are practically soundproof. Maybe it's because most of the shouting is in Russian.

There is a guard at the end of the hall. He wears camouflage and carries a semi-automatic. We are definitely not in the United States anymore, I realize as I sit on a hard chair, swinging my legs back and forth, trying not to bleed on Russia's really nice rug.

"I didn't mean to do it," I mutter after a while.

"I know," Alexei says. He stays perfectly still, listening to the words that filter underneath the door.

"It was an accident," I say. "He should know better than to go around grabbing people."

"He was trying to help you!"

"I was fine," I say, the words automatic now. I don't have to mean them. I just have to make everyone else believe them.

But Alexei has never been like everyone else.

"What happened back there?" he asks.

"You were there. You saw it."

"What did *you* see?"

I recoil, but Alexei can't know about the visions or the flashes or the memories. He can't possibly have guessed that I saw my mother – that I heard her voice and felt her touch. I'm not seeing ghosts. The embassy is not haunted. But *I* am. And sitting on that hard chair, I know the truth – that what I saw three years ago will haunt me for the rest of my life.

I don't realize I'm rocking back and forth until Alexei places his hand on my back. I freeze, then pull away.

"Don't touch me," I warn him.

"Whatever you say, Gracie."

"Don't call me Gracie."

"OK." Alexei slowly nods. "It's OK. At least, I hope it's OK."

When Alexei looks at the closed door I realize I'm not the only one who's afraid.

"What aren't you telling me?" I ask, but Alexei says nothing. "Alexei, what is going on?"

"Things have been sort of…tense…lately." He keeps glancing toward the door.

"We're the United States. You're Russia. Things are always sort of tense."

"It's gotten worse."

Diplomatic relations are like an iceberg. About ninety

per cent of them exist beneath the surface, unseen by the world at large. But they're always there. And if you're not careful, they can sink you. I know that I didn't just fall into a photo op. I fell into treacherous waters – and made things even worse.

"Gracie," my grandfather says when he opens the door a few minutes later.

I stand and limp toward him. There is still dirt on my clothes, and the palms of my hands are red.

"I'm sorry," I say for what feels like the millionth time.

"Don't tell me, Gracie." Grandpa stands back and points at his Russian counterpart. "Tell him."

The man is my grandfather's age, but his hair is thinner and not quite as white. He has taken off his tie, and blood stains his white dress shirt. There is a bandage on his neck where the rose bushes scratched him. His left eye is already starting to blacken, and he glares at me as if I came at him with a switchblade.

"Mr Ambassador," I tell him, "I'm so very sorry for my carelessness. It was an accident. I guess I just don't know my own strength."

I try to force a laugh. I desperately want it to be funny, but the glaring man doesn't think so.

It doesn't have to be a big deal! I want to shout, but it's no use. The Russian ambassador is bleeding and it happened on US soil – at the hands of a US citizen – so I take a deep breath and lower my head.

"I am sincerely sorry."

The Russian ambassador nods and then leaves. I might

feel relieved except Alexei's father is coming toward me. "Very well," he says. Then he snaps, "Alexei. Come."

When Alexei stands and starts down the hall, I realize something: he's in trouble, too.

Alexei's father stops at the end of the hall and glances over his shoulder, back at me. The look on his face is obvious. I've been in the country less than eight hours and already I've corrupted his son.

"Good night, everyone," Alexei's father says. "I trust that this incident will not follow us into tomorrow."

"Grace, are you OK?" Ms Chancellor asks, dragging me from the Russian embassy and onto the street. We don't even wait on Grandpa, who is, presumably, still saying his goodbyes inside. "Are you injured?" she asks, but my answer is beside the point. She's too busy looking at me like I'm broken.

"I'm sorry. I didn't mean to–"

She holds up a hand to stop me, the universal signal for *don't waste your breath.*

"Exactly what were you doing in the garden?" she asks.

"I wanted to go for a walk."

"I thought you were going to unpack."

"Yeah. I was, but…"

"But what?"

"I wanted to get some air."

"Some air?" She puts her hand on her hip and whips off her glasses. "You wanted some air so you decided to attack the Russian ambassador during the middle of the annual tree-planting ceremony? Do you know why your grandfather plants a tree with the Russians every year?"

"I didn't *attack* him. It was an accident!"

"It is to symbolize our renewed commitment to cooperation and hope for the future."

"It was an accident," I say again, softer this time. "I had to get some air, get out of that room, and…"

"And what?" Ms Chancellor snaps. "Please, Grace, tell me what was so urgent that you made a man bleed."

I can't tell her the truth. I'm too exhausted to make up a lie. So I don't say anything at all.

After a moment, Grandpa joins us on the street. He looks tired, older than I remember. Of all the changes I'd been expecting, this wasn't one. I mean, old is old. I'd never really thought of it as something that has degrees. But his hair is whiter. His skin is a little looser. And his eyebrows are definitely bushier. I wonder for a minute how I must look to him.

"I'm sorry," I say before he can start in on whatever lecture is probably coming. I'm too tired to listen.

"I know you are, Gracie," he says as if he's seen me every week for ages, like it hasn't been years. He puts his hand on my shoulder and steers me toward our gates. "So, how's your brother?"

"Fine," I say.

"He's a West Point man now, I hear."

"Yes, sir."

"I bet your father's busting his buttons over that one."

"He's very proud of Jamie," I say as I look down at my dirty hands.

No one is proud of me.

"How was your flight?" he asks, his tone so conversational that he might as well be talking about the weather, inquiring about my health.

Then I realize that, no, that is the last thing he would ever ask about. Even small talk is a minefield now, so I just shrug and say, "My flight was fine."

"Eleanor tells me you don't like your room."

I cut my eyes at the woman. "I didn't say that," I lie.

"She's dead, Grace. She's not going to need it."

Some people would call my grandfather callous, unfeeling. Cold. In truth, he's none of those things. And he's all of those things.

"Your momma would want you to have her old room," he goes on, and I see the soft, gooey center of his diplomatic shell. "She was happy here. You'll be happy here. You've got to let her go, Gracie."

Let her go. The words jolt me to a stop. I spin on him.

"You think I don't know she's gone?" I shout. "I was there, remember? I watched her die. And now *you're* telling *me* to let her go? No. You don't get to stroll back into my life and tell me how to deal with anything. Not now. Not after three years."

Grandpa shakes his head. "That was your father's doing. When he and your brother came for the funeral... we had words. After that, he didn't want you and Jamie to come visit for a while."

"Planes only go one direction?"

"Your father felt that it might be best if you had some space, because..."

He trails off then, but I recognize the silence that follows.

"Because I went crazy," I fill in. "It's OK, Grandpa. You can say it."

"Because you were having a hard time."

"So that's the term we're using now." For some reason, I have to laugh. "How...diplomatic."

"Grace," Ms Chancellor says, her voice a warning.

"Do you want to hear about the fire?" I ask him, ignoring her. "I was there. I remember everything," I say, but I don't elaborate. I may be crazy, but I'm not stupid. There are words I have stricken from my vocabulary completely.

Murder.

Arson.

Homicide.

Scar.

I know it's no use, and so I do not mention the man I saw – the one who didn't appear on a single surveillance camera and wasn't seen by any other witness. It's no use to talk about the scar that was on his face – the one that was so clichéd and manically sinister that everyone assumed my mind had pulled him straight from central casting.

I don't tell my grandfather that my mother's antique store was ransacked. I don't say that when the building burst into flames, it sounded like a bomb.

These are the things I never say to anyone anymore. Not because I don't want to say them – I want to scream them. But these are the things that no one else can bear to hear.

"It was an accident, Grace. Your mother died in a terrible, tragic accident." His voice cracks. Tears well in his eyes.

"I'm not crazy." *My* voice stays steady. *My* eyes don't tear up. For one split second I feel victorious. But I haven't won a thing.

"Go to bed, Gracie." He steps through the embassy gates, past the marines who are constantly standing guard. "You've had a long flight and a long day. Tomorrow will be longer. Lots to do."

"Good night, dear," Ms Chancellor tells me, the lecture over.

I don't say anything back. I just shuffle, dirty and cold, toward the doors.

I can sleep anywhere. Planes. Trains. Sofas. Lawn chairs. Call it the upside to life as an army brat. Never having a home means, I guess, that everywhere is your home. There is absolutely no place I'm anxious to return to. But this is different.

I'm not trying to fall asleep in someplace new; I'm in a place that's old. And that's why I find myself lying in my mother's bed, staring up at the pink canopy overhead and studying the shadows that dance across the walls as the wind blows through the limbs of the tree outside my window. When at last I fall asleep, I dream I'm trapped, my wrists bound. I toss and turn. Even my subconscious wants to figure out a way to break free.

"Hey."

The voice is soft in my head. I think for a moment that Alexei has invaded my dream, so I turn over, mumble some insult.

"Hey," the voice says louder.

And then a hand lands on my bare shoulder. I don't even bother waking, not really. My brother goes to West Point. My father is an Army Ranger. Asleep Me can handle this.

Still groggy, I roll over and grab the hand. And before I'm even off the bed, the boy is on the floor. When I finally find myself fully awake, I'm standing over him.

"Grace!" he half yells, half whispers.

"Tell me why I shouldn't kill you."

My hair is falling into my eyes. The old T-shirt I'm wearing is about three sizes too big and hangs off of me weirdly, leaving one shoulder bare. I probably look as freaky as I feel. And I'm glad for it.

I wrench the boy's hand farther back, holding his thumb with my other hand.

"I can break it."

But the boy doesn't scream. He doesn't cry out. He just looks up at me. And smiles.

"Hi, Grace. I'm Noah," he says. "I'm here to be your best friend."

I've never lived anywhere long enough to have a best friend before. Maybe that's why I let him off the floor and don't protest while he fumbles around my room in the dark.

"Come on. Get dressed," he tells me. "We have to go."

"Go where?" I ask. "Who are you? Am I going to regret not breaking your hand? Because it's not too late. I can still totally break your hand."

"I know you can." He looks at the piles of clothes, grabs whatever is lying on top, and throws it at me. "Here. Put this on."

"That's a duffle bag."

"OK. Then put on something else. But that's a really nice bag. It would really bring out your" – he gestures to me oddly with his hands – "personality."

It's kind of funny. He's kind of funny. But I don't laugh. Instead, I ease closer and ask again, "Who. Are. You?"

I know better than to shout. There are always guards on patrol in the courtyard and by the gates. My grandfather's suite is on this floor. And I'm fairly certain Ms Chancellor probably has my room bugged, wired, and booby-trapped. Yelling is a bad idea.

"Sorry." The boy holds out a hand. He has spiky black hair and dark eyes that catch the moonlight as he tells me again, "I'm Noah," sounding only slightly annoyed. "Noah Miguel Estaban."

"Noah Estaban?"

He shrugs. "Mom's Israeli. Dad's Brazilian. What can I say? I am Embassy Row personified. You really lucked out in the best friend department."

"I didn't realize one had been assigned to me."

"Sure. My mom and Ms Chancellor are sorority sisters or something. Anyway, I'm supposed to mold you in my diplomatic image. Now hurry up. We've got to go."

"Ms Chancellor *asked* you to break into my room in

the middle of the night, then drag me out of the embassy and onto the dark streets of a foreign city?"

"Well, technically she asked me to show you around. Exactly when and how she left up to me. And I say there's no time like the present. So come on. We're late." He looks at me impatiently. "Get dressed."

I stare back and then something occurs to him.

"Oh, you need me to turn around? Here. I'll turn around."

Three minutes later, the embassy is dark and Noah and I are making our way down the halls. There are mosaics on the ceilings and gold-embossed angels by the stairs. I know that most modern embassies are more like fortresses – barbed wire and cement blocks, born out of the war on terror. But not in Adria. This country is like the land that time forgot, and even here, on what is technically US soil, it shows. The building was originally built by a spice baron in 1772. It became the US embassy at the end of World War I. And it was the only real home my mother ever knew.

As I follow the boy with the spiky black hair and dark brown eyes, I feel like a thief. A trespasser. And I'm a little afraid to admit that I like it. I even like Noah. But when we reach the side door, I stop.

He looks back at me. "What's wrong?"

I can still hear my grandfather's words rattling around in my head. I can feel the scathing glare of a few very ticked-off Russians. And I know that I have two options:

I can be the person everyone wants me to be.

Or I can be the person they all expect me to be.

"I can't go," I say. "I just got here. I can't..."

"It's OK," Noah tells me. "Consider it part of your training. Besides, you're with me."

Then, as if to prove his point, Noah pushes out the door and marches toward the gates.

"Hey, Martin," he says to the marine stationed there. The marine takes his hand and shakes it like Noah is his oldest, dearest friend.

"Be good, buddy," the marine tells him.

"I always am," Noah says. "Oh, this is Grace. She's with me."

"I'm the one who lives here," I protest, but the marine just takes me in.

"Welcome back, ma'am," he says.

"Thank you," I say.

And then we are off, free...or so I think, right up until the point when Noah stops by the gate and holds up a finger.

"OK," he says. "First lesson."

Noah broadens his stance, taking his place firmly on the embassy side of the threshold. "In the United States," he says. Then, with both feet, he leaps onto the sidewalk. "Out of the United States." Quickly, he jumps back toward me. "In the United States." Another jump across the threshold. "Out of the United States. In. Out. In—"

"Is this the part where I hit you?"

Noah raises one finger. "You could. But you might

want to do it while you are" – he leaps back to stand beside me – "*in* the United States."

I put both hands on his chest and shove gently, pushing him out into the dark and empty street. Noah only laughs and catches his balance, then glances back at me.

"Diplomatic immunity, Grace. It's not all it's cracked up to be."

I join him on the other side of the fence and let the embassy gate slam behind me. Martin the Marine's laughter is the only sound as we disappear into the shadows, walking uphill on a narrow street lined with mansions.

Noah is taller than me, with long, lanky legs that wobble like he's a puppy that's still growing. He practically bounces down the street, arms thrown out wide as he says, "This is Embassy Row!"

"I know," I tell him, but it's like he doesn't even hear.

"Named for the rows of embassies that line the street." He makes a gesture like a flight attendant pointing out emergency exits. "Newcomers to the city are often fascinated to learn that Valancia is actually laid out like a gigantic circle, ringed by the ancient wall that has protected our fair city from intruders for more than seven centuries."

"I'm not a newcomer," I say, but Noah talks on like the world's most overenthusiastic tour guide.

"Embassy Row actually lies on the outer perimeter of the city circle, with many of the properties backing up against the wall itself. The land here was originally farmland that was supposed to help feed the city in the event of a siege, but eventually the wealthiest citizens of

Valancia chose to build their estates here. At the end of the First World War, the homes were gradually bought up by the various nations with whom diplomatic relations in Adria are oh so important. Forty-seven in all – and that's just on the row. There are a lot of other, smaller embassies and consulates within the city."

One of the mansions is as white as the sand on the beach that stretches from the sea. It has high walls and reinforced gates. Noah points to the blue-and-white flag that flies from the highest tower as we pass.

"I live in that one."

"Israel," I say. "Not Brazil?"

"Only on the weekends." Noah shoves his hands into his pockets. "Mom and Dad weren't exactly suited to matrimonial harmony."

Noah walks on. If there's more to the story, then he isn't in the mood to share it. At least we have that much in common.

"Each embassy is the sovereign ground of the country it represents. Each country is sacred."

We walk through the glow of antique streetlights that are still – even in the twenty-first century – fueled by gaslight. And, suddenly, I realize that the city hasn't changed in three years; in fact, it hasn't changed in three hundred. So I walk down cobblestones that are slick with the damp night air. I wish I'd brought a sweater.

"Thanks, Noah." I stop beneath a streetlight. "This has been the most enjoyable-yet-totally-redundant tour I've ever been on. Truly. It was swell. But it's late and I'm jet-lagged, and now you can tell Ms Chancellor that you have done your duty, and go back to doing whatever it is you do when you aren't busy kidnapping the new girl."

I slowly back away, toward the embassy and my mother's bed and whatever bad dreams await me.

Noah looks slightly hurt as he calls, "Where are you going?"

"Back to the good ol' U. S. of A."

"You can't leave," he tells me. "We're almost there."

"Almost where?" I ask.

Noah points to the end of the row, to a dark, winding path that leads straight up a steep incline and then disappears into blackness. In the stillness of the night, I hear music, a pounding bass keeping beat like the crashing of the waves. It's a sound that knows no language. It is the same in every place in the world. And I know what awaits us long before Noah tells me.

"No." I shake my head.

"Come on. You've got to come."

"No, thank you," I try again in my most diplomatic tone.

"Hear me out," he says as I start to turn. "Grace, wait."

"No." I move out of the glare of the streetlight, going back down the long, sloping street.

"Come on. You've got to meet people eventually. Everyone is there and—"

"You don't have to tell me about the party, Noah. I know that party. I've been to that party. In Fort Sill and Fort Benning. You should have seen the bonfire they did at Fort Dix. I got second-degree burns from that one."

"Come on, Grace," he says, but I walk on. I'm almost to Italy when he calls, "Are you chicken?"

Noah has been my best friend for twenty minutes. Already he knows me too well.

The path is overgrown and winding and steep. Thorny bushes scrape my legs. Low-hanging branches catch in my hair. Noah tries to be chivalrous and hold the branches and vines out of my way, but the poor guy just ends up half eaten by a bush, and I have to rescue him. I wish I'd brought a flashlight. In the dense overgrowth there is no moonlight. We stumble, practically blind.

"So what's the occasion?" I ask him. Despite the rough terrain and steep incline, I'm not even a little out of breath. "I hope it's something special to be worth all this trouble."

"It's the last day of school, first day of summer; full moon; you're here – take your pick."

"Me?"

The brush is a little thinner overhead, and the moon slices across his face. It's the first good look I've gotten at him. I can see his freckles.

"New blood, Grace," Noah explains, his voice soft beneath the ever-stronger pulse of the music. "The sharks can smell it. Now come on. It's time for the real tour."

When Noah takes my hand it's all I can do not to pull away. Not to run down the hill, back to the embassy and the canopy bed, not to lash out again for reasons he can't possibly understand. But he's looking at me like I'm a normal girl, and that stops me. No one has looked at me that way in a long, long time.

He leads me up the winding path. It grows wilder with every step, and I know the smart thing would be to turn around and go back to the safety of the embassy. But the sense of déjà vu that has been haunting me for hours is slowly fading. I realize Noah might be leading me to the only place on Embassy Row where my mother's memory will not follow.

"What is this place?" I ask when I realize just how high we've climbed.

"Technically? It's *nowhere.* I mean, once upon a time it was the grounds of one of the embassies, but then the country sold the land back to Adria and this happened."

Noah gestures to the overgrown path that surrounds us.

"Oh, it's *lovely,*" I say in my best Ms Chancellor voice.

Noah laughs. "Just you wait."

"Wait for what?"

"Until you see *this.*"

He pushes aside one last branch and steps from the moss-and-leaf-covered ground onto solid stone. Overhead, the canopy of the trees disappears, and I look out onto a plateau that stretches for thirty yards in front of us. Beyond that, there is nothing but the deep-blue sea and the largest moon that I have ever seen. It's as bright as any of the streetlights, there at the top of the city.

"Welcome to the secret side of Embassy Row," Noah tells me as I ease forward to take in the scene. The music is louder, but so is the crashing of the waves against the rocky shore. I inch forward and look straight down over a cliff that is at least a hundred feet high. Probably higher.

"Easy, there," Noah says, taking my arm and pulling me gently back.

I feel the mist in the wind coming off the water. The air is damp and salty. My hair clings to my forehead, and even though I haven't slept in two days, I am wide awake in the middle of the night, standing on a cliff with a boy who, technically, broke into the US embassy and absconded with the ambassador's granddaughter.

"Bet you didn't see *that* when you were a little girl," Noah says with a smirk. He seems entirely too pleased with himself. He doesn't know the half of it. I look back to the overgrown path, waiting for my mother to follow, but, for once, she's not there.

I scan the cliffs and the sea and then let my gaze fall onto the land beneath us, the massive wall that encircles the city, the flags that rise above the mansions on the row, waving through the spotlights that streak through the night sky. And then a cold chill seeps into my bones.

"Wait, if that is the US" – I point toward the familiar flag that flies in the distance – "then that's Russia, Japan, Italy, and" – I look down at the embassy closest to the cliffs – "that makes this..."

I shift my gaze onto Noah, who shoves his hands deep into his pockets. He rocks back on his heels. "Iran."

"We're in Iran!" I don't even try to hide the terror in my voice, but Noah pushes my fear aside.

"Technically, Iran sold this land back to the city at the same time they gave up diplomatic relations with Adria. Iran still owns the building, of course. But the land is fair game." He points down to the base of the cliffs, the small stretch of beach that reaches from the sea to the back of the abandoned building.

"It's a shame. It's the only embassy with private beach access. I tried to talk our ambassador into buying it, but for some reason the Israelis didn't think the Iranians would be up for a real estate swap."

"Fancy that," I tell him.

Noah gasps in mock surprise. "I know!"

"So the local teenagers come up here to party…in what used to be Iran?"

"What can I say? We're resourceful. But, Grace…" He steps closer to me. "We do not go past the fence. I mean, we could. But we don't. Because none of us are superexcited about starting World War Three. *So we do not go past the fence.*" He stares at me, as if waiting for a protest that never comes. "Say it with me, Grace. *We do not go past the fence.*"

"Noah."

"Say it."

"We do not go past the fence," I tell him.

"Because we do not want to start World War Three."

"We do not want to start World War Three," I add.

"Good girl."

Noah smiles and takes a few steps closer to the party. For a second, he can't quite meet my gaze. It's a look (or, rather, a non-look) that I know well.

"So what did Ms Chancellor tell you about me?" I ask.

Noah shrugs a little. "Not much."

"You flare your nostrils when you lie."

"I knew that," he says, nostrils flaring again.

The clouds are gathering over the moon, and for a moment we are shrouded in shadow, there atop the rocky cliffs. Someone changes the music and it's quiet for a split second. But that is all it takes for me to see it – the look that fills people's eyes when they think they know the truth about me and what happened. About my mom's death and what I did – or didn't – see. It isn't fear; it's pity. And I hate that even more.

"I'm not crazy," I tell him.

"I know that, too," he says. This time it's obvious he's telling the truth. Or at least he thinks he is.

"Do you want to ask me about it?" I ask as the music comes back on.

Noah takes my hand. "I don't even know what you're talking about."

He leads me toward the party. It isn't much, as big, rowdy shows of adolescent rebellion go. As we walk closer, I feel the gazes of three dozen strangers land upon me. Noah drops my hand. This isn't a date. We aren't a couple. Only then do I register that people aren't staring just at me.

"On our left," Noah starts slowly, speaking low into my ear, "we have the wealthy locals." He points to a small group of kids speaking Adrian and Spanish and Arabic. They wear expensive watches and nice clothes and immediately stop talking when we pass, glare after us as if we aren't supposed to be there.

"The gifted locals." These kids nod at Noah, but don't speak to me. They are in skinny jeans and T-shirts for bands that I don't know. "Popular embassy kids." We pass another small pocket of kids, who are sitting around the fire. It looks like a miniature, more beautiful version of the United Nations. There are probably half a dozen countries represented in that one small group alone. A girl asks a question in Spanish. A boy answers her in French. But the looks they give me are universal. I am the new girl in every possible language.

"And, finally, embassy kids who just really want to go home." Noah points to the last group. Here, the kids stand on the outskirts of the party, shifting their weight from foot to foot, constantly checking their phones.

"So the unifying factor is...what?" I ask. "You all go to the international school?"

"Correction." Noah raises a finger. "We all go to the international school. Or we will come fall. Tonight, we are the children of summer."

He raises his hands dramatically, gesturing to the fire and the groups of talking teens, the cliffs and the crashing waves of the sea that sweeps out below us.

"The children of summer?" I try to tease.

"It sounded better in my head."

"And where do you fit into all of this?" I glance back at the carefully sequestered cliques.

"I am a man without a country. Or I'm a man with too

many countries – you pick. Ultimately, in both global politics and the high school power hierarchy, they amount to the same thing. Do you want some water or something? Wait here. I'm going to get you some water."

I nod, and Noah wanders off into the night, leaving me alone with the wind and the sea and, finally, with a small voice that says, "Hi."

For a second, I think I must have dreamed it. I turn, looking for whoever spoke, but it's like the word came from the wind.

"Hi," the voice says again. "I'm down here."

And then I see her, on a ledge that sticks out from the cliff below me – not clinging, not frightened, just sitting there, staring up at where I'm standing. It's the girl from the wall outside my window. Again, she is so pale and solitary that I think for a moment she might actually be a ghost. I can't help but glance around, wondering if I'm the only one who can see her.

"You're the new American," she says.

"So I've been told."

"Do you want to see a trick?"

"Sure," I say.

She gets up, and no sooner is she on her feet than she begins to run straight for a tree that's growing out of the side of the cliff, and I can do nothing but stand, dumbfounded, as the girl jumps straight into the air and grabs its lowest limb. The force of her momentum pushes her around the branch, swinging in a broad circle not once but twice before she lets loose of the limb and flies through the air, landing safely right in front of me as if it's as easy as falling off a log.

"Wow," I say. "That was...Wow."

"I was going to be a gymnast. But now I'm not. Too big," she explains, even though, to me, she looks positively tiny.

Then I feel the need to say what people are always saying to me: "That looked really dangerous. Maybe you shouldn't do that anymore."

The girl shrugs. "I'm Rosie. Germany. Twelve."

The way she says it, I know these are the facts that matter here, the embassy-kid equivalent of name, rank, and serial number.

"Grace. United States. Sixteen," I tell her. She nods as if we've bonded. And I guess perhaps we have.

"Do your parents know you're here?" I ask.

Rosie crosses her arms. "Do yours?"

"Well, Mom is dead and Dad is getting shot at, so I don't think they're in a position to care. Now it's your turn to answer the question."

"Did you know there are five hundred kilometers of tunnels beneath the city?" Rosie asks as if I hadn't spoken at all. "At least that much. There may be more. I bet there's more. The Romans built them. People died down there all the time. There are bones and everything. I can show you if you want. I'm kind of an expert."

Before I can respond to this, I see a beautiful girl coming toward us. She's got olive-colored skin and striking black eyes. But there's something else about her.

She reminds me of someone, I think, but I can't quite imagine who.

Before I can say a word, the pretty girl starts shouting.

"No. No. No. Get out. Get out now! Don't pretend you didn't hear me. Get. Out. Now."

For a second I just stand, stunned. Then I realize that she's not talking to me. She's talking...behind me.

I turn and see Rosie at my back, my white-blond shadow. She's so small she must have been pretty unnoticeable there, but the girl with the perfect cheekbones isn't fooled.

"You don't belong here," the pretty girl snaps.

"Excuse me?" I tell her.

"I'm not talking to you," she says in a tone that makes it clear I'm too inconsequential to bother tossing aside. "I'm talking to *that*." She points at Rosie, who stands defiant, not giving any ground.

The girl looks around me. "You're not welcome here."

"They aren't your cliffs," Rosie shoots back.

"But it's my party," the pretty girl corrects her.

"Funny," Rosie quips, "I didn't see your name on it."

"Listen here, tiny blond person, I've warned you before, and you are testing my patience. *Auf Wiedersehen.*"

"Hey," I say. "Leave her alone."

When the dark-haired girl looks at me now it's like she's seeing me for the first time. She scans me from head to toe, taking in my sloppy ponytail and dirty old sneakers. I'm ready for whatever insult she might hurl my way, but instead she crosses her arms and says, "You're new."

"Did you figure that out all by yourself?" I reply.

"I guess I should introduce myself. I'm Lila. And I'm—"

"Oh, I know who you are," I cut her off, and she smiles a little, pleased that her reputation has preceded her.

"You do?" When she tosses her hair it catches the moonlight, so pretty it's almost fake. A joke. But she's as serious as she can possibly be.

"Of course I know you," I say, and her eyes soften. I can almost hear her thoughts, contemplating giving me a makeover, molding me in her image. I am the *Before*, I know. She is most certainly the *After*.

"I've attended seven schools in ten years," I explain. "So you can rest assured I know you. You're the girl who thinks being cruel is the same thing as being witty. You think being loud is the same thing as being right. And, most of all, you're the girl who is very, very pretty. And also very, very...common. Trust me. There's at least one of you in every school." I watch her features shift. "Oh. Wait. Did you think you were *unique*?"

When her face hardens, I can tell she isn't hurt; she's offended. I snicker a little, unable to keep it in. "Oh my gosh, you *did*, didn't you? You thought you were special. I'm so sorry."

But I'm not sorry.

I am standing on ground where I have never stood before, looking at a stranger. But this moment is so familiar to me that I could script out every gasp, every insult, every cajoling sneer.

I even know what she is going to say before she opens her mouth to tell me, "I don't like your attitude, new girl."

And that turns my snicker into a laugh. It has to. It is the absolute best weapon I have in this situation.

So I laugh louder. "Oh my gosh – you're serious. You really think I should be scared of you. Oh, that's so sweet." This confuses her. Her dark eyes narrow. "And kind of pitiful." I reach out to pat her hand. "I'm sorry. You just aren't a very big deal to me. It's OK."

The girl pulls her hand away before I can touch her again.

"No one told me the new girl was a freak!" she spits out.

"There you go," I say, my voice dripping with mock kindness. "Keep your chin up. Eventually, you will meet someone who cares about your opinion. I'm so sorry I'm not her."

For a moment, there is silence on the cliffs. That must be why the voice carries to me so clearly, why there's no mistaking it when I hear, "Lila, are you OK?"

I turn at the sound and see another girl behind us. And before I even realize what I'm saying, I blurt out, "Megan, is that you?"

Of course it's her, I realize. But I can't help myself. Megan looks different. In fact, she looks...like Lila. Well, not *like* Lila. Megan's mother is Indian American, and she's also shorter than Lila by a head. But they both wear silk scarves wrapped around their necks and bejeweled headbands in their hair. Short skirts and at least a dozen bracelets on their wrists. Megan is the same girl I used to know, just shinier. Much, much shinier. Embassy Row might not have changed, but Megan has, I realize as she steps closer.

"Grace?" Megan sounds stunned. It's like she'd never thought she'd see me again – like maybe she'd heard that I was dead or comatose or worse.

She no doubt heard I was *worse.*

And the awful part is that it was true. And Megan knows it. I liked this party a lot more when I was surrounded by strangers.

"I didn't know you were back," she says.

"Surprise." I force a smile and feel whatever momentum I'd had against Lila seep away. The cliff's edge feels closer than it should.

"You two know each other?" Lila asks, confused.

"Grace used to spend summers here. With her grandfather. The *ambassador.*" Megan emphasizes the final word, and I see its meaning land.

My grandfather is the ambassador for the United States. He's also Megan's mother's boss. That makes me important on Embassy Row. This fact makes Lila shift, but it doesn't make her like it.

"You were friends with *her*?" Lila asks Megan in a whisper that she totally wants me to hear.

I look at Megan, and Megan looks at me. Her mother is important at the embassy. Well liked. Every summer of my childhood I would arrive at Embassy Row and Megan's mom would bring her over. Day after day.

Megan would ask if I had any dolls. I would ask if she knew where my mother had hidden my slingshot. She would invite me over for tea parties. I would ask her to keep lookout while I followed Jamie and Alexei over the wall.

We were not friends.

We were simply what becomes of kids who are thrust together so often that, eventually, they run out of reasons not to go play.

I keep looking at her now, realizing that neither one of us has a clue how to answer Lila's question. And, if that is the case, then the answer is most certainly no.

"Listen," Lila finally says, to me this time, "you're new, so allow me to spell it out for you. This is an important place. Our parents are important people. Everyone here is significant in some way. I'm not in charge because I want to be. I'm in charge because somebody has to be."

The scary thing isn't what she's saying – it's that she means it. It's that, on some level, she might even be right.

"Do you know what happens if someone gets hurt at our party?" Lila asks. "If your little German friend does a backflip and lands on the Japanese ambassador's daughter? What if the Australians or the French bring alcohol and then the South Africans try to drive home and get into a car wreck with the Egyptians? That could happen, you know. And believe me when I say none of us are ready for the consequences." She crosses her arms and steadies her nerves, quite certain that her place in the hierarchy has been restored. "There has to be order. There have to be rules. It's not my fault everyone looks to me to make them."

"Congratulations," I tell her with a slight bow. "I hope you and your power trip will be very happy together. Now, if you'll excuse me, it's time for me to go."

I turn, searching the crowd until I see Noah. "Grace," he says, coming cautiously forward with two bottles of water in his hands. "Hey. Maybe you and I should—"

"Get out of here, loser," Lila says, spinning on him.

"OK." I try taking a deep breath, but my blood has begun to boil. "Now you've done it."

"Done what?" she asks with a snarl.

"Messed with my best friend."

This time it's Lila who laughs. "He's not *your friend.*" She crosses her arms. "He's *my brother.*"

I shoot a glance at Noah, who shrugs. "Twin brother, to be specific."

And finally I know who Lila looks like.

Lila reaches for me – to do what, I do not know. It's like she's moving in slow motion. She is smaller than Dad, slower than Jamie. She is no contest for me, but her hand never reaches my shoulder.

Before I know what is happening, a small blond blur bolts between us. Rosie grabs at Lila, pulling the beautiful blue-and-white scarf from around her neck.

"You!" Lila snaps.

"Leave her alone!" Rosie yells, and I pull her back.

"OK. Everybody leave *everybody* alone," I say.

"Here, give me that," Megan snaps at Rosie. She grabs

at the scarf, pulling it from Rosie's grasp. But the wind gusts at just that moment, and the scarf flutters, flying free. For a moment all we can do is watch as it floats over the cliff's edge and down the hill. It is soaring over the trees and out to sea when the wind shifts and blows it toward the lone dark building on Embassy Row. There is nothing but a cumulative gasp as it catches on the roof, flapping in the breeze over what is technically still the country of Iran.

"OK. This is bad," Noah says. His eyes are wide and filled with terror. "This is very, very bad."

I feel the mood shift around me. Lila is pointing to the night sky as if in disbelief. Rosie shakes and says, "I'm sorry. I'm so sorry," over and over so silently it is like she's locked in a very bad dream.

And then Noah grabs hold of me and Rosie and starts trying to pull us toward the path.

"Noah?" Rosie looks at him.

"Go home, Ro," he says calmly. "You were never here. We were never here. Everybody!" he shouts. "Party's over!"

"She was here!" Lila shouts, pointing at Rosie. "That little terror was here and it's her fault."

Megan steps toward her. "Lila, it's—"

"Do not talk to me!" Lila snaps.

"OK, Lila, let's go." Noah takes his sister's arm. "Go home, Rosie, Megan. Everybody just go!"

I have this habit. It's not a good one. It's not like I'm proud of it or anything, but sometimes I find things funny when they really, really aren't.

It's a scarf on a pole on an abandoned building, I think as I look at the panicking people around me, and I don't even try to hold my laughter in.

"Grace, come on," Noah says, reaching for me.

"It's a scarf," I say. "A *scarf.*"

I've been awake for almost forty-eight hours. I'm jet-lagged and exhausted, tired of these people and their drama.

"It's not like it's an international incident." I look from Lila to Megan to Rosie, and then finally I let my gaze linger on Noah, who eases closer, lowers his voice.

"Actually, Grace, it kind of is. We're Israeli. And *that* is Iran."

When I look back at the blue-and-white scarf, I realize that, from a distance, it bears a striking resemblance to the flag of Lila and Noah's home nation.

"The Israeli ambassador gave that scarf to our mom. In fact, he gave scarves like it to *all* of the women on his senior staff," Noah says. "If anyone sees that up there..."

Lila grabs Megan and the two of them move toward the trees. Most of the others have already started the climb down the overgrown path.

"So don't let anyone see." I shrug. "Go get it."

"We can't!" Noah snaps. He's not mad. He's scared. And I know that being friends with me is already far more trouble than he bargained for. "We can't just traipse into Iran anytime we feel like it."

"I can get it," I say.

"Really, Grace?" Noah asks. I can hear his impatience, his nerves. "What can you do?"

"This," I say.

I don't stop for anything. Not for protests, not for logic. I don't care about the height of the cliffs or the rocks that line the shore.

I run as hard and as fast as I can toward the ledge and then I reach out my arms, swan-diving into the sea.

Adria has the deepest shoreline on the Mediterranean, and that's how I know the fall won't kill me. Still, my stomach stays on the cliffs even as my body hurtles through the salty air. I feel free and just a little bit aware that I might be wrong. I know, deep down, that I should be terrified. But I'm not. So I close my eyes and breathe out as I hit the water. Cold swallows me. My lungs burn. And that is how I know I'm still alive.

By the time I crawl out of the water and onto the sandy beach, they've turned off the music. Or maybe I just can't hear it from here. There is nothing but the sound of the waves crashing onto the beach and then receding slowly back to sea – like an infantry trying to take the shore, pushing against it wave upon wave, going nowhere.

The wind is cold, and it hits me, chills me through my jeans and wet shirt. I push my hair out of my face, and realize that I survived the fall, but pneumonia might totally get me. And I decide that that's OK.

Noah was right. The Iranian embassy's property actually stretches right out to the beach. I stumble along soft, wet sand fit for a five-star resort. When the clouds shift I see a crumbling fence failing to keep the world at bay.

The boards are rotting. A weather-beaten sign announces *Keep Out* in five different languages as it dangles by a single nail over a place where the sand has been washed away. This is where I cross, crawling slowly, carefully, on my stomach like all new recruits are taught to do during basic training. I used to run that obstacle course just for fun every chance I got. It feels strangely just like coming home as I slowly slither, inching into the sovereign nation of Iran.

Inside the fence, I wait for something to change. A light to flip on. A siren to sound. For a moment, I stand silently in the dark, heart pounding in my chest, but nothing changes. No one comes. I am alone as I cross the final stretch of private beach toward the high stone wall that surrounds the entire city and, with it, the back of the mansion.

An iron gate hangs between the wall and the base of the cliffs. There is an arching doorway that actually leads *through* the massive wall that rings the city. This old passageway is why the Iranians are the only embassy on the row with private beach access. The passageway was probably well hidden five hundred years ago, but the Iranians were no doubt more concerned with reaching the beach than keeping out invaders, so they left it there, exposed for all the world to see. Whatever guards were once posted there are now long gone.

Once I break that barrier, I know there will be no going back, no good excuses. It should bother me, I'm certain. If I had good sense. If I had the proper amount of fear and respect for authority. But I'm not thinking about Ms Chancellor and her warnings; I'm too busy thinking about Lila and her smirk.

I step into the courtyard.

There are a few chairs and tables. Trees line the wall, but mostly the space has been taken over by grass and weeds and bushes that have grown, unchecked, for decades.

I hear a flapping noise, the gentle metallic sound of a chain banging against metal. Even in the dark, it's easy to see the blue-and-white scarf that has wrapped itself around a flagpole on the very top of the building.

I search the back of the four-story structure, but there is no fire escape, no ladder that I can see. There's not even a drainpipe or tree that I can scamper up. But there is a broken window. A few stray shards of glass cling to the inside of the frame, so I'm careful as I reach to unlock it, slide the broken section up, and ease my way inside.

The floorboards are rotten, at least in the place where I'm standing. I have no way of knowing when the window broke, but it's probably been years. Decades even. Rain and sand have collected here, and when I start to move,

I feel the floorboards shift. I smell mold and dust and abandonment. I almost feel sorry for the building.

When I ease away from the window, the floor starts to feel more solid. There are once-marvelous chandeliers above me, dusty and dim. Part of me wants to reach out and try a switch but I know better. At best, there is no electricity to the building. At worst, there will be and the sight of a light burning will bring about all the things I'm here to stop. So I creep on carefully, silently, through the dark.

I pass through a long room with a dining table that seats thirty. In the parlor, there are dusty paintings and furniture covered with dingy white sheets. Room after room I see, all of them furnished and lived in, yet empty and abandoned. It feels as if a very large family simply picked up and left for the season, as if they were going to come back just as soon as some mysterious drama were over. But, I guess, some dramas never do end.

When I reach the broad, sweeping staircase I move faster. It feels like the US embassy, so my feet grow more certain as they run, taking the stairs two at a time.

The full moon slices through the windows, the only light in the dark, dusty space. I break through cobwebs as I reach the second story and then the third. That's where I find a smaller, more utilitarian staircase, so I take it to the highest floor.

Here the ceiling is lower, the rooms smaller. If I'm right, then the flagpole is directly above me. There has to be a way to reach it, so I glance out a window and find a small metal landing. I ease carefully outside and see a ladder rising from the landing to the roof.

I'm careful as I climb. The ladder is old and hasn't been used in ages, but it holds my weight. The worst part is that I'm now on the side of the building. Someone could see me from the Italian embassy next door; I could be spotted from the street. So I move as quickly as I dare up the side of the building, then climb out onto the flat section of roof where the flagpole stands.

From here, the sea is gorgeous. I turn to my left and take a second I don't have to scan down the long line of embassies. I can make out thirteen flagpoles all in a row, waving in the glow of their spotlights, ringing the wall like soldiers.

A security car is driving down the street, a searchlight washing over the exteriors of the embassies, their fences and gates. When it flashes onto the roof of Iran, I fall, crashing hard onto my stomach, lying perfectly still upon the roof. I move my head slightly, just enough to see the top of the beam of light catch the bottom of the scarf's fluttering edge. And then the light is gone.

I wait a second, then bolt to my feet and start untangling the scarf from the pole. But it's so twisted and snagged that I have to pull the tiny knife that my father got me for my birthday from my pocket and saw away at the silk.

Soon it's in my hands and I'm wrapping it around my wrist over and over before I climb down the ladder so quickly I almost lose my grip.

I throw my leg over the windowsill and scurry back into the embassy's fourth-story hallway, slam the window closed behind me, and start to run down the stairs.

I'm going too quickly. I'm going to fall. *Someone is going to hear me*, I think, before I remember I'm alone. And yet I cannot shake the feeling that I'm wrong.

I listen for my mother's voice, but it doesn't come. I have no memory of her here, in this building where I have never been. But I swear that I hear footsteps, that someone's on my tail.

When I reach the main landing, I turn and rush down a hallway, toward a narrow alley I saw from the roof. I have to get out of here. I have to give Lila back her scarf and return to my own embassy, my mother's bed. There are ghosts inside these shadows, I'm certain. I can feel them. So I run faster.

I hurl myself around a corner, then skid to a stop, breathing hard, staring down at a massive, gaping hole in the floor. The boards are rotten and broken. What was probably once an incredibly expensive Persian rug hangs over the edge, like a piece of asphalt not quite taken by a sinkhole. Down below, I see water glistening, hear the *drop, drop, drop* of more water falling into a huge, ornate swimming pool that lies in the basement.

I stand on the precipice, listening to the water drip – my heart pounding.

When a voice says, "We shouldn't be meeting here," I can't be sure that I'm not dreaming. The man speaks in Adrian, but it's the language my mother spoke to me just like her mother spoke it to her. Without trying, I understand every word.

"In Adria, the walls always have ears," someone else answers. "What better reason to meet in Iran?"

The man's laugh is low and dark. Perhaps it is the decaying building, but it sounds sinister and menacing. I expect there to be sharks circling in the swimming pool, a cable with acid dripping onto it, ready to plunge me to my death.

I step back, but I move too fast and the floorboards creak beneath my feet. For a moment, I think I'm going to crash right through the rotten wood, onto the men below me. But I don't fall. Instead I stand perfectly still, waiting.

"What was that?" one of the men asks.

"Your nerves are not what they used to be, my friend," the other man says.

And then one of the men walks to the pool. He looks down into the almost-still water. Silently, I gasp but force myself to stand motionless, knowing that if he looks up, he'll see me. And if he sees me…

I refuse to think about what happened the last time someone saw me.

For a long moment, the man keeps his gaze locked on the pool, almost like he's lost in thought.

"Are we going to have a problem?" the unseen man asks.

"I have no reason to think so," the man by the pool says.

"But if a problem develops…"

"Then I will deal with it." The man places his hands in his pockets and turns to his companion. "I always do."

The basement is dim – the hallway only lit by moonlight. The whole building is a kaleidoscope of dark and light blending into swirling shadows. But for a second I see him clearly – I really do. Dark hair speckled with gray. A nice suit. A strong jaw.

A scar.

I am absolutely certain that I see a scar.

And that is why my hands shake. My lips tremble and I squeeze them together, swallowing the cry that is rising in my throat, fighting against the tears that fill my eyes.

And then I *do* hear my mother's voice. A haunting cry. "*Grace, no!*" she tells me.

It is the last thing she will ever tell me.

As soon as the Scarred Man steps out of sight I stumble backward. Somehow, I make myself inch slowly, quietly, down the hall. When I reach the broken window I hurl myself through it, and then my feet begin to move faster and faster, running back the way I came, through the overgrown courtyard and the broken gate, back across the soft, sandy beach.

I hate my footsteps, how easy it will be for someone to see where I've been. But I don't dare stop to smooth the sand behind me.

I'm on my stomach, belly-crawling back beneath the wooden fence, onto public land, when my shoulders leave the ground completely. Suddenly, I'm slammed into the rotting fence. I can feel the raised letters of the *Keep Out* sign through my wet shirt as I look up at the big, blue eyes that stare at me.

I tremble as Alexei says, “Grace, what have you done?”

I can't feel the pavement anymore. Alexi is gripping my arm so tightly that my fingers have started to tingle. He doesn't speak again, though. He just half drags, half carries me down Embassy Row. My mind is still back at that swimming pool. When I start to shake, I blame my wet clothes, the cold wind. I don't dare say a word of protest. I let Alexei drag me along.

"Grace!" someone yells.

I stop, but Alexei tugs me harder. "I am taking you home," he says through gritted teeth.

"Grace!" Noah's footsteps are heavy and loud on the street behind us. When he finally catches up, he cuts us off and then leans over at the waist, panting. "Are you OK?"

"I'm fine," I tell him.

"She won't be when I'm finished with her," Alexei snarls.

I see Lila then, and Megan. They ease out of the

shadows in front of the German embassy. Rosie must already be inside.

Lila isn't looking at me, though. "Hi, Alexei," she purrs as she eases closer.

"Hi." Alexei's voice is gruff. He never loosens his hold on my arm. "I'm taking Grace back to her embassy. I'd suggest you all go home as well."

"How did you find me?" My voice cracks and I can't stop shaking even with the heat of Alexei's hand on my arm.

"Megan called me. She was worried."

And now I know the answer to my question: Megan is definitely not my friend.

"It was that or call my mom," she says, defiant.

But Noah just keeps looking at me.

"I can't believe you're OK," he says. A nervous laugh escapes his lips, but it's too loud on the quiet street, so he pulls his hands down to cover his mouth. It doesn't hide the look in his eyes, though. Relief. "You're OK," he says again. "When you jumped I thought—"

"Say good night, Grace," Alexei tells me with a tug on my arm.

It takes all my strength to hold my ground and push the now torn and ragged piece of silk in Lila's direction.

"Here's your scarf," I force out.

"Thanks," Lila says, but she keeps looking at me as if whatever's wrong with me might be contagious.

Then I tug myself free of Alexei's grasp and push ahead of him. Overhead, the streetlights flicker and fade.

I'm shrouded in shadow as the street curves and I pause, press myself against the fence that surrounds the US embassy. I'm almost home. Or, the building that will pass for home for the foreseeable future. I'm almost safe.

And maybe that's why I stop. I lean against the stone and the cold comes. My clothes are still wet. My hair has started to dry, and it clings to my face and to my neck. I want a hot shower, to feel the ocean and the sand washing off of me, pouring down my back.

"What were you thinking?" Alexei asks when he comes around the corner and finds me. But before I can answer, my brother's best friend studies me anew. Alexei places a hand on my arm and I know that I am rocking slightly, back and forth. The others round the corner, and I see the looks on the faces that stare back at me, and I know what they are thinking.

I know because I've seen them before. The worried looks and cryptic glances. I can almost hear the whispers that will follow in my wake.

When Alexei speaks, he sounds like Jamie. "What is wrong with you?"

But this time I know better. This time, I lie.

"I'm fine. Just cold. Tired."

"Grace—"

"Leave me alone, Alexei." I try to push past him. Adrenaline is coming back in a heady, overwhelming rush. My voice is ice. "I am not your problem."

"You're Jamie's problem. And since Jamie isn't here..." He lets the words draw out, smiles at me – a look that is part dare, part charm, and I hate him for it. For how easy life must be for him. I wish I were bigger, stronger. Male. I wish I could make people stop worrying about me and my so-called frailness. And if they can't forget to worry about me, then I wish they would just forget about me completely.

"You don't get to boss me around just because I'm a girl, you know."

"No." He eases closer. Part of me is happy for the warmth, but the rest of me wants to cut that part out, toss it in the sea. "I get to be the boss of you because you're Jamie's kid sister and Jamie isn't here."

"Well, that's his problem."

"No. It's my problem." Alexei leans closer. I shake harder. "Do you have any idea where you were? What would have happened if someone – anyone – had seen you in there?"

I do know. I know exactly, but I can't give him the satisfaction of hearing me say the words. Besides, the lecture is coming no matter what I say. If there's one thing my life has taught me it's that the lecture is *always* coming. That's why I don't tell him about the men; I don't dare mention the scar. It will be like it never happened.

With any luck, even *I* will eventually forget that it happened. Even if I know it did.

"I paid the neighbors a visit. Sue me."

"I'm going to do far worse than that," Alexei snaps. Then he softens. "You are the daughter of a major in the United States Army. You are the granddaughter of the

United States' foremost ambassador to Europe. You cannot break into embassies of hostile governments, Grace. I didn't realize someone had to spell that out to you, but I'm spelling it out now."

"Leave me alone, Alexei," I say, my voice cracking. I hate how badly I'm shaking. I want to pull my treacherous tongue right out of my throat.

"There's something you're not telling me," Alexei says. He could always do that – see through me. I used to think it was Jamie, letting him in on all of my tells. But Alexei has grown up on this curvy street. He knows all the languages. Even mine.

"What is it, Grace? What is it you aren't telling me?"

I think about the men in the basement, the voices, the ominous drip, drip, dripping of the water. And, again, I shiver. I do not say the things that I have sworn to never say again.

Instead I say good night.

Alexei doesn't stop me when I pull away and start toward the gate, but I can hear his footsteps behind me, echoing my own.

"You're following me," I say.

"Yes, I am."

"That's really annoying."

"I'm sure it probably feels that way, yes."

I stop. "I can take care of myself." Overhead, the gas in the streetlamp surges. It grows brighter, harsher. There are no shadows anywhere as he looks at me.

"That's exactly what worries me."

He doesn't say another word as I step toward the gate and the marine who stands there, keeping guard.

No one questions my appearance or the hour – they're tasked with keeping threats out, not teenage girls in.

I don't pass a soul as I race up the stairs and into my mother's room, closing the door firmly behind me.

The window is open. The cold wind blows inside and I rush toward it. I don't ever want to feel that wind again. But as my hand lands on the frame, I see Rosie standing on the wall, looking at me. Slowly, she raises one hand in something that's not quite a salute, not quite a wave.

I wave back and close the window, then silently draw the shades.

When I wake, it takes a long time to remember where I am. Then I move my arms, trying to assure myself of where I'm *not.* The bed is soft and warm, so I know that last night I didn't have an incident. But I also know that what happened wasn't a dream. Oh how I wish it were a dream…

The Scarred Man was there.

I lie perfectly still, trying to control my breathing, desperate to convince myself that I could have been seeing things. I could have been hearing things. After all, I was jet-lagged and exhausted, compromised by adrenaline and subpar lighting. I try to tell myself there was no Scarred Man last night – that I have absolutely nothing to fear. But that's before I roll over and kick the woman sitting on the end of my bed.

"Good morning, Grace," Ms Chancellor says. She's wearing a purple suit today, but it's almost a carbon copy of the same one she wore yesterday. "It's time to get up, dear."

"And what time is that?"

"Almost seven."

I huff and roll over. I was sneaking into a hostile country just five hours ago. But I can't tell Ms Chancellor that.

"I'm jet-lagged," I say, pulling my pillow over my head to block out the light that streams through the window. She must have opened the shades.

Ms Chancellor pulls my pillow away. "The best way to combat jet lag is to put yourself on your new time as quickly as possible. Now, come on. Up. Up. Up."

She's laughing as she says it, teasing. She really wants to be my friend, I realize, and suddenly I feel sorry for her. She doesn't know what a terrible thing it is she's asking for.

"Is *he* up?" I ask, pushing myself upright.

"Your grandfather has always been an early riser. Well, he has been for as long as I've known him. I'm afraid he can't join us for breakfast, though. He had an early meeting at the palace."

"Well, if he was needed at the *palace*..."

Ms Chancellor forces a smile. "Why don't you get dressed, Grace? Come downstairs. There is something you and I need to discuss over breakfast."

When Ms Chancellor leaves, I go into the bathroom. My mother kept snapshots tucked inside the mirror's frame. There are probably a dozen, and I have no choice but to study them as I brush my teeth.

Mom and the grandmother I never knew. My mother and her best friend, smiling on the beach. Mom with me as a little girl, sitting at Grandpa's desk. Part of me wants to yell and scream and throw every piece of my dead mother out the window. But I just put my toothbrush in the cup beside hers. I pull my hair onto the top of my head and go downstairs.

When I reach the doors to the dining room, Ms Chancellor is standing behind a chair at the head of a table that probably seats at least forty. Maybe fifty. I don't stop to count. I'm too busy staring at the silverware, and then wondering if you can still call it silverware if it's actually made of gold.

"Come in, Grace," Ms Chancellor tells me.

"I usually eat in the kitchen."

"Come in," she says again. "And close the doors."

"Yes, ma'am."

I'm careful to do exactly as she says as I walk around the edge of the room, as far away from the ornately set table as possible.

None of our plates at home even match, I realize. One of the many downsides of moving every six to eighteen months of your life. I learned from an early age to never own anything I didn't want to end up in a million pieces at the bottom of a box.

"I thought you were getting dressed," Ms Chancellor says, and I look down at the T-shirt I slept in, my yoga pants with a bleach stain on the hem. I bring my hand up to touch the ponytail that sits lopsided on the top of my head and regret every decision I've ever made. Ever. Which makes this a perfectly average morning. Just with better silver- (or gold-) ware.

"Oh. Right. Sorry. You know, I think I left an iron on upstairs, and I—"

"Grace, if you have used an iron within the last six months, I will eat that fork," Ms Chancellor says.

"Which one?" I try to tease. "You've got a lot of forks to choose from."

"*From which to choose*, Grace. Do not end your sentences in prepositions, dear."

"Of course. I totally see what you're getting at. I mean, at what you're getting."

I force a smile and move to the head of the table, take hold of the chair, but before I can pull it back, Ms Chancellor singsongs, "*Not that chair.*"

"OK," I say, moving to the chair beside it.

"And not yet," Ms Chancellor says, moving to the head of the table. "You may sit after the head of the table sits, Grace. Never before."

"OK," I say as she sits down regally. When she nods, I take the chair beside her.

"Have you ever studied etiquette, dear?"

"Yeah. My dad and brother were super big on that. Right after they covered the proper cleaning and storage of military-grade side arms, of course."

"Grace." The word is a warning.

"What?" I ask.

"I'm serious."

"I know. I'm sorry." And the bizarre part is that I really am. I want to be good, to use the right fork and wear a pretty linen dress to breakfast. I want to be the girl in the pictures upstairs. But I can't be. That girl is dead.

"Your arrival here is quite good timing. Did you know that?" Ms Chancellor takes the napkin and places it gently in her lap.

I mimic the gesture as I tell her, "Uh...no. I didn't know."

It hadn't seemed like good timing to me.

I don't pick up my gold fork until Ms Chancellor picks up hers. I mimic everything, right down to the small sliver of ham she slices and puts in her mouth.

"Oh, well, Adria is a place that takes its traditions very seriously. History matters here, in the best possible sense. And one of the traditions that matters most is about to be upon us."

"Oh." I prepare to take another bite. "What would that be?"

"Every year, the ambassadors who are stationed here must visit the palace and present their credentials to the king. It's a very old, very important tradition."

"OK," I say, then risk a sip of water.

"Always wipe your mouth before you take a drink, Grace."

"OK," I say one more time, not fighting it. I'm just happy to, at last, be eating.

"As it happens, the presentation-of-the-credentials

ceremony is tomorrow night at the palace."

"That's nice," I say, still unclear what any of this could possibly have to do with me.

"Oh, it is *very* nice." Ms Chancellor chuckles a little. "In fact, technically, it's *a ball*." I wipe my mouth and reach for my juice as Ms Chancellor finishes, "And you are going to be your grandfather's date."

That is when I spit juice all over Ms Chancellor and her pretty purple suit.

"No."

I don't wait for Ms Chancellor to stand before I bolt to my feet. It's all the proof they should need that they are after the wrong girl. I drop my linen napkin on the floor for good measure.

"No. Just no," I say.

"Grace." Ms Chancellor is trying to come after me, but I'm moving too fast. I have always been fast. "Grace, hear me out."

"I'm sorry," I say, turning briefly to glance at the woman behind me. "I mean no, *thank you.*"

When I reach the doors, I try to throw them open – but there must be some kind of trick to the latch, because they don't budge.

"The tradition is three hundred years old."

"Then they know how to do it without me!"

"It is an essential part of maintaining our place in

diplomatic society! Without it, the United States would no longer have diplomatic status here."

"All the more reason to leave it to the professionals," I tell her.

Ms Chancellor takes my shaking hands, pulls them away from the door. "Grace, you are officially the lady of this house. It is your duty to be by your grandfather's side at events like this. Like it or not, your country needs you."

She knows how to play me – I'll give Ms Chancellor that much. Honor. Country. Code. These are the things that have been drilled into me all of my life.

"Grace" – she grips my shaking hands harder – "it has been a very long time since your grandfather has had someone by his side. The other ambassadors, they bring their spouses. Their children. But your grandfather... Please do this. For him. For your mother. Or, better yet, do it for yourself."

She's looking at me now – not at my stained yoga pants and messy hair. She's looking at *me*, as if maybe a part of me actually does resemble the girl with the pink canopy bed. Like maybe I might belong here after all.

But she's wrong. And I don't have the heart to say so.

"I..." I start slowly. My voice is more of a whisper than a scream. It's harder than it should be to admit, "I don't know what to do."

Ms Chancellor smiles. The doors pick that moment to slide open, and I see Noah standing there. He must have been holding them closed all this time.

"That is why I'm here," he says.

Before I can do anything, Ms Chancellor is embracing Noah in a hug. He wears a polo shirt with a navy blazer and khaki slacks. His hair is slicked back and his posture is perfect. He looks like diplomacy personified, and I can't help thinking that this is a boy who knows his way around the goldware.

"Thank you so much for coming," Ms Chancellor says, then turns to me. "Grace, this is Noah Estaban. He's offered to help us. Plus, I thought you two should know each other."

"I—" I start, but Noah quickly holds out a hand, cutting me off.

"Hello, Grace. It's so nice to finally meet you," he says. When Ms Chancellor looks away, he winks.

"Oh. Yes. It's nice to meet you, too," I say.

"Noah's mother is one of my dearest friends and one of the most cultured women I know," Ms Chancellor says.

"But she wasn't available, so I'm afraid you're stuck with me," Noah quips and flashes the kind of grin that grown-ups love. "Don't worry, Grace. I've been doing this stuff for years. A bow here. A curtsy there. You'll do fine."

"Yes. Because you know me. I *live* to curtsy."

Ms Chancellor ignores my sarcasm, and Noah offers me his arm.

"Stick with me, kid."

I know I don't really know Noah. One moonlit excursion doesn't count for much in the grand scheme of things. But I look at the boy beside me, so confident and comfortable. He's different from the boy on the cliffs. He's not in either of his countries, but I can't shake the feeling that Noah is back on his home turf.

"Shall we begin with a waltz?" Ms Chancellor asks.

"What do you say, Grace?" Noah eyes me. "Shall we?"

There's no furniture in the room next door. I know why as soon as Ms Chancellor leads us inside, walks to an old-fashioned record player, and drops the needle on a vinyl album. It scratches to life, and soon we aren't two twenty-first-century teens being drawn into an archaic tradition. No. We are two young people transported back in time. The grand room makes sense. My messy hair is all but forgotten as Noah places his hand at the small of my back.

"Yes. Very nice. Very nice," Ms Chancellor says. "Now, Grace. Chin up. Shoulders back. And follow Noah's lead."

"Hear that, Grace?" Noah asks. "Follow my lead."

When we start to dance, I don't protest. Noah is pretty good at this. At least, I do more stepping on his feet than he does stepping on mine.

There is a parquet floor beneath my feet and antique sconces on the walls. The record is decades old, and for a moment I feel timeless, weightless, and unafraid.

When we make it to the other side of the room, Noah leans a little closer and lowers his voice.

"So last night..." he starts, and it all comes rushing back to me.

The cliffs.

The party.

The Scarred Man.

I'm starting to shake as Noah goes on. "We aren't going to have a repeat of that little performance anytime soon, are we?"

"Did Alexei feed you that line or did you come up with it all on your own?" I ask.

We dance a little more. From the other side of the room, I can hear Ms Chancellor chanting, "One two three. One two three."

"What you did was dangerous. You know that, right? It was insanely, ridiculously, freakishly dangerous."

I stare up at him. "It was a calculated risk."

"Chin up, Noah. Shoulders back!" Ms Chancellor chides.

"Besides, if I'm not mistaken, I kind of saved your sister's hide," I tell him. It's meant to sting, but he smiles instead.

"Thank you." He glances away. "Don't do it again. But thank you."

"*You're* not the one who owes me," I point out.

He nods. "Yeah, well, Lila is…Lila. I'm just grateful that she didn't eat me in the womb."

"Grace, dear, the waltz is not what one would call a humorous dance," Ms Chancellor scolds when I start laughing.

"Noah?" I say once I've regained my composure.

"What?" Noah asks.

"Do people ever go in there?"

"Where?"

"*There*," I say.

"In the *Iranian embassy*?" Noah whispers, glancing to where Ms Chancellor stands on the far side of the room, thumbing through a stack of records. "Is that what you're asking? Do people ever go *in the Iranian embassy*?"

"I take that as a no."

"No. That's an *are you out of your mind?* Wait – what am I saying?" he asks with a shake of his head. "You jumped off a cliff. *Of course* you're out of your mind."

"It's just…" I can't find the words – or maybe the strength – to finish.

"It's just what?" There's an edge to Noah's voice. He's known me less than twenty-four hours and already he knows he should be worried about whatever is going to come next.

"I heard something." As I say it, the music fades away. In my mind, I can hear the creaking floor, the scurrying vermin. And the voices. I can see the man with the scar.

I cannot forget the man with the scar.

"When I was in there," I go on, "I thought I *heard something*."

"The place has been abandoned for years. The whole building is probably falling down. Half the rats in Valancia live in there. I'm sure you heard a lot of things."

The needle scratches. The music stops for real this time. In the silence I whisper, "Voices, Noah. I heard voices."

"You did not hear voices."

"But—"

"No one goes in there, Grace. No one. And that includes you. OK?"

"OK," I tell him.

"OK," Ms Chancellor parrots the word but not the tone. She slaps her hands together, obviously pleased with our morning thus far. "I believe we are ready for phase two."

Noah says goodbye even though I beg him to stay. I'm far less likely to kill Ms Chancellor if there's a witness.

"No boys allowed for phase two," Ms Chancellor teases as she pulls me toward the open doors across the hall. "Look at these, Grace. Aren't they beautiful?"

She honestly sounds like a schoolgirl as she walks toward the racks of clothes that fill what is usually a formal living room. Now the furniture has been pushed aside. There are long rolling racks covered with dresses. Stacks and stacks of shoe boxes.

But the worst part isn't the rows of clothes and shoes. It's the girl who stands on the opposite side of the room, staring at me.

"Megan!" Ms Chancellor throws open her arms. "Hello, dear." She gives Megan a big hug, then pulls away. "Did you see Grace is back with us?"

Megan did see me. She saw me jump off a cliff and

crawl under an Iranian fence. Megan has seen plenty. And I can't help but hold my breath, waiting on her answer.

"Hi," Megan says, turning to me. "Welcome home."

Home. The word hits me. I've spent all my life thinking that I didn't have one, but now that I'm back I can't deny that I've spent more of my life on Embassy Row than in any other place – that maybe it wasn't just my mother's childhood home. In a way, it's mine, too.

"Thanks," I tell Megan. Then I turn to the rows and rows of dresses. "Where did you get these?"

"All the designers, dear," Ms Chancellor says. "It's the event of the season in Adria."

"Then I shouldn't go," I say, looking only at Ms Chancellor, trying to make her understand.

"Nonsense," Ms Chancellor says before stage-whispering to Megan, "Grace doesn't think the ball sounds like very much fun. What do you think we're going to have to do to convince her?"

"Obstacle courses help," I say. "I'm really, really good at obstacle courses."

"I bet you do an excellent belly-crawl."

Megan's voice is flat. Our stares lock. This is how things are going to be, I can tell. Her knowing something that can destroy me. Me waiting for her to either throw the grenade or put the pin back in.

"Yes," I say slowly. "I'm a good person to have around in a crisis."

If Ms Chancellor hears the undertones of our exchange, she doesn't show it.

"What about this one for Grace?" Megan asks, selecting a gown that is long and puffy and very, very pink. "The color will look good with your skin."

I want to glare at her. I am as pale as ice in winter except for when I'm angry or embarrassed, and then my cheeks go red.

In other words, my cheeks are almost always red.

Megan has maybe the prettiest skin that I have ever seen. Her hair is sleek and black, perfectly straight and constantly shiny. My hair is thin and shoulder length and looks like the stuff you pull out of the dryer after doing a load of yellow towels.

But Megan just holds the dress up against my skin as if to prove her point.

"Oh, I love that," Ms Chancellor says.

The dress is the color and texture of cotton candy, with a tight bodice and a long, full skirt. There must be acres and acres of fabric.

"That's called a princess cut," Ms Chancellor says, eyeing me over the top of her glasses. *But I'm no princess*, I want to say.

"I've never seen you wear pink before, but I always thought you should," Megan tells me, and something in the words makes me panic. *Always thought you should.*

That's when I realize that Megan knows me.

Even worse, Megan *knew* me.

Before.

There is a privacy screen set up in the corner of the room. I freeze as I recognize it, as I remember.

"Grace..." My mother steps out from behind the screen, then spins around. Her dress is long and white with beautiful black lace covering the bodice. She actually does look like a princess. "What do you think?"

"So, Grace..." Megan's voice is too loud. I shudder. "What do you think?"

"What?" I say, remembering where and when I am.

"The dress?" Megan's arms look like they are filled with cotton candy. "Do you want to try it on?"

"It won't fit," I say. "See, it's dragging on the floor."

"That's a train, dear," Ms Chancellor tells me, and she and Megan share a chuckle at my expense.

"You have to try it on," Megan says.

"I don't have to do anything," I counter.

"Sure you do. It's as easy as, say, jumping off a cliff." Megan crosses her arms, and I know she's got me, so I go behind a screen and try to wiggle into the contraption. But there are so many straps and zippers and hooks that Megan has to come help me.

While I slip out of my clothes, she takes the dress off the hanger. It puddles on the floor like a pale-pink volcano.

"So, how have you been?"

Is she asking for Ms Chancellor's benefit or her own? I honestly don't know, so I say, "Fine."

She helps me step into the dress then work it up over my hips.

"I'm sorry about your mom," she says as she finds the zipper.

"Thanks."

"I thought I'd see you at the funeral, but..."

"Yeah. Couldn't make it. Got tied up." If she hears the bitterness in my voice, she ignores it.

"Suck in."

I do as she says.

"Did you get my letters?" she asks.

"Yeah. Thanks," I say. "I was going to write back, but..."

"It's OK. I know."

And the scary part is that I think she really does.

When Megan speaks again, her voice is a whisper. "So are you going to tell me what happened last night?"

"You were there. You saw what happened."

"No. Last night...that wasn't you."

"The last time you saw me I was jumping off the wall, Megan."

Megan's gaze burns into me. She isn't backing down. "You were always a daredevil, but you never had a death wish. The girl I knew was always running toward something. Last night...you were running away."

"Megan, I'm fine," I say again, but Megan just shakes her head.

"No, you're not."

She pulls the zipper up. Smooths the fabric into place. And then she walks away. I hear the door open and close, and there is no doubt in my mind that she is gone.

"Grace?" Ms Chancellor calls over the screen. "Grace, let's see the dress."

"No." I shake my head, emphatic, as if she can see

me. I can handle stressful situations. I am equipped. Prepared. Drop me into a war zone and I'll be fine. But this is different.

"Grace, tomorrow night is very important for your grandfather." Ms Chancellor's voice is low. Her words sound mildly like a threat.

"Then he should ask me!" I don't mean to shout – but I can't stop myself. The dress is too tight and I can't breathe.

"He should talk to me," I go on. "He doesn't want me here. And he really doesn't need me at some fancy party where all I'll do is embarrass him."

Ms Chancellor doesn't bite back. She doesn't snap. She just steps calmly forward and pulls me from behind the screen. "He wants you here, Grace. He has been alone in his duties for a very long time. And he is going to want you with him tomorrow night."

She stops and steps back, points to the full-length mirror that someone has leaned against the opposite wall. I can see the girl who stands there. Long, billowing pinkness over very pale skin. The same shade of pink fills my cheeks.

Ms Chancellor smiles. "And he is going to want you wearing this."

The next day is a blur of dress fittings and dance lessons and trips to various salons with Ms Chancellor. Some of her instruments of torture are hot. Some are cold. Some are hard and some are soft. All are dangerous, I decide.

If the army knew about curling irons, basic training might look very, very different.

It's almost six when we make our way downstairs.

"Stand up straight, Grace," Ms Chancellor tells me, as if I have any choice in the matter. My dress is so tight I couldn't slouch if I wanted to. I'm pretty sure they're going to have to tie me to the hood of the car to get me to the palace.

"You look lovely, dear," Ms Chancellor tells me with a smile. Her dress is long and black. She wears a shiny blue wrap around her shoulders and has piled her auburn hair on top of her head. I can't quite decide if her sapphire earrings are real or not, but then I know they must be. Ms Chancellor is simply *not* the kind of woman to put up with imitations.

"You look nice, too," I tell her. I am gripping the rail too tightly. I really don't want to fall.

"Thank you, Grace." She smiles at me and takes my free hand. "It's going to be a wonderful evening."

And I know she means it – she really does. This is her world. Her domain. Politics and intricate back-alley deals, trade alliances formed over champagne and shrimp cocktail.

"Well, there are my girls!"

My grandfather has a big, booming voice that fills any room. It floats up the stairs and greets us.

Then he throws open the door. "Let's go."

They don't tie me to the hood of the stretch limo that waits outside. But I wish they would. I half sit, half lean along the seat, my back to the driver. Grandpa and Ms Chancellor sit across from me. They don't touch. But there is an easiness between them, a comfort borne from twenty-five years of late nights and early mornings, good times and bad.

"You clean up real good, kid," Grandpa says, but he's not looking at me. He slaps Ms Chancellor's hand. "Now, how about me?"

"You look like a man who has never quite mastered the bow tie." She takes his shoulders and turns him to face her. "Here."

As Ms Chancellor goes to work on his tie, he shifts his gaze to me.

"You, too, Gracie. I almost didn't recognize you with the dirt washed off. No casts?"

"Not yet, sir."

"Good." He eyes my dress. "So how many people had to force you into that thing?"

"Just her. But she's stronger than she looks."

Ms Chancellor pulls his tie tight. He grunts.

"Tell me about it," Grandpa says.

"I'll have you know, William, that Grace is very excited to be taking part in her first official function."

"Her first!" Grandpa sounds almost nostalgic. He turns and looks out the tinted window at the scene that is rolling by. Ancient buildings and cobblestone streets. Bicyclists and fruit stands. As we climb higher and higher toward the city center, we can glimpse more and more of the sea.

"My first came six months after I got here. There I was, fresh off the boat, just a junior State Department employee at the time, and I was told to go to the palace. The king's father was on the throne then. He was a big man, powerful. World-class polo player, they said, but if you ask me, so few people play polo, how hard could it be to be world-class, really?" Grandpa considers this for a moment and then talks on.

"Anyway, the president was supposed to visit that day, but something came up at the last minute and he needed to cancel. And instead of calling on the king himself, the ambassador at the time sends *me*, hat in hand, up to the palace to make our apologies."

Grandpa laughs a little at the memory. I try to imagine him as a young man, insecure and frightened, but the mental picture simply doesn't fit. I can't see him as anything but a senior statesman.

"So the palace officials put me in an elevator and take me down to the basement. I thought I was going to an office or a study or something – probably to see an aide. But no. It was the pool. Hot springs run underneath the whole city, you see. And there is the king himself, climbing out of the water. Naked as the day he was born. Ha!" Grandpa slaps his leg. Ms Chancellor demurely covers her smirking lips. "Then His Royal Highness proceeds to stand there stark naked through the whole talk. Lots of bowing and apologizing on my end. And then the king – the *naked king* – says, 'Oh well. I guess I have time to get back in. Why don't you join me?'"

“What did you do?” I ask.

“What could I do? I joined him!”

“So you took a bath with the king of Adria?”

“I did indeed, Gracie. I did indeed.” He gives a very mischievous grin. “So just keep that dress on tonight and you’ll be ahead of me.”

“I promise I’ll try.”

Those are the words that are still in the air when the limo slows and turns through the palace gates. When a uniformed man opens the limo’s door, I glance down at the red carpet that runs to the palace’s massive doors. Grandpa exits the car first and offers his arm to me.

“You ready, Gracie?” he asks with a wink.

I smile and look up at the white-haired man who, to me, is little more than a stranger.

“Absolutely,” I lie.

"Ambassador William Vincent of the United States of America!"

The small man has a huge voice. It booms through the ballroom, over the low din of chatter and the faint sound of the string quartet playing in the distance. He wears a red jacket with military medals I don't recognize, a rank and regiment I don't know.

Grandpa and I have been standing in line for ten minutes. I've already lost the feeling in both of my big toes. But now that we've been announced, I'm expected to walk. And smile. I can see Noah on the far side of the room. When I catch his eye, he gives me a low, exaggerated curtsy just like Ms Chancellor made me practice.

I want to laugh, but it's not funny. Falling flat on your face in front of seven hundred people rarely is.

Slowly, Grandpa and I make our way down the very long receiving line. Shaking hands. Repeating names.

Smiling. It feels like my jaw might fall off. I wish my lips were as numb as my toes.

"Your grandmother used to do this with me, Gracie," Grandpa whispers while we're waiting to be introduced to the royal family. "And after your grandmother passed, your mother took this walk with me every year."

"I know," I say as we ease slowly down the line.

"No matter where your father took her, she always came back and held my arm for this night."

"I know," I say again.

"What I'm trying to say is that it's nice to, once again, have the woman in my life by my side."

He means it. I can tell. And for one second I forget about the women in tiaras, the crowds that are watching the procession. I'm looking only at the old man with the white hair. For the first time in Adria, I don't feel entirely alone.

"Your Royal Highness."

It takes a moment for me to realize that my grandfather is no longer speaking to me – that he isn't making a joke, mocking me and my princess-cut gown. But then I see her and I forget everything I was thinking.

Her dark hair is pulled back in an elegant pile of curls that are topped by a diamond tiara. Her dress, I note, is *not* a princess cut, but I don't stop to comment on the irony. I'm too busy staring at the woman in front of me, wondering if she might be the most beautiful person that I have ever seen.

When my grandfather bows, I remember to curtsy.

I lower my eyes and my head. My job in this moment is simple: *Don't fall down.* I'm doing pretty well, but I know better than to get cocky.

Then the princess reaches out and takes both of my grandfather's hands in hers.

"I'm still not used to hearing you call me that, Mr Ambassador," the princess says.

Grandpa laughs – actually laughs – and tells her, "It would have been a strange thing to yell when I was telling you girls to stop sliding down the banister."

Then the princess laughs, too. My grandfather takes her gloved hand and kisses it. And the moment is so strange – so surreal – that I almost forget what I already technically know: that Princess Ann wasn't always the wife of the future king of Adria. Once upon a time she was just a regular girl in Valancia. And she was my mother's best friend.

Then Grandpa seems to remember I'm beside him. "Your Royal Highness, may I present my granddaughter, Grace?"

I do my best curtsy. I try out my most serene smile. I don't trip or fall or knock anyone down, but I'm certain I've done something terribly, terribly wrong because the princess is staring at me, stunned. And it looks like she might be crying.

"You look like your mother," she says softly, then turns her gaze to my grandfather. "She is exactly like Caroline."

Grandpa's hand is at my back. "I know."

Then the princess's hands are in mine and she is leaning close to me, kissing both of my cheeks, saying, "Hello, Grace. I am so glad to see you again."

Again? Her wedding was on the cover of every magazine in America. When she finds a new favorite designer, it actually affects the stock market. She is one of the most famous women in the world. And, even with all my issues, I'm pretty sure if I'd met her I would remember.

But Princess Ann merely tilts her head and says, "But perhaps you don't recall. It has been a long time, after all. Not since you were perhaps three? Maybe four? We all went to the beach one day. You and your brother rode the carousel. Your mother and I lay on a blanket and laughed for hours. It was a happy day." The woman smiles the same smile I've been seeing on the covers of magazines for years. But then the smile fades. "I never go to the beach anymore."

I wait for the memory to wash over me, but it doesn't come.

"Your mother, Grace..." I can feel the line growing behind us. We should have moved on by now, but Princess Ann still holds my hands. "I miss her so. I am very glad to see you."

"I live here now," I somehow manage to blurt.

She smiles. "Then perhaps we will ride the carousel together sometime soon."

Moving down the line again, I feel half a step behind my body. I no longer think about my sore feet or my tight dress. My mind is too busy imagining Princess Ann and my mother sliding down the embassy's banister and lying on the beach. I finally realize why the girl in my mother's pictures looks so familiar.

I curtsy when my grandfather is greeted by Ann's husband, the prince. His mother. And finally the king himself, but in my mind I'm on the carousel. I'm waiting to hear my mother laugh.

"Mr Ambassador," the king says, taking my grandfather's hand.

"Your Majesty," Grandpa says with a low bow. In his free hand, Grandpa carries a very formal-looking scroll of paper. It is secured by a red ribbon and sealed with wax. "Please allow me to present my papers of appointment on behalf of the President of the United States."

Solemnly, the king takes the scroll and carefully hands it to an aide.

"It is my pleasure to accept these credentials and welcome you back to Adria, my friend."

When the two men shake hands again, they really do look like friends.

Then Grandpa bows again. I curtsy. And both of us walk away.

"Are we done?" I'm asking as Ms Chancellor approaches.

"Cakes are done. People are *finished*," she says in the sing-song tune I'm coming to know quite well. But she's not angry. If anything, she's beaming. "You were wonderful."

"I just stood there," I point out.

"And you did it *very well*."

"Do you feel like pushing your luck?" Grandpa asks.

"Not exact—"

"Mr Prime Minister!" Grandpa says it with such gusto he's almost shouting. There is a small group of men standing in a circle, talking, and Grandpa walks straight toward them. I don't have a second to object before he says, "Allow me to introduce my granddaughter, Grace."

"Hello, Grace," the man in the center of the group says, turning to take me in. He's tall, his tuxedo classic. I watch the way he glances from my grandpa to me.

Is this the one I've heard about? the prime minister's look says.

Yes. Go easy on her, Grandpa's smile replies.

"Welcome to Adria. How long will you be with us?" the prime minister asks.

"Grace is here to stay," Grandpa tells him, beaming.

"Excellent. You know, I've been saying for ages that we need someone to keep this old man in line," the prime minister jokes.

"I think she's up to the task," Grandpa says.

I know he and the prime minister are talking about me, but at no point do I get the feeling that they are talking *to* me. I might as well be a statue. A work of art. I am simply something to be commented upon.

I see Alexei and his father only a couple of feet away. I smile but Alexei just walks on, as if he doesn't see me at all.

"So, Grace, how do you like our little nation so far?" the prime minister asks.

"It's very nice," I say and risk a glance around the massive room. The ceiling is at least fifty feet high and the walls are lined with portraits, many of which are older than my own country. "I've never been to the palace before."

"Oh, really? Well, there's a lot of history here, Grace." He walks to one of the oldest portraits and points up at a portly man in a crown. "Fredrick the First. He was a knight who stopped here on the way home from the Third Crusade at the end of the twelfth century. But it seemed that Fredrick was not yet finished fighting, because he landed on our shores and won Adria from the Mongols who ruled it then. Before the Mongols, for a short while there were the Turks. Before the Turks, the Byzantines and the Romans. But Fredrick built the wall, so Fredrick and his heirs got to keep it. Unless you consider..."

The prime minister walks down the long line of paintings and points at another portrait. This one is of a woman.

"Queen Catalina. She was the eldest daughter of the king of Spain, but she was betrothed to King Fredrick the *Third* when she wasn't much older than you are. She married at seventeen, I believe. Her husband died in his sleep five months later, and Catalina ruled for sixty years." He leans closer. There's a glint in his eye as he adds, "If you ask me, she killed him."

We walk silently down the gallery, the portraits looming large over us – kings and queens still keeping a watchful eye over the land so many people had died for.

"What about them?" I ask, pointing to the only portrait

in the room that shows an entire family.

"Oh, well, in many ways, they are our most famous royals." The prime minister laughs, but it is not a joyful sound. "That is King Alexander the Second, his wife, and their two sons. There was a daughter, too, but she was just a baby at the time – so young they hadn't even commissioned a portrait of her yet. Alexander ruled during a terrible famine. The wells were dry. The crops were dead. And almost the entire region was at war. The people were hungry and frightened, and they grew to distrust the monarchy. One night, the royal guard rebelled. They left their posts and threw open the gates. The people stormed the palace and dragged Alexander and his family from their beds."

"They were murdered?" I ask.

The prime minister nods grimly. "Power has always corrupted, my dear. Even the *promise* of power. It is a hard thing to look at through a fence for hundreds of years without wondering what it would be like on the other side."

"But Adria still has a royal family?" I say, confused.

"We do indeed," the prime minister says. "That great tragedy began what is known as the War of the Fortnight. In the end, the rebels surrendered and the king's brother took up the throne. The monarchy was restored – this time *with* a house of parliament and a prime minister." He gives a slight bow, as if the tale had conjured him out of magic.

"So just like that it was over? The rebels just gave up?"

"Yes, dear."

"But why?" I ask.

For a long moment the prime minister looks at me as if the answer should be the most obvious thing in the world. When he speaks again, his voice is soft.

"*It rained.*"

I look back at the painting of the dead king and queen and the two little princes who were dragged from their beds. For the first time I realize how perilous peace can be. I appreciate the tightrope that my grandfather has spent his whole life trying to walk. And now, more than ever, I grow terrified that I am going to make us all fall down.

"Now, Grace, if you'll excuse us for a moment, I need to borrow your grandfather. Official business," the prime minister says. "Man stuff."

Before I can say anything else, Ms Chancellor takes my arm. "I believe it's time for us to go powder our noses."

"He said *man stuff*," I tell her as we walk away.

"He did indeed, dear."

"Are you OK with that? Tell me you are not OK with the phrase *man stuff.*"

"I am not," she says through a too-bright smile.

"But—"

"But Queen Catalina bided her time and ruled for sixty years, my dear."

"So you're going to kill the prime minister in his sleep?" I ask.

She never softens her smile. "No. But that doesn't mean I don't appreciate the power of patience. Now, if you'll excuse me, I see the Chinese ambassador and I need a moment of his time."

I have new respect for the woman who is walking away from me. Her hips sway beneath her long black gown. Her blue wrap catches the light. She is a guest at the palace, but there is no doubt she is the belle of the ball.

I feel exceedingly glad she's on my side.

I also feel very much alone as I stand in the crowd of people, looking up at a painting of two dead little princes, wishing that I could talk to Jamie.

I could call him, send him a text. But it's not his voice or his words that I miss – it's him. It's not being alone. It's having someone to step in between me and the strange looks, to change the subject and tell me that I'm doing fine.

But I shouldn't miss my brother so badly. It's almost like I've conjured him – or someone just like him – out of thin air because instantly I feel a hand on my arm. I hear Alexei say, "Hello, Gracie."

Jamie is the only person I allow to call me Gracie. Sure, other people (like my grandfather) do it too, but Jamie is the only one who has my explicit permission. I'm tempted to remind Alexei of this fact, but as soon as I turn to face him, all I can think is that Alexei is here. Alexei is looking at me. And Alexei is wearing a tux.

"You look very lovely this evening."

His accent is heavier as he says it. And being all slicked and shaved and tuxedoed like he is, a more gullible girl might be impressed – she might even swoon a little. But whatever swooning I'm doing is entirely tight-dress related. I swear it is.

"Hello, Alexei. I was just going to powder my nose, and—"

"Not so fast."

I'm turning away when he catches my arm, pulls me to him. His arm goes around my waist. His other hand takes mine and before I realize what is happening, we're dancing.

"I'm not talking to you," I tell him. "And you're not talking to me either if that look you *didn't* give me a while ago is any indication."

"Whatever you say."

"In fact, I'm sick of you."

"OK."

"I'm just–"

"You seem to be struggling with the concept of 'not talking,' aren't you, Grace? Or perhaps my English is not as good as I think it is."

We're spinning, and I watch the ballroom pass. The royals in their receiving line, the musicians, the long tables filled with food. I know there are other couples around us, but they feel like distant blurs. Only Alexei is solid and sure. Between my tight dress and aching feet and swirling head, he may be the only thing keeping me steady.

And I kind of hate him for it. Or maybe I just hate myself.

"You do look nice tonight, Grace. Being clean and

bruise-free seems to agree with you. Are you enjoying the party?"

True to my word, I stay silent.

Alexei gives a short laugh and talks on, his accent thicker.

"Most posts aren't like this, you know. Embassy life is not usually so…glamorous. But Adria is different, my father says. It is like the old days here, with their balls and their beautiful embassies. Some say it is because it is good for tourism – that it is an act and they have an image to protect. But I do not know. In any case, you and I are very lucky that our families are posted here."

"I'm not listening to you," I say, looking over his shoulder and refusing to meet his gaze. "I don't have to pay attention to you. Or mind you. Or care about your opinion." Finally, I do find his eyes. I'm staring right into them when I say, "You are not my brother."

I expect this to hurt Alexei, wound him in some way. But he just laughs at me like I'm hilarious with my attempts to be my own person.

"I am your brother's proxy, Grace." He pulls me tighter. "And in the diplomatic corps we take proxy responsibilities very seriously."

Alexei has known me for most of my life. And he still sees me as a child. But it could be worse, I realize. He could see what I turned into.

The song ends and we stop moving, but Alexei is still holding me.

"Grace, I…" he starts, and then he drops me.

I don't fall. But when his arm leaves my waist I stumble for a moment, struggling to stay upright while my numb feet find their place beneath me.

He's looking around like he's been caught sneaking out, breaking into Iran, doing the kind of stupid stuff that is usually reserved for me.

"What was—" I start.

He cuts me off. "I must go, Grace. Excuse me."

He gives me a real, actual bow and pushes away just as the quartet begins to play again. I can't stop myself from calling out, "You really have a hard time making up your mind, you know?"

But Alexei is already gone.

I step off the floor that is filling rapidly with dancing couples. It's like a minefield of swirling, moving silk and sparkling sequins. I'm more than a little relieved to make it to the edge.

I scan the room, looking for Alexei, but he is nowhere to be seen. Even when Noah approaches, I can't stop looking.

"Well, if I didn't know any better, I'd say you were a lady," Noah teases, but I'm too busy scanning the crowd, looking for answers.

"Where did he go?" I ask.

"Who?"

"Alexei. He was here and then he just disappeared."

"Oh, *Alexei.*" Noah doesn't sound surprised. He eyes me skeptically. "*Et tu,* Grace?"

"What?" I ask, distracted and annoyed.

“Nothing.” Noah shakes his head. “There he goes.” He points to the big, sweeping staircase. Alexei’s figure is unmistakable as he climbs.

“Just remember who your best friend is!” Noah says as I turn to leave. But then I stop and spin back for a moment, stand on my tiptoes, and give Noah a kiss on the cheek. He blushes, happy.

“Save me a dance,” I tell him, even though I’m pretty sure it’s the pink dress talking, not me.

And then I turn and dash off through the crowded hall.

The carpet on the stairs is rich and red, and so lush that it feels like running through a forest covered with moss as I chase after Alexei. He doesn't look back, and by the time I make it to the landing he is nowhere to be seen. So I hold my billowing skirt in both hands and dare to run a little faster down the long corridor.

The ceiling is at least twenty feet high. The stones are a dark gray, and I know even without reaching out that they will be cold to the touch. Outside, the sun is finally down and the lights of the city shine like fireflies through the darkness. Beyond the wall, the sea stretches out, dark and vast, and I know why – once upon a time – it would have been easy to think the world was flat.

The music is so faint it's like someone left a radio on somewhere in the depths of the palace. I am so alone in that wide hallway that it's easy to forget there are hundreds of dancing, laughing people just a floor away.

Alexei, I want to call out, but I do not dare. I can feel eyes upon me as I walk past even more portraits of the kings. A few queens. They are practically life-sized, the frames towering over me, filling every inch of the wall. I almost expect them to speak and tell me to go back to the party or at least point me in Alexei's direction. But they stay silent in their frames. Whatever secrets they are hiding, they do not say a thing.

The hall leads to another massive room. Formal furniture and a fireplace so large that I could walk inside it without even bending over. There are more portraits and chandeliers, but no Alexei. So I step back into the hall, turn, and keep going.

The music is gone now. The party all but forgotten. There is a force I cannot name that is pulling me forward. I want to call out for Alexei. And I'm afraid he'll hear me. Both.

When I turn another corner, I hear a door creak open, but it does not close.

I freeze and lean against a large piece of antique furniture, pressing myself and my enormous dress against the wall, suddenly all too aware of how far I've wandered, the trouble I will be in if I get caught.

But I do not move. I cannot leave. I just slow my breathing and listen.

"I need to talk to you," someone says in Adrian. And in my mind I feel cold and wet, like my dress is an ocean and I'm drowning inside it.

"Not now," the second voice spits back.

Someone is in the hallway. Someone is coming closer. "This isn't the end of this!" the first voice says. The second man laughs.

It is a cruel sound, high and haunting. And I am certain of one thing: I have heard it before.

"Of course it isn't," the man says at last. "If I'm right, then it is only beginning."

I'm not sure when I started shaking, but I'm terrified they'll hear me. I'm terrified they'll see me. Just like when I overheard them in Iran.

Because if there is one thing I'm sure of, it is that these are the same voices that I heard in Iran.

I push myself farther into my little corner. I'm trying to disappear, willing myself to become one with the stone and the wood. And maybe the palace hears me and grants my wish because the wall behind me starts to move, pushing slowly inward as I push slowly back.

It's a closet, I think as the blackness envelops me. I move into it as quickly as I can. The hem of my train catches and snags as I push the door silently shut behind me. There is still enough light coming in through a crack in the door for me to see movement in the hallway.

I shift and peek out. The floor creaks.

The dark figure outside spins and looks. "Who's there?" he asks.

My breathing is so heavy I bring a hand up to cover my mouth. A slice of light cuts across my face, and the man is so close I can smell his cologne. He turns and looks up and down the hallway, as if somehow he knows that he is not alone.

He stops and opens the door of the cabinet I had been leaning against. His shadow crosses my face.

And that is when I see him – really see him.

He is no more than a foot away this time. Unlike the Iranian basement, the palace hallway is well lit. I will never again be able to convince myself that it was a trick of the light, a figment of my mind.

No. The man has dark hair speckled with gray. He wears a well-cut tux with gold cufflinks, an expensive watch, and a long black tie. His profile is handsome and perfect and strong with the exception of the jagged scar that runs from his eyebrow to his jaw.

The scar that is very real.

The scar that is perfectly clear.

The scar that has haunted my dreams every night since the moment my mother died – from the moment the Scarred Man killed her.

I press my hand against my mouth and swallow the cry that is rising in my throat. I don't want the Scarred Man to hear me. To find me.

To kill me.

I press myself against the closet wall because my head is spinning and I'm afraid I might pass out. There isn't enough air in the closet, in my chest. There isn't enough air in the world.

But there also isn't time to panic. Now is the time to think and process and act. Now is the time to survive.

"*Grace, no!*" I hear my mother call.

My mother would want me to survive.

I don't know how long I stay in the closet. A minute. An hour. A year? When I finally push my way outside and retrace my steps I half expect to return to a different party. But the quartet is still playing. The people are still talking and dancing, not caring at all that the man who killed my mother is here.

He's here! I want to scream and claw and wail until someone hears me. Until someone finally cares.

But the words don't come. I've said it all before, after all. I've described the Scarred Man to my father and to Jamie. I told the military police and the cops from town. I told the doctors all about him.

Once, I even wrote the details in a note and sent it to my grandfather. But I never got an answer to that letter. Maybe he never got it. Or maybe he just didn't want to be one more person to tell me I was crazy.

It was an accident.

There was no Scarred Man.

You have no idea what you really saw.

But I do know. I know what, and I know who, and I know that I was right that night in the Iranian embassy.

The Scarred Man is in Adria. I've finally found him. But I don't dare let him find me.

"Grace, your dress is ripped," Noah says. He has been here for a long time, I realize. Talking to me. Trying to tease me into dancing or eating. But he's not teasing anymore. "Grace, what happened to your dress?" Then he rethinks, asks a better question. "Grace, what happened to you?"

"I... I..."

"Grace, look at me!" Panic is seeping into Noah's voice. I want to tell him that it's going to be OK – that I'm going to be OK. But I can't lie to Noah. Not even when I know it's what he wants to hear.

"Ms Chancellor," Noah says, calling her over.

"Well, hello there, you two," Ms Chancellor says. "Don't you look handsome, Noah? You make a very striking pair."

There's a twinkle in her eyes, and I know what she's thinking. She's playing matchmaker. She's practically naming our children, taking credit for Noah and the most excellent influence he has been upon me.

"I was just telling the ambassador of France all about you, Grace. Her niece is visiting next month and I told her that you and I would love to..."

But then Ms Chancellor looks at me. She must see the panic in my eyes, the way all the color has drained from my face. I'm sure I no longer share the rosy hue of my pink gown. I must be the color of paper.

"Grace, are you OK?"

I try to speak, but the words don't come.

"Noah, take her home," Ms Chancellor commands, but Noah is one step ahead of her. He already has my arm and is guiding me to the door.

"I need to go home," I mutter.

"I know," Noah says. "Come on. I'll take you back to the embassy."

"No! I need to go home," I say, but then the realization comes: my mother was my home. My mother is dead. And the man who killed her is wearing a tuxedo and an expensive watch and going to parties. The man who killed her is at this party.

"Where's my grandpa? I need to talk to my grandpa."

"He's busy, Grace. Come on."

We make it outside and Noah says something to one of the uniformed men. The car with US flags is coming toward us. Noah is leading me to the door.

"You're going to be OK, Grace," Noah tells me. "You probably just ate something funny or..."

I climb into the car, but before Noah can join me, I slam the door and tell the driver, "Go! Just go."

The car is not on fire.

I know this like I know my name. My age. My social security number, and that I have brown eyes. I am certain of these facts, and yet I forget them. The black leather interior fades away. The divider between the driver and me is up, and I'm alone in the strange red glow that is coming off the instruments in the backseat. I blink harder and harder, and I know that I'm not crying. My eyes are just trying to wash away the smoke that isn't there.

I bang my head back and slam my hands over my ears, but still I hear the cries.

"*Grace, honey! No!*"

"No." I toss.

"No!" I yell.

"*Grace*," my mother's voice comes again. "*Honey, run!*"

"No. No. No."

The limo's windows are black, like mirrors in the

night, but I can see through them into the small shop my mother ran back in America. Rows and rows of antiques and first-edition novels. Dusty and cramped.

A *tinderbox.*

That was the word the fire marshal had used.

So much old, dry wood. So many flammable things.

She never stood a chance. Not after the second-floor balcony collapsed. Not once the fire moved into the walls.

"*Grace, run!*"

"No!" I yell.

I can hear the glass cracking. I can feel my fists begin to bleed. Oxygen crashes through the broken window and the fire booms, knocking me to the ground, burning my hair and my lungs.

"Stop!" I yell, clawing through space and time at the blaze that started three years ago and, in a way, never has gone out.

"Stop!" I yell and start to scream.

"Are you OK?"

I look up at the driver. The limo isn't moving and the divider is down.

"You did yell for me to stop, didn't you? You've got to lower the divider for me to hear you. Or press the intercom."

"Yes. Yes. I want – I need..."

I don't bother to finish. I just climb out of the car and start down the street, holding up the skirt of my puffy pink ball gown, the train cinched within my fists. Running.

My shoes are gone, forgotten on the floor of the car,

and I feel the damp cobblestones through the thin tights that cover my feet. Feeling is starting to return to my toes. They go from numb to cold to bleeding, but I just run faster.

Gas surges through the streetlights overhead, growing brighter, then dimmer, then brighter again. The flames flicker and I have to stop.

My breath is coming harder than it should. My dress is too tight and so, so heavy. My head is spinning, too. When I slam myself against a wall, the gasp that comes is too shallow, too quick. I need a paper bag to breathe into but all I have are acres and acres of fluffy pink fabric.

I close my eyes and tell myself that I will not have a panic attack. I will not let them find me. I will not say a word.

Overhead, the streetlight flickers and goes out and all breath fails me. I slide to the ground. It must have rained because the stones are damp. My dress will be not just ripped, but ruined. But breath is more important to me. All I can care about is trying not to die.

When I close my eyes *I hear the gunshot. I see the small circle of blood that starts in the center of my mother's chest. Just a drop of something dark – like she should have used a napkin. But it has already started to spread. She stumbles back, unsteady.*

And then the balcony falls. The sound is so loud. There are so many sparks – so much dust and flame and damage.

"No!" I think I might yell.

And then the man is on the street. He looks at me with cold indifference. He smells like smoke. Soot and ash cling to his brown leather jacket.

I retreat backward, away from the growing heat of the blaze. I stare up at him.

"My mother," I say. "She's dying!" I scream.

But the man just looks at me. "She's dead."

And then he turns and walks away so slowly.

In the distance, there are sirens. Someone will have seen the smoke. The shop has a security alarm. People are coming to help, but the man is not here to save anyone, least of all me.

He stops when he reaches a dark sedan car, turns and looks back at the burning building. The whole street is orange and red. I need no other light to make out the massive scar that covers the left side of his face. I swear that I will never forget that face as long as I live.

I swear that, someday, I will see that face again.

"Grace?" I hear the voice in the darkness. When the glow of the lamp returns, I can see the dark figure on the other side of the street.

Instinctively, I move backward, clawing against the sidewalk, desperate to put every possible inch between me and the man who is moving steadily closer.

"Grace, are you OK?" Alexei says, and I curse him. I hate him for disappearing during the ball and now for showing up here – when I'm crying and broken and low.

I can't let him see me like this. He'll tell Ms Chancellor or my grandfather. Or, worse, he'll tell Jamie. And then it will start again. It will be just like *After*. With the pills and the shrinks and the looks.

I can never go back to After.

I push myself off the sidewalk and begin limping down the street. My toes are raw, but at least I'm free of the uncomfortable shoes.

"Grace, stop." Alexei sprints across the street and tries to block my path.

"Go away," I tell him.

"No." The way he says it, he must think the idea absurd. He must think *I'm* absurd. "What is wrong with you?"

"My feet hurt," I say. "High heels – they're even worse than advertised."

The streetlights flicker, and I jump. I'm not afraid of the dark, but of the way the fire flits and moves, like it is a living, breathing thing. And then I remember that it is. It really is. It lives. It breathes. It kills. But it did not kill my mother. She was dead long before the fire took her.

"Here." Alexei is taking off his tuxedo jacket and placing it around my shoulders. I want to push it off, turn triumphantly, and walk away. But the jacket is still warm from his body and the heat seeps into my skin. It feels like sinking into a hot bath. I want to soak in it for as long as I can.

He takes my arm, keeps me there as he asks me, "Where did you go tonight? Why did you leave?"

"Me?" I snap before I even realize what I'm saying. "You're the one who disappeared! You went upstairs. Were you there?" I shout. "Answer me, Alexei!

Were you with him?"

"With who?" he says, but then shakes the words away. "Let's get you home. We have to—"

"I'm not crazy!" I'm shouting so loudly that dogs bark. Lights go on in windows, shopkeepers stirring from their beds. But I cannot keep the words inside.

"You want to hear that, right? I mean that's what they told you. That's why Jamie is so worried about his crazy kid sister. Because – news flash – *she really is crazy.*"

The last part I say softly. They're the words I have been carrying for so long that they have a weight of their own. Physical. I should feel lighter now that I've released them, but there is no relief from the truth.

"Guess what, Valencia!" I shout. "The fire wasn't an accident! My mother didn't die from smoke! Did you hear that, Alexei?" I'm taunting him. "She was murdered. She was shot."

"Grace, come on. Let's get you home." He's looking at me like I've been drinking, and I can't blame him. My dress is ripped and my words slur. *I'm not myself,* I think, but then I realize something even scarier: I am exactly myself.

The look in Alexei's eye tells me he is right to be afraid of me. And I was very right to hide it.

"She was murdered, Alexei," I say, softer. His jacket falls from my shoulders and lies like a puddle in the street. "She was. She really was. And I saw the man who killed her."

Then the panic comes again. I try to breathe deeply,

to think of calm and soothing things. But the wind is cold on my skin and the light that fills the street is the color of fire, and I can't stop it.

"I saw him," I say as his arms go around me.

"What happened tonight, Grace?" Alexei whispers.

"I saw him!" I yell again.

"Jamie told me what you think you saw—"

"He was there. He's here. I saw him," I say one final time, but I doubt Alexei even hears me. His arms grow tighter as my legs grow weaker, and then he is sweeping me up into his arms.

As I curl into the warmth of his chest I know that I should fight and protest, talk about my rights as a strong, independent woman. But the fact that I don't have the strength to walk anymore undermines any argument I might make.

The attacks, when they come, are awful. But it's what comes after that leaves me broken, riddled with shame. They are everything I hate. I am the thing that I despise: weak and docile and frail.

I am so frail, it's like I have no muscle, no bones. I am nothing but a pounding head and a thousand electric wires pulsing inside a pale-pink gown.

I am nothing as I say another final time, "He's here."

I wake to the sound of voices, muffled but raised. Like they belong to people who are trying to yell as quietly as possible. For a second, I'm confused. The sky beyond the window is still dark, and then I reach down and feel the soft pink gown that I'm still wrapped inside. A tuxedo jacket lies across me. It smells like Alexei. And that's when I know why the voices can't stop shouting.

"Someone should have brought her home," Grandpa says.

"We tried," Ms Chancellor explains. "Noah said he would escort her, but she left him at the palace."

Slowly I sit upright on a bed that's not my own. I place my feet on the rug and creep toward the door as softly as I can.

"Is she hurt?" Grandpa asks, but the question is met by silence. "Is she?"

It takes a moment for Alexei to say, "I don't know.

I've never seen Grace like that. She was not herself." Then Alexei mumbles something in Russian. "I have to tell Jamie."

"No!" Grandpa snaps.

"He is my best friend, sir. It is my duty."

"I know it feels that way, young man," Grandpa says, softer now. "But, please, let us handle it. Her father…well, we all thought the worst of it was over."

"With all due respect, sir," Alexei says slowly. It's like he's almost afraid when he finishes, "the worst of *what*?"

I'm almost to the door. It's open just a crack, and I can see Alexei in the small sitting room that constitutes the outer chamber of my grandfather's suite. His tie is undone and his sleeves are rolled up. He looks like he's seen a ghost. Then I realize with a start that he has – he's seen the ghost of me. Of the girl who was never supposed to follow me across the ocean.

"Grace has had a difficult time of it, young man," Grandpa says with a slap on his back. "She's not the same Gracie who used to tag after you and Jamie, I'm afraid."

"Yeah," I say, pushing open the door. "Seeing your mother murdered in front of your eyes will do that."

"Grace." Ms Chancellor spins on me, shocked. "We thought you were—"

"Unconscious?" I guess. "Insane?"

"Resting, dear." She starts toward me but suddenly stops. "You should be resting."

I look right at my grandfather.

"I saw him tonight, Grandpa. I saw the man who killed

her. The man with the scar. He was there. He was at the palace and… I saw him." I take a deep breath. "I saw the man who killed my mother."

For a second, no one speaks. Not one of them dares to move. It's like they are afraid of me. I'm a house of cards and any quick movement – sudden breath – might send me crashing to the ground.

"Somebody say something!" I shout.

Grandpa turns slowly toward Alexei and takes his hand. "Thank you for bringing her home, young man. We will see to Grace from here."

That's Alexei's cue. There's no doubt he's been dismissed. And yet he stands there, looking at me. It's like he doesn't trust himself to leave me alone. Or, more likely, that he doesn't trust me to *be* alone.

"It's OK," I tell him. "I'm fine."

I'm not fine, but no one says so. He just walks to the door of the sitting room.

"Good night, everyone." He looks at us all in turn. For just a second, his gaze lingers on me. "Sleep well."

And then he's gone. Not for the first time, I want to chase after him. To see where the boys go when they disappear. But Ms Chancellor closes the door firmly behind him, and I know that I can't follow. They don't want him to hear what comes next. Like most streets, on Embassy Row you never let your neighbors hear you fighting.

"Gracie," Grandpa tells me, his big Southern voice booming in the small room. "Now, I don't know what you thought you saw tonight—"

"I saw him. I saw the Scarred Man."

"You saw no such thing!" Grandpa yells, but then he seems to regret it. He's a diplomat. He knows there is a time and place for strength and a time and place for tenderness. But heads of state are one thing. It's been a long time since he's tried to raise a teenage girl.

"You were tired, sweetheart. Confused. You don't know what you saw," he tells me.

"How do you know? You weren't there. You haven't been anywhere near me since she died."

This wounds him, I can tell. And that alone makes me happy.

"Grace, dear, let's take you to your room. Get you out of that dress," Ms Chancellor tries. "You'll feel so much better after a hot bath and—"

"I don't need a bath!" I'm shouting now. I can't help it. "I need someone to listen to me! I need someone to *believe* me."

I cross the room in two long strides and then I'm gripping my grandfather's waistcoat. I have to make him see me – see that I'm not lying. See that I'm not the girl they'd warned him I'd become. I have to make somebody understand.

"He's real, Grandpa. And he's here. I saw him!"

"There is no Scarred Man, Gracie."

"You don't know that," I snap.

"Of course I know that. Who do you think paid for the doctors?" As soon as the words are out, he regrets them.

I recoil. "I'm sorry. I never meant to be such an

expensive inconvenience," I say, letting him go. I no longer want to touch him. I don't even want to look at him.

"Now, Gracie, sweetheart. Hear me out. You were so young."

"I was thirteen," I counter, but he talks on.

"It was traumatic. You were confused. Your mother…" And then his voice cracks. He can't look at me anymore. "Your mother's death was an accident, Grace. It was terrible and tragic, but it was an accident all the same."

"I know what I saw," I tell him.

"The police scoured all the footage from the nearby security cameras. There was no sign of any man. There was no evidence of foul play."

"The bullet wound in her chest seemed like pretty good evidence to me," I say.

"You know there was no bullet wound, Grace. We've told you that. I saw the autopsy report myself, and the coroner's findings were very clear."

"But—" I start, but then my grandfather interrupts with a shout.

"It was an accident!" His face is red. I can't tell if he wants to scream or cry. Probably both. I am talking about his daughter, after all. "It was an accident, Gracie. An *accident*."

When he says the word one final time, it is almost a whisper.

"Think about it, Grace." Ms Chancellor's voice is soft. She tries to smooth my hair, but I jerk away. "You're still jet-lagged. I know you haven't been sleeping well. You're exhausted."

"I know I'm exhausted! That's why I didn't say anything when..."

When I saw him in Iran, I think, but dare not say.

"When what?" Grandpa snaps.

"When I was at the party," I finish meekly. "But now I know it was him. I know it."

"Forget about the Scarred Man, Gracie. Make your peace. Let her go." He tries to calm himself. At least his voice is softer when he turns to look out the window at the city lights, the small sliver of inky black sea. "I've had to let her go."

I could protest. The words are rising up inside my throat. I want to throw open the window and yell out into the street – run around the wall, announcing the truth to the entire city. But no one will believe me.

"Can I go to bed now?" I ask. I try to smooth the skirt of my dress that was so pretty once. So lovely. But it's ruined now. There's no use in standing there, being reminded of it over and over.

The Israeli embassy looks different in the light of morning. The building itself sits farther back than the other embassies on the street, but the Israelis have built a new wall that juts up directly against the sidewalk. It is the only embassy on the row that has two.

"Hi," I greet the guard outside the main gates. The guard studies me but doesn't say a thing. "I'm here to see—"

"Grace?"

When I turn, I notice a small pedestrian-only gate along the side of the building. That is where Noah stands, looking at me through the bars. It's like I'm visiting him in prison. Or more like he is visiting me.

There is a loud buzz and then Noah pushes on the gate, comes toward me.

"Well, hello, Cinderella," he says with a roguish grin. "I should have known you would come back, looking for your slipper. The ladies always come back. But you're too late. I'll have you know the Dowager Countess of Capri was all over me last night after your untimely exit."

"That's nice," I say.

"Not really. She's my grandmother's age. But feistier. Way, way feistier."

Noah gives a whole-body shake like someone has just walked over his grave.

"So, where'd you go?" For once, Noah sounds serious.

"Back," I say. I don't tell him back to where. He doesn't have to know I'm not talking about the embassy – that I'm talking about going back to the darkest corners of my memory. Going back in time.

"Can we go somewhere?" I say.

"I'm already going somewhere," he tells me, holding up the backpack he carries as if it's proof.

"Where?"

"Brazil. We're staying at Dad's tonight. Lila's already there. Come on. Walk with me."

"But is there somewhere else we can go? Someplace private?"

My voice doesn't sound like my own. I keep looking at my hands. In the past twelve hours my cuticles have become the most fascinating things ever. I can't look anyone in the eye anymore. I'm afraid of what else I might see.

"Grace, you're scaring me."

Slowly, I force myself to find his eyes, hold his gaze.

"That's OK," I tell him. "Because I'm terrified."

*

I don't know where we're going. Not exactly. But when we cross to the other side of the wall, my feet seem to take me automatically to a place I haven't seen in ages. Once upon a time it was probably lovely, but the years and the salty sea air have taken their toll. And now the carousel with its horses and knights and dragons sits abandoned, paint fading, its melody long since silent.

"What is it?" Noah asks when we get there. "What's going on?"

He drops his backpack, and I step up onto the carousel, run my hands along the back of a white horse that no longer rises or falls.

"My mom used to play here when she was a little girl. It was her favorite place in the whole city. She would bring Jamie and me here at least once every summer. We'd pack a lunch and eat it over there – on that big, flat rock. Last night, in the receiving line, Princess Ann said she came here with us once when I was little. I don't even remember. Isn't that weird? There are some things about my mom that I think about every hour of every day, but some…it's like I've blocked them out completely. That's strange, isn't it? I wonder if it's always like that?"

"Grace, I—"

"I found him, Noah," I say, and to his credit, Noah doesn't ask who – he doesn't demand answers. He must already know me well enough to know that I have to say this in my own time, in my own way. He must know me well enough to know that I'm afraid this truth might kill me.

"I found him," I say again. "I found the man who killed my mother."

At my words, Noah actually stumbles back. He trips a little over his own backpack, rights himself, and tries to play it cool.

"I didn't realize he was missing."

"I'm serious, Noah."

"I am, too," he says. "I mean… I don't know…what happened? I thought your mom died in an accident or something. A fire."

"That's what they say."

"But…"

"But I was there. I saw it happen."

"You saw your mom die?" Noah's eyebrows are raised. He can't hide his surprise or his pity.

"It was late and it was dark, but yeah. I saw it."

"That was…what? Three years ago? You were twelve?"

"Thirteen."

"Wow."

"Don't start, Noah." I walk around the white horse, take shelter behind a dancing bear.

"I'm not starting anything," he says. "It's just—"

"Yes, it was dark," I snap back. "Yes, I was young, and it was traumatic. Yes, I have never been the most reliable girl in the world, but I know what I saw. And I'm telling you, I saw a man with a scar on his left cheek shoot my mother. I heard the bomb that burned her shop to the ground."

My breath is coming hard, but this isn't an attack. It feels different. I feel different. The shock is over and all that remains from the night before is my overwhelming anger.

"I saw his face that night, Noah. I have seen his face every night. And last night – I'm telling you that last night I saw *him*."

"You saw *him* or you saw a man with a scar?"

I don't give him a reply. I don't dignify what he's said with a response. I do not dignify *him*. I've already heard the speech so many times that I know it better than he does. I have no desire to hear it again. I'm off the carousel and strolling back the way we came almost before he can realize what he's said and done.

"Grace, wait. Grace!" Noah calls after me. "I believe you!" he shouts, and that stops me. "I'll go with you to tell your grandfather."

"I already told him," I say.

Noah nods, steps closer. "Good. Good. Now he and Ms Chancellor can—"

"They don't believe me. They think I made him up. They've always thought I was making him up, and now..." Noah gives me a look. "I'm not!"

"I believe you! It's just...why doesn't your grandfather believe you? I mean, it's not like you make a habit out of accusing scarred men or anything, right?"

I must stand a little too still for a little too long because Noah asks again, "Right?"

"Of course not," I snap. "It's just easier to tell me I was

seeing things. It's easier for him not to believe me, but if you don't believe me either, then—"

"I believe you!" Noah insists again. "I do. OK?" He eases closer, places his hand on my arm. I shudder but don't pull away. I get the sense that he's probably trying to comfort me, but neither of us are sure how that is supposed to go, so he just keeps his fingers on my elbow, like a really distant, really awkward hug.

"I do believe you. But, Grace, what are we supposed to do?"

I didn't sleep last night. Not because of the crying, or the trauma, or the flashbacks. Not even the humiliation of having Alexei witness one of my attacks could distract me from the thoughts that filled my mind once the shock and terror finally faded.

"Grace..." Noah starts slowly.

"We're going to find him," I say, certain and strong. I will tear the great walled city down stone by stone if that is what it takes. "You are going to help me find him."

There are seagulls overhead. I can hear their cries and the breaking of the waves against the shore. Down the beach, a group of little kids is sitting in a circle on the sand. Even though they're far away, the song they're singing catches on the wind and carries toward us.

Wait, little princes, dead and gone
No one's gonna know you're coming home
Wait, little princes, one-two-three
No one's gonna know that you are me

It is the 'Duck, Duck, Goose' of Adria. I'd totally forgotten it until now, but the haunting melody comes back. I can remember our mother singing it as Jamie and I played in the yard. When the song ends the kids all stand and chase each other wildly around. I want to join them. Those words have always made me want to run.

Noah rubs his hand over his face, mumbles something that is a cross between Hebrew and Portuguese. Then he shrugs and gives the long sigh of someone who has learned not to argue. "Just tell me what to do. Wait...do we know what to do?"

He doesn't look at me like Jamie or my father, like Grandpa or Ms Chancellor. Noah isn't looking at me like I'm seeing things, hearing things, too fragile and grief-stricken to live.

In short, for the first time in three years, I'm talking about the man who killed my mother with someone who isn't looking at me like I'm crazy.

And that is why I trust him. That is why I say, "Come on."

"Hello, Grace. Noah." It's clear from the way Ms Chancellor is looking at us that she thinks her plan is working – that we've come to ask her to arrange the wedding, maybe be godmother to our child. "To what do I owe the pleasure?"

Ms Chancellor is carrying a stack of files and walking through the embassy in a pair of impossibly high heels. I've noticed this about Ms Chancellor: she's almost always moving. And she's almost always doing it while wearing shoes that would make me want to stay perfectly, utterly still.

"I was hoping you could help me," I say, following her up the stairs.

She rests her left hand on the smooth rail but glances quickly back.

"Of course I will if I can."

"After last night…" I begin.

This, at last, stops her. Ms Chancellor pivots on the

balls of her feet, looks down at me from two steps ahead.

"Your grandfather and I have already spoken about this, Grace, and I'm afraid I—"

"I'm not talking about that," I hurry to say.

"You're not?"

"She's not," Noah adds. Ms Chancellor slides her gaze onto him. At least there's someone on my side she can trust.

"No. Grandpa was right," I say. "I'm sure I was just tired. This is all so new to me. I probably just got overwhelmed."

"Yeah." Noah moves to join me. "In fact, Grace and I were talking about how overwhelming it all can be. So many new people. Not to mention all the protocols and the rules and—"

"And the people," I blurt. "There are just so many new people. It was—"

"Overwhelming," Noah interjects.

"Yes," I say. "Overwhelming."

Ms Chancellor crosses her arms, file folders pulled tightly against her chest. "I see."

Noah moves forward. "So I was telling Grace about the directory. I thought that she could take a look at that – maybe memorize a few names and faces and then—"

Ms Chancellor spins and starts back up the stairs, Noah chasing after her.

"I don't know what you're talking about, Noah."

"I know you keep a book. A file. Something with pictures and names and job titles and the lowdown on all the players. Come on, Ms C. I know you have something like that."

"You know no such thing," she tells him.

"Then you'd be the only embassy on the row that doesn't have one." It's a good point, and I can tell by the look on Ms Chancellor's face that he's got her.

"Come on, Ms Chancellor," Noah says, easing closer to the place where she now stands at the top of the stairs. "Tell me, would you rather have Grace getting her information off the street? Or here, in the safety of her own home?"

Ms Chancellor looks between us, a slight crinkle in her brow. We amuse her, I realize. Up until my arrival, her job was probably all conference calls and paperwork.

"Actually, Noah, I prefer Grace get all of her information from *you.* Now, if you'll excuse me, I have to go drop these files off in my office and then go have tea with your mother, Noah. Grace, I'm sure everything is going to be fine. And that, right now, is the best I can offer."

She starts to walk away but turns back, eyes me over the top of her glasses. It's like looking at Clark Kent and getting a glimpse of Superman. I'm almost sure she sees through me.

"Are you certain you're feeling OK today, Grace?"

I smile.

I lie.

"I'm great."

*

The sun is lower when Noah and I step into the courtyard.

"So what's Plan B?" I ask him.

"Wait," Noah says. "I was supposed to come up with a Plan B? I don't have a Plan B. I mean, I guess I could just start randomly going up to strangers, asking if they've seen a big, scary guy with a scar on his cheek. I'm assuming he's big and scary. I didn't really ask about that part."

Noah rambles when he's nervous. It's one of many things I'm starting to figure out about him.

"Can you get the directory from Israel or Brazil?" I ask.

Noah shakes his head. "I doubt it. I don't have that kind of access."

"They'd have a guest list for last night inside the palace, right?" I say. "Invitations, security checks? Everyone went through a metal detector. There have to be cameras. Facial-recognition software. They have to have that, don't they?"

Noah looks at me like maybe I'm off my meds. Which I am. But that is totally beside the point. "I guess so."

"Well, who do we know at the palace?"

"Who do we know at the palace?" Noah can't help himself; he laughs a little. "Correction. Who do we know who would hand over classified security footage and facial-recognition results? Well, there's got to be a super long list. Hey, the king seems like a good guy. I bet we can call him up and ask for a favor."

"Well, we've got to do something! Can we hack the palace's computer server?"

"Of course!" Noah actually hits his forehead with his palm. "Why didn't I think of that? I'll get right on it."

"What about the embassy's servers?"

"Who are you?!" Noah cries, like I'm morphing right in front of his eyes. He doesn't know this version of me has been around since the cradle. "More importantly, who do you think *I* am?"

Poor Noah. All he wanted to do today was go see his dad, and look at what I've done. I've tried to turn him into an international hacker and all-around spy.

Man, I find myself thinking, *I wish I knew a spy.*

I hear the gate behind me open, and soon Megan is coming toward us. She's in pink shorts. A pink top. There is even a pink headband keeping her glossy black bangs out of her eyes while her glossy black ponytail swings back and forth, keeping time. She's been for a jog, and her dark skin has a glow that is…well…pink.

For a second, I think Noah might actually gag on his own tongue.

"What are you two talking about?" Megan asks.

"Nothing," I say, just as Noah blurts, "Hi, Megan!"

It's like he's just worked up the nerve to talk and now the words come rolling out. "You look…sweaty. But in a good way. The good sweaty, is what I mean."

"Thanks," Megan says, the word clipped, like she's not exactly certain what to make of either the compliment or the boy who's given it.

I expect her to walk inside, to roll her eyes and go do whatever it is that popular, beautiful people do. But Megan just stands there, arms crossed, looking at me.

"Are you going to tell me what you're up to or not?" she asks finally.

"Not," I say. Not because I'm worried that she'll tell someone. I'm worried she'll tell everyone.

"That's too bad," Megan says, pushing past us. "I thought I heard you trying to figure out how to hack into the palace's mainframe."

"That's what you get for thinking," I say with a shrug. "I hear it can give you spots. Nasty business. Best to avoid it altogether."

And then Megan turns on me.

"I never did anything to you, Grace! I never did anything at all. I've been trying to be your friend since we were six years old, but I'm not good enough for you, I guess. I've never been good enough for you. Well this is me, deciding to stop trying."

I'm still reeling from her words when she spins and starts toward the door. She's almost inside when Noah calls out "Wait!" and she actually does.

Noah seems as surprised by this as I am. When she looks at him, his cheeks turn red and he starts to talk too quickly.

"It's just that we're looking for this guy and we know he was at the party at the palace last night, but we don't have any way of finding him and—"

"I can find him," Megan says matter-of-factly. Then she looks at me. "If that's OK with you."

But all I can think is *Megan wanted to be friends with me?*

I think back on all the times the two of us were thrust together: companions of last resort. I always thought she resented having to come play with me. And as a result, I hated having to play with her. But maybe we were both wrong. Maybe we were just two proud and stubborn little girls who were just too proud and stubborn.

"I know you just got back from your run and you're all…sweaty," Noah says. I elbow him in the gut. Hard. "But we really need your help."

Megan crosses her arms. "So what's it going to be, Grace? I can help you. Or you can stand here, being too bullheaded to let me. It's your call."

I've known Megan almost all my life. This is the first time I've ever liked her.

"Whose office is this?" Noah asks three minutes later.

"Someone who is currently having tea with a good friend in Israel," I tell him.

"Ms Chancellor?" Noah sounds like he might hyperventilate, so I hurry up and close the door. "We just broke into the office of… OK. Not going to panic."

"Yeah. That's what not panicking looks like," Megan says, pushing past him and taking a seat in Ms Chancellor's plush leather chair. As soon as she touches the computer, the US State Department seal pops up on the screen along with a prompt for a username and password.

"She's got to keep her password written down around here somewhere," I say, looking at the meticulous desk.

"Ms Chancellor? I don't think so. Besides, I don't need

it." Megan's sparkly pink fingernails are a blur as they fly across the keys. Sixty seconds later she announces, "We're in."

We're looking at a new screen now. It's nothing like I've ever seen before. This isn't the official US Foreign Service desktop. This is something different. It's like we're inside the computer's brain, and Megan is its master.

She spins on us, watches our expressions change.

"Don't let the glitter fool you." She wiggles her shiny nails in the air, then taps her temple. "I'm up here."

"I see that," I say as Noah whispers a very soft, "*I love you.*"

"What?" Megan asks.

"Nothing," Noah says, then pulls back and walks to the other side of the desk.

"Now, what is so urgent?" Megan asks me.

But I'm still flummoxed by what I've seen.

"How did you…?"

"My mom is the chief operations officer for the CIA stationed in Europe," she tells me. "I pay attention."

"I see that," I say.

"Now what do you need?"

"I need to know everyone who was at the party at the palace last night."

"Is that all?" Megan asks, like the least we could do is try to challenge her.

A few minutes later she's hitting print, and soon I'm looking down at a list of names. Hundreds of them. My hands start to tremble as I realize that one of them must belong to the man who killed my mother.

I can feel Noah looking over my shoulder.

"Is there any way to cross-reference that list with embassy ID photos or something?" he asks. "We don't have a name. Just a face."

"You need pictures?" Megan seems a little upset that we didn't mention that in the first place.

"Yes. Why? Is that a problem?" I ask.

"No. It just means we're looking in the wrong place."

Megan goes to work, and three minutes later I'm looking at a screen filled with nothing but people in formal attire walking slowly toward a camera, yellow dots covering their faces.

"What is that?" Noah asks.

"That is the palace's facial-recognition program chronicling everyone who entered the gala last night." Megan leans back and crosses her arms. She knows that we're impressed. *She* is impressed. And I have to admit she has the right to be.

"Can we get a copy of that – without anyone knowing we have it?"

"I already emailed it to a dummy account." She scribbles out a username and password. "Anything else?"

"*Marry me?*" Noah whispers.

If Megan hears him she ignores the question. She just keeps looking at me as I shake my head slowly back and forth.

"That was..." Words fail me. I don't like to owe favors and I hate to be caught off guard. Thirty minutes with

Megan and I am both. Embassy Row is turning into a far more dangerous place than I ever thought it could be.

Walking out of the embassy, Noah's long, lanky legs carry him up ahead. For a moment, Megan and I are alone.

"Well, thanks," I say, and reach for the scrap of paper, but Megan tugs it away, just out of my reach.

"So are you going to tell me now?" she asks.

"Tell you what?"

Megan spins on me, stopping and blocking my way.

"I'm sorry about your mom, Grace. And I'm sorry about what you've been through. But this" – she holds up the paper, accentuating the point – "whatever this is. It won't bring her back."

"It's not—"

"You don't want to tell me what's going on? Fine. But don't lie to me. OK?"

"OK," I say.

She hands me the paper. "And, Grace? Whatever this is…be careful."

Megan pushes through the gates and starts down the sidewalk. I feel as much as see when Noah comes to stand beside me.

"You ready?" he asks.

I smile and try to convince myself the answer is yes.

Brazil is totally dark when we get there. Noah leads me through a side gate to a small door at the back of the building. It's smaller than a lot of the other embassies, but it's always been one of my favorites. So many of the buildings on Embassy Row are palaces – fortresses. The Brazilian embassy always looked, from the outside at least, like a home.

Noah knocks on the door. When no one answers he uses a key and lets himself in. As far as I know there are no keys to the US embassy. Just a whole lot of marines with semi-automatic sidearms.

"Come on," Noah tells me. "We can work upstairs."

"Are we supposed to be here?" I ask him.

"I told you. I have dual citizenship. It's my night with my dad."

"I mean, the place seems empty."

"It's not," Noah says with a smile.

"Then where is everyone?"

Just then, as if on cue, there's a massive, thunderous roar. Whoops and applause and cheers in Portuguese.

Only then do I realize that the building isn't dark. Not exactly. The lights in the hall are out but there is a faint, flickering glow coming from a room not far away. Slowly, Noah and I creep toward it. As we pass, I can see the light is from a television that is so large it practically covers one wall of the big room. Inside, it seems like the entire Brazilian delegation is gathered around it, watching a soccer match that could be taking place anywhere in the world.

One man sits in the center of the crowd. Even among what has to be at least thirty people it's impossible not to notice him. His skin is dark and smooth. He has broad shoulders and the kind of super intense gaze that could make most girls melt.

But I am not most girls.

I only go a little wobbly.

When he sees Noah and me, he nods and smiles in our direction.

"Oh my gosh," I mutter to myself. "That guy is hot."

"That guy's my dad." Noah says it like he's said it a lot. "The ambassador."

"Oh." I can't quite hide my embarrassment. "Should I say hi and introduce myself or something?"

"Are you kidding?" Noah sounds like I've just suggested I go jump off a cliff. Again. "That's his old team playing. We do not interrupt my father when his team is playing."

"Your dad was a soccer player?"

Noah looks disgusted. "*Footballer.*"

"Oh. Right. Sorry."

"And, yes. National team, World Cup, Olympics – you name it. He was, as you Americans say, a stud. Clearly it runs in the family. Now, come on." He points toward the stairs. "Let's get to work."

"What about him?" Noah asks several hours later. I don't know what time it is, but I'm sure it must be late. There are shouts periodically from downstairs. The game has ended and a new one has begun, but the embassy is still mostly dark. We haven't actually laid eyes on Lila yet, but I can hear her moving around in the room next door, noisy but unseen. Like a very entitled, very tortured poltergeist. I'm half afraid she'll float through the wall at any minute.

"Grace?" Noah says, pulling my attention back to the screen.

I look at the image on the laptop, lean closer to the man who is there in black-and-white. He is looking in the wrong direction and we can't tell whether he has a scar or not.

I shake my head. "Too short."

Noah hits a button and the footage advances to the next man in line. "This guy?"

"No scar," I tell him.

"OK. How about..."

"I'm telling you, he was Caucasian. Six one or two. He moved like a guy who knew what he was doing. Like he had training and was sure in his skin. You know what I mean?"

"No." Noah shakes his head. "I really don't."

"I've seen it all my life. I grew up around those guys. Special forces – I can spot them from fifty paces. You can't have that much power in your body and not let it affect the way you move. I'm telling you, he looked like..." I trail off, shiver a little. I make myself look Noah right in the eye when I finish, "He looked like a killer, Noah. He is my mother's killer."

"OK," Noah says calmly, then stands. I can tell he's tired of sitting, staring at the screen. He's tired of feeling helpless and he's not the only one. "But maybe he–"

"I saw him!" I snap before Noah can join the long list of people who have told me that I am delusional.

"I know," he hurries to add. "I know. I was just going to say that maybe he's not in here."

"I thought everyone had to go through that checkpoint."

"All the *guests* did. But maybe he wasn't a guest. Or maybe he found a way around the main doors. He could have posed as a waiter and then changed into a tux in an air duct or something."

"This isn't a spy movie," I tell him. It feels like maybe he's not taking it seriously.

"I'm just saying that he might not be in here, Grace. And that's OK."

I stand now, too. "It's not OK! I've got to find him, Noah. I've got to..."

"What?" Noah presses closer to me, looks down right into my eyes. "*What?* No, I'm serious. Let's think this through. Let's say you do find him – then what happens? Really, Grace. I'm asking."

I stumble slightly back. "And then I make him pay."

"And what does that entail? Tell me *exactly* what you are going to do."

"I'm going to prove what he did. I'm going to prove…"

That I'm not making this up.

The lights come on in the hallway. There's more laughing now, talking. The matches must be over – the party breaking up – because the Brazilian embassy is coming awake even as the rest of Embassy Row is going to sleep.

Noah reaches past me, carefully closes the laptop.

"Come on," he tells me. "We've just been looking for one day. Tomorrow we can make it two."

I gather my things and Noah walks me to the street. He seems oddly protective in a way I've never really known before. Noah doesn't think I'm a little kid; he doesn't want to lock me in my room and keep me away from the dangers of the world. Noah isn't like Jamie – not like Alexei. He just wants to make sure that when those dangers find me I'm in a position to take care of myself.

"You really do believe me, don't you?" I ask when I reach the small gate that opens onto the sidewalk and the short walk home.

"Of course I believe you."

"And you really are my friend."

Noah grins. "Looks that way. Is that going to be a problem?"

"Just an unexpected development." I shake my head.

Noah closes the metal gate behind me. "Yeah, well… welcome to Embassy Row."

I start back up the hill, toward the US flag and my mother's bed and a building full of people who would never spend a day helping me, even if they didn't think it was a wild-goose chase.

"We'll find him!" Noah yells through the fence, watching me walk away. "He's out there somewhere. And we'll find him."

I have to smile. He's such a dork. But I'm starting to realize the one good thing that's happened: he's my dork.

The wind is strong, blowing off the sea, and, overhead, the flags all stand like soldiers in their spotlights, cracking and popping in the breeze. I think about what Noah is saying. We're not looking for a man. We're looking for a needle in an international haystack.

"We'll find him!" Noah yells again.

I laugh and turn and wave. I'm sure he cannot hear me when I say, "No. We won't."

I'm not sure how long I wander through the city. I'm not trying to get lost. I don't want to get in trouble. But even though I know the shortest route back, I cannot bring myself to take it.

So I turn down shady alleys and wide promenades lined with darkened shops. I climb so high up a windy street that I can see over the wall and watch the sea. The moon is so bright here – I'd forgotten how much bigger it always seemed, like a spotlight shining down from Heaven. I wish it would shine upon the Scarred Man, but he doesn't cross my path. The moon cannot lead me to him no matter how far I'm willing to go.

When the bells of the national cathedral chime midnight, I make sure I'm already on the other side of the embassy fence. The marine on duty raises his eyebrows – he knows I'm cutting it close. But I'm pretty sure the marines all like me. I'm a military kid. A member of their tribe. Besides, at the very least, my presence here has the potential to break up the monotony of their days.

I'm through the residence's entrance and halfway across the black-and-white floor when Ms Chancellor's voice catches me off guard.

"Not quite so fast."

I freeze, turn. Ms Chancellor is still in her suit and heels, and I can't help imagining her sneaking downstairs for a midnight snack. In heels. Skiing down the Alps. In heels. Skydiving. In heels.

"I'm in," I say, forcing a grin. "Midnight curfew observed."

"Grace, if I could have a word, please?" She asks it like a question but doesn't wait for an answer. She just trusts me to follow her up the stairs.

"I get it, OK?" I'm saying. "I'm here. I'm shutting up. I'm going to bed like a good little girl."

"Oh, sweetie."

I don't know what's more concerning, Ms Chancellor's words or the look on her face. When she stops at the top of the stairs, I'm seriously worried that she might try to hug me.

So I take a step back. "I'm nobody's sweetie."

She takes off her glasses and tilts her head. "Do you really believe that's true, Grace?"

"What are you talking about?"

Then Ms Chancellor eases away. She must know I'm on the verge of jumping onto the railing and sliding away, bursting through the doors, and never, ever coming back.

I'd rather live in a war zone with my father than with people who call me sweetie.

"Did you know I knew your mother?" Ms Chancellor asks, sinking down to sit on the top step. It's oddly casual. It doesn't suit her. "Oh, I know that *you and I* never had much reason to interact when you came here as a girl, but I joined your grandfather's staff not long after your grandmother died. Your mother was about your age at the time. And she and I became very close. We stayed quite close."

"So?" I say.

"So I was there the day your mother met your father. And I was there when your father asked your grandfather if he could marry her – that took some time to sink in, needless to say. I was with your grandfather when he learned that Jamie had been born. And when you were born. And, so, Grace…I know that you were *her* sweetie. And I know that now – even though she's gone – you are not alone."

"OK. Whatever. Fine."

It's dark, but I can feel Ms Chancellor staring at me – I feel it like a physical touch, and the sensation is almost too much. I'm tired of having so many emotions coursing through me. My nerves are raw and bleeding.

"You've been busy today." Ms Chancellor fiddles with her eyeglasses and I wonder if she knows that we were on her computer. Did Megan run and blab? But it isn't like that, I remember. She doesn't have to know what I've done – what Noah and I are still doing. She just has to know me.

I climb the final step and come inches from her. My voice is a whisper as I lean down and say, "You can't change what I saw."

"I know that," Ms Chancellor tells me. "But I can help you to deal with it."

I start past her. "You had your chance to help."

"You lost your mother, Grace!" Ms Chancellor calls after me. I can feel my anger growing, rising even as Ms Chancellor's voice stays cool. "You lost her in a terrible and horrific way. And that is why your grandfather and I have decided that perhaps you should talk to someone here. Like you did after the accident."

"Someone like a shrink?" I ask.

"Someone who can help you to come to terms with what happened. Put it behind you. Move on."

She's not asking me if I want to do this – if I think it is a good idea. She's already made up her mind. Or, worse, she's already made up *his* mind.

"I want to see my grandfather," I say, starting down the hall.

"He's not in his room."

I stop, spin on her. "Then where is he?"

"At the moment, I'm afraid he's—"

"Let me guess." I cock an eyebrow. "Busy?"

"He has guests, Grace."

I have to laugh. "It's after midnight. What kinds of guests does he have after midnight?"

Ms Chancellor doesn't answer. She just glances down almost involuntarily at the closed doors of the large formal sitting room that is on the opposite side of the foyer.

I don't wait to hear more.

"Grace!" Ms Chancellor yells as she struggles to her feet, but she doesn't have a prayer of catching me as I race down the stairs. The marines couldn't stop me. Not a battalion of Sherman tanks.

There is only one thing on this earth that could stop me in my tracks and that is the sight of the doors sliding open.

I hear laughter. Talking. A whiff of cigar smoke slips from the room and rises up the stairs.

I'm staring through the haze of it when a man steps into the foyer. He is tall and broad shouldered, his dark hair closely cropped. He could be anyone. Through the cigar smoke, he is simply Generic Man Number Three. And perhaps I would just keep running were it not for the way he moves, a series of efficient, fluid steps, easy perpetual motion inside a well-tuned body. The kind of body that has been prepared and honed and trained.

From my place halfway down the stairs, I'm shrouded in shadows. But I can see the man. I can hear laughter. Some more men join him in the foyer. They are slapping backs and shaking hands.

"I'll see you next week at your place, Pierre!" Grandpa calls to one man, who laughs and speaks in heavily accented English.

"And I expect you to bring my money so that I can win it back."

Through the sitting room's doors I see a table covered

with brightly colored plastic chips and playing cards. Poker night. My grandfather has been hosting poker night.

Ambassadors fill the foyer. I recognize the prime minister and several of the men I saw at the palace.

The G-20 summit is nothing compared to the power that has been assembled around my grandfather's poker table. The men say their goodbyes, their breath no doubt smelling like cigars and Grandpa's good Tennessee whiskey.

There are at least a dozen men, but no women. It's like peeking behind the curtain of some ancient, all-powerful boys' club. There is so much testosterone swirling in the air that for a second I lose sight of the broad-shouldered man.

I move a little closer, stand on my tiptoes, try to see better.

The prime minister moves toward the door, raises his hand in a goodbye wave. "Until next week, my friend," he tells my grandfather.

Someone opens the door.

The prime minister starts to leave.

But not before the man holding the door for him turns back to my grandfather, offers a nod of his head.

The light from the porch flashes across his face, and I can see the dark, soulless eyes, the high cheekbones. And the scar that runs from his eyebrow to his jaw.

"Grace." Ms Chancellor's hand is on my arm. I realize, faintly, that I'm sliding, trying to sit on the cold stairs. My grandfather and many of his guests are still in the foyer, and I know we cannot have a scene. I cannot cause an incident. Now would be an inopportune time for a distraught teenager to yell "Murderer!" and go running down the stairs.

I know what she's thinking. But she doesn't have to worry about that. I'm too busy shaking.

"*Grandpa knows him.*"

I look up at Ms Chancellor. She must see the betrayal in my eyes – the hurt as I say it again. "Grandpa knows him!"

"Come, Grace. Let's wait for your grandfather upstairs."

"Grace, I know you must have questions..."

Grandpa doesn't even say hello when he reaches his office. He doesn't ask what I was doing out until midnight, or who I was with – none of the typical questions an adult authority figure is supposed to ask. He's already been briefed by Ms Chancellor. He is ready for this fight.

Which is a good thing because I'm already up and shouting, "*You know him?*"

"Now, Gracie..." Grandpa starts slowly. His tie is loose and the top button of his shirt is undone. When he walks to the small rolling tray by the window and pours himself a drink, I can tell it isn't his first of the night. The way things are going, it almost certainly won't be his last.

"I told you what I saw. I came to you and *you know him.* You knew him all along and you told me I was seeing things!"

"No." Grandpa's voice is sharp. He's not doing the

folksy Southern-gentleman act anymore. This is the man who negotiated the Treaty of Caspia. This is the man who championed the development of the EU. This is why the president and the prime minister and a half dozen other world leaders call him their friend.

I'm supposed to be intimidated. But I'm not. I'm disgusted.

"I told you, Grace Olivia, that you did *not* see the man who killed your mother. And you didn't."

"Who is he?" I demand.

Grandpa takes a slow sip of his whiskey. When he speaks again, his accent is stronger than I have ever heard it.

"He is a man I've known for years. He's a friend."

"*Who is he?*" I shout.

Grandpa's voice remains soft. "His name is Dominic Novak. He's the head of security for the prime minister. He is a decorated war hero and a key advisor to one of the most powerful men in Europe. He is trusted and respected and... He's just a man with a scar, Grace. It doesn't make him evil."

"I know not all people with scars are evil," I snap. "I'm not living in a cartoon. But I also know—"

"You know *what*?" Exasperated, Grandpa throws open one of his desk drawers and pulls out a file. "Tell me what you know, Grace. Because I remember when you just *knew* you saw your mother's murderer two years ago in Santa Fe." He pulls a photograph from the file – a face I thought I'd never see again.

"Or the man in the airport in Chicago." He pulls out another picture. And then another. And another. "This one was a corporal at Fort Meade, wasn't he?" My grandfather keeps pulling photographs out of the file folder, dropping them onto the desk. One scarred man after another. "And let's not forget the priest in St. Louis. You were positive it was him. Even after we found out he'd been in South America when your mother was killed. Even then you shouted and insisted and—"

"OK!" I yell. "Enough!"

"You said these men killed your mother, didn't you, Grace?" Grandpa asks, and I stand silent. "*Didn't you?*"

I stop shaking and look him in the eye.

"I'm right this time. I saw him."

"Well, let me tell you what *I* see."

He takes a step toward me, gestures with the hand that holds the glass. Brown liquid sloshes over the side and stains his expensive rug, but my grandfather doesn't notice. Or maybe he just doesn't care.

"I see a girl who witnessed an horrendous thing and never let herself deal with the trauma. I see a girl who, upon seeing a man who has a scar – *any* man with a scar – jumps to a terrible conclusion. But, most of all, Grace" – his voice is heavy and tired – "I see a girl *who has said all of this before.*"

"I know how it looks. I know–"

"You don't know anything!" My grandfather's voice is so strong, so loud, that I half expect the windows to shake, the security alarms to go off. "My Caroline is dead!"

It is the first time in three years that I have heard him say my mother's name. It is the first time I have ever seen him cry.

"She died in a terrible, tragic accident. And if I thought… If I thought that there was someone who needed to be punished for that, I would do it." His voice grows low, gravelly. Desperate. "So help me, I would do it myself."

Grandpa is staring at me now. And for the first time I can't fight the feeling that a part of him hates a part of me. For bringing this memory to his door. For looking a little too much like her. For taking his daughter away from him all over again.

"Dominic is a good man, Grace," Grandpa says, finally tearing his gaze away from me. "The best of men. I would trust him with my life. I would have trusted him with my daughter's life." He waves me and my crazy, irrational worries away. "He would not have hurt her."

I feel embarrassed and indignant. Both. But I don't argue anymore. "Why didn't you tell me that last night?"

"I did." Grandpa takes a sip, then shrugs. "Or I tried to. Don't bother Dominic, Grace. Leave the poor man alone. Stay out of the affairs of the prime minister. These are busy people in troubling times. None of us need more worries or stress or wild, unsubstantiated theories circling around."

I have to laugh a little. "You really don't trust me, do you?"

Grandpa studies me. "Of course I do."

But the words are too slow, the eye contact too fleeting.

"For a good diplomat, you really are a very bad liar," I tell him, then leave before he can say another word.

"Noah," I say, shaking his shoulder. "Noah, wake up."

He rolls over, mutters something in Hebrew that I can't translate but is probably the Israeli equivalent of "Ten more minutes, Mom."

I shake his shoulder again and he swats me away, like a fly.

So I slap him.

"Grace!" Noah shouts. Then he seems to remember where we are and lowers his voice. "What are you doing in my room?"

"So you can break into *my* room, but I can't pay you a call?"

"I was… I had… I mean…"

"Relax," I tell him. "Lila let me in. She's super cheerful in the mornings."

"Yes." Noah drags his groggy body out of bed, swings his feet onto the floor. "You know, keep this up and I'm going to get a reputation."

"You're wearing Spider-Man pajamas. I think your reputation can handle it. Now come on." I toss a pair of jeans in his direction. "Get dressed. We've got to go."

"Go where?"

But I just step into the hall and wait for him to change.

"Grace..."

The breeze is cool, but Noah's voice is colder. We stand close enough to touch on a sidewalk, staring across a busy street at a building that is three floors tall. A black wrought-iron fence and two guards are positioned between the front door and the sidewalk opposite us.

It's just an ordinary street in a lot of ways. Buses pass. Café owners are busy setting up their sidewalk tables. I can smell the day's fresh bread. It is a perfectly lovely morning in every way but one.

And that is why I stand, not moving. Now is not the time to be careless or rash or... *Grace-like.* Now is the time to make the exact right move at the exact right time. Now is when I have to be patient.

"Grace," Noah tries again. "That's the prime minister's residence."

I take a sip of coffee and never let my gaze leave the door. "I know."

"And I'm pretty sure the prime minister doesn't have a scar on his face."

"I know."

A bus passes, temporarily blocking my line of sight.

It's all I can do not to panic until my view is restored. But a split second later I'm looking back at the same tall, black iron fence. The same empty sidewalk. The same polished gold door knocker. I can't help myself. Part of me just wants to cross the street and ring the bell – tell the prime minister that he is being guarded by a killer.

But then another, scarier, thought occurs to me: *Maybe he already knows.*

"So I'm pretty sure that the prime minister could not have killed your mother," Noah finishes, proud of himself.

"I know the prime minister didn't do it," I tell him.

Noah actually sighs with relief.

"Good. Because for a second there, I thought you were going to say—"

A streetcar is coming, its bell ringing in the air. When it passes, I look across the street, stare at the man exiting the prime minister's residence, and say, "He did."

I know the way people look at you when they think that you're crazy. Call it a byproduct of being me. So I know that Noah hadn't thought I was making it up – that my mind was playing tricks on me or it was just the trauma speaking. But he still sounds surprised when he mutters, "It's him."

Surprised and a little terrified.

Looking for a killer from the safety of your bedroom inside a foreign embassy is one thing. It's quite another when the killer is about to cross the street and head in your direction.

"It's really him," Noah says again.

"Yes," I say. "It is."

"We have to do something," Noah says. "We've got to go tell your grandfather or…I don't know."

"I *did* tell my grandfather. He said that the Scarred Man's name is Dominic Novak. He is the head of security for the prime minister and a generally upright dude. He says that I am crazy."

"He didn't say that, Grace," Noah guesses.

Noah is sweet and nice, a little naïve. I have to shake my head as I tell him, "They *always* say that."

When the Scarred Man crosses the street, he comes within five feet of us, almost close enough for me to reach out and touch the scar on his left cheek. For a second, I'm tempted to do just that – to make sure it's real. It was one thing to look at it through a small crack in a door. But I'm standing on a sunny street now. I can hear birds singing and the bells of the trolleys in the distance. Everything around me is alive. But as soon as I see that scar, I think of death.

"Grace," Noah says very, very slowly, "is he still behind me?"

"Yes…no. He's moving now."

"OK." Noah draws a deep breath. "OK. Good. Now we can go get someone or do something or—"

"There is no one to get, Noah."

"But someone has to do something!"

"I know." I reach into the bag I have slung across my body and pull out the walkie-talkies I got for my twelfth birthday. "That's why we're going to follow him."

Noah and I stick together, trying to mimic the Scarred Man's pace. It's erratic, though, like he knows someone might be back here. And then I realize that, yeah, he probably does.

"Just so I'm clear," Noah says, his voice lower than it needs to be, "this man is the head of security for the leader of a small but prominent European country."

I might glare at him a little because Noah pulls back, wounded.

He throws up his hands. "What? I just thought someone should point out the obvious."

"OK," I tell him as the Scarred Man turns onto another busy street. Noah and I wait a beat then follow him up the hill.

"The obvious," Noah goes on, a little out of breath, "being that he is probably some supersecret assassin or something. And I'm not as tough as I look."

"That's OK," I tell him. "I'm way tougher than you look."

Noah levels me with a glare. He's not teasing as he says, "Don't you think we might be out of our league?"

I can't tell him that he's wrong. Or that he's right. I can't tell Noah any of the things he probably has a right to know, mainly because I don't want to lose him yet. I don't want to skip ahead to the part where he pities or distrusts or even hates me. I like that he is different from everyone else I've ever known in that one essential way.

We're passing by an antique store and for a moment I stop. Frozen.

I see my mother's face in the glass, hear a little girl ask, "Momma, do you like that locket?"

But my mother doesn't answer. She will never answer me again.

And that is why I turn to Noah and say, "We're the only league there is. Right now, you and I are all we've got." I mean it. I mean it so much more than he will ever know.

When the Scarred Man turns down another street, I start to follow. But this street isn't busy like the last. It's narrow – not much more than an alley lined with apartments and houses. Quiet and sleepy, this is the kind of street where a trained operative would know if someone were on his tail.

"We've got to split up."

"What? No! I'm not leaving you."

"That's why I brought the walkie-talkies," I tell him, already stepping into the street.

"Grace, wait!"

"Just go to the end of the block. Wait there. I'll tell you where to meet up and then you can take my place and we can tag-team it – like that."

"Grace—"

"I'll be OK, Noah," I tell him. I press the button on the walkie-talkie. "See?" My voice echoes in stereo. Scratchy and haunting. "I'm OK."

Part of having the world think you're crazy means you

always have to remind yourself of the truth. Always. Especially if you don't necessarily like what you have to say. And right now I'm alone on a street so narrow only the noonday sun can shine upon it. I'm walking thirty yards behind the man who killed my mother, pecking at my phone, trying to act like a normal, harmless, well-adjusted teenage girl.

But I am none of those things.

And I am anything but OK.

"Hey, Grace," someone says an hour later. I jump, startled. Did she just appear out of thin air? Or was I so hungry and tired and focused on my target that she has been following me for thirty minutes and I didn't even notice?

In any case, I try to sound as calm as possible when I say, "Hi, Rosie."

The tiny girl eases closer. "Whatcha doing?"

"Sorry, Rosie, but I'm a little busy at the moment."

I start to ease around the corner, needing to be ready if and when Noah tells me it's my turn. But mostly I just need Rosie to get away from me. It's bad enough I've already corrupted Noah; I can't stand the thought of putting Rosie in danger, too.

But Rosie is holding back a laugh. "Oh, I can tell."

I'm just about to ask what she thinks is so funny when Noah's voice comes ringing out of the walkie-talkie I'm holding behind my back. "Grace, we have movement on the south side of the building. I repeat, we have movement, and it's coming your way."

I look at Rosie. Rosie looks at me.

"Grace," Noah says after a moment. "Grace, do you read—"

"Go ahead," Rosie tells me. "Answer him."

Slowly, I hold up my walkie-talkie. "I read you." I can't take my eyes off of the small girl with the very self-satisfied smile.

"You're doing it wrong," Rosie says.

"Sorry, Rosie. I wish I could stay, but I–"

"But you're trying to follow one of the most security-conscious, not to mention paranoid, men in Adria," Rosie tells me. "*And you're doing it wrong.*"

For a moment I just stare at her. I don't have a clue what to say. All I know is that I will *not* tell her that she's crazy – that she's making it all up. I will never use that as a weapon against another human being as long as I live.

Rosie looks at my slack jaw, my dazed expression. "I've spent my whole life tailing after people who think they're more interesting than me, Grace."

"But–"

"I'm not an idiot! I'm just twelve. I'm a twelve-year-old girl and neither of those facts are my fault."

I was thirteen when I saw my mother die, when I told my story. When I started "having a hard time," as my grandfather likes to say. Would they have locked me up if I'd been thirty? If I'd been a boy? It's a question I do not dare to ask.

"Grace?" Noah's scratchy voice cuts through the air. "Grace, are you there?"

Before I can stop her, Rosie pulls the walkie-talkie from my limp hand.

"Noah," she says into it. "This is Rosie. Hang back twenty meters and do not cross the street. We're going to get ahead of him."

She hands the walkie-talkie back to me. "This is how you do it."

I am a natural tree climber, swimmer, and window-crawler-outer. Turns out, what Rosie does best is disappear.

She's small enough that she weaves, totally unseen, through the crowded market. She blends in easily among the tourists that gather outside the palace. And when the man with the scar stops cold and turns, he walks right past her – *and Rosie lets him* – as if both of them are exactly where they are supposed to be.

For the most part, Noah and I do as we're told. When she says to get on a streetcar, we get on. When she tells us to split up and wait on opposite corners outside the national cathedral, we do that, too. We are students of a twelve-year-old ninja. And we have a lot to learn.

When the Scarred Man comes out of the church and turns onto a street I've never really seen before, I am the one who is closest, so it's my job to follow.

The Romans built this part of town and I'm walking on cobblestones a thousand years older than my home nation. The world has changed. Wars raged and governments rose and fell, but the streets of Valancia have stayed exactly the same. Curving, twisting, climbing.

As I follow the man who killed my mother up the winding street, there is a moment when I realize that I am not afraid. I'm actually happy that there is something real that I can do. If I can see him I can follow him. And if I can follow him I can find proof of what happened three years ago. And then I can do what they've been telling me to do ever since that fateful night: move on.

There's laughter on the street behind me. A little girl holds tightly to her brother's hand.

"*Jamie, come on!*"

"*There's nothing down there, Gracie.*"

"*But I saw Momma come this way.*"

"*No. See, Grace, Mom isn't here.*"

"Grace?" Noah says. "Grace, are you there?"

We've ditched the walkie-talkies and are on a three-way cell phone call. There's a micro-receiver in my ear. I feel like James Bond. That is, if James Bond ever went into the field with twelve-year-old former gymnasts.

"Do you have eyes on him?" Rosie asks.

"Not yet," I say as the street curves slightly. I ease silently around, waiting for a clean line of sight. "I..." – I stagger to a stop and no longer try to muffle my voice – "lost him. I lost him."

"What?" Noah snaps.

"It's a dead end," I say. "The road curves and then it just...stops. It stops right here."

"He must have doubled back," Rosie tells me. "You must have missed him."

"Did you look away for a while?" Noah asks. "Were

you distracted by something?"

For a second I can't answer. I think about the memory.

"No… I mean, I didn't miss him," I say, looking around at the empty street that had been growing gradually more and more narrow. Where I stand it's not much more than an alley, and I am alone. There is no way I missed a car or a pedestrian. It would have been obvious.

The Scarred Man didn't double back. The Scarred Man *disappeared.*

I stand there for a long time, looking at the empty alley, and thinking about that little girl who was certain she had seen her mother come this way. Not for the first time I have to wonder where my mother went and why I couldn't follow.

The Scarred Man is boring.

At least that's what he pretends to be over the next three days. When he isn't at the prime minister's side, he sits at a sidewalk café drinking a single cup of coffee and reading the morning paper. He looks at books he doesn't buy and shops for groceries that he leaves in the store to be delivered later. He certainly never has any clandestine meetings where he talks about killing my mother. At least not that I can detect.

Eventually, Rosie gets bored and Noah gets busy, and only my mother's memory is with me, looking in shop windows and eating gelato on hot days.

I try following the Scarred Man again on my own, but I lose him in the market. It feels as if Dominic is not the only one who has disappeared down a dead end. There is absolutely nowhere else for my investigation to take me. So that's why I'm standing on Embassy Row on an overcast day, looking down the street to where it curves out of sight. I am looking for another angle.

And then I spot Alexei.

He's alone as he leaves the Russian embassy. He walks next door and talks to one of our marines, who shakes his head, then laughs. Alexei laughs, too. The whole thing feels surreal. I feel almost guilty – like I shouldn't be spying on Alexei.

Alexei who disappeared inside the palace.

Alexei who was upstairs right before the Scarred Man met with some mysterious accomplice.

Alexei who saw me at my lowest and who I will never, ever forgive for witnessing my shame.

Maybe I think he's involved somehow. Maybe I'm just here for practice. Or maybe I simply like the way Alexei looks from behind. I'm not thinking about *why* as I watch him walk away.

Alexei doesn't see me. I watch him pass on the other side of the street, wait until he's up ahead and then step out to follow him. I don't know what I'm hoping to gain. I only hope that there's nothing more that I can lose.

When Alexei turns and starts up one of the steep streets that leads to the palace and the city center, I don't think twice. I turn the corner…and run right into Lila.

"What are you doing here?" she huffs.

Over her shoulder, I see Alexei's father has joined him on the street. He's yelling at his son. Alexei skulks forward, almost like he's in trouble. But that can't be possible. Alexei is the Russian Jamie. Alexei can do no wrong.

"Are you listening?" Lila snaps.

"No, actually, I'm not," I tell her. Lila crosses her arms. She's not trying to play nice, and neither am I.

"He's not here," Lila tells me before I've said another word. She jerks her head toward the gate that is slamming shut behind her. "Noah's the reason you're here, right?"

That's when I realize that I'm actually on the corner in front of the Israeli embassy. It sits at the intersection of two of the busiest streets in Valancia but Lila doesn't care about that.

"Our dad is playing in some charity football tournament and he's making Noah play, too."

"Noah plays soccer?" I ask, genuinely stunned.

Lila scoffs at my ignorance. "It's *football*," she tells me. "And everybody knows my brother plays. It's the one thing he's halfway decent at. So, like I said, my brother is busy."

"Uh…OK."

Megan is coming down the street, and when she sees me and Lila together, for a split second it looks like she wants to run. Save herself. And I can't say I blame her.

"Hi, Megan," I tell her. We haven't spoken since the day she broke into Ms Chancellor's computer for me.

"Is everything OK?" Megan asks.

Lila laughs.

"I'm fine," I say. Alexei and his father are already far up the hill, climbing toward the palace. "In fact, I was just going."

"Not so fast," Lila tells me. She steps onto the sidewalk,

blocking my path. "I've been meaning to talk to you."

"Whoa. *You* have been meaning to talk to *me.* Oh my gosh!" I gush with mock enthusiasm. "I've been hoping this day would come. Are we going to be BFFs? Because I'd really love to be your BFF. That last *F* is for *forever*!" I add with a wink and a whisper.

"Does anyone think you're as funny as *you* think you are?" Lila asks.

"That depends. Does anyone ever think you have as much power as you think you have?"

"Listen." Lila draws a deep breath, as if calling a temporary truce. She steps slightly closer, lowering her voice and giving more power to her words. "You need to stay away from my brother."

"The brother you hate?" I ask.

"The brother who had enough trouble before you showed up."

"What kind of trouble did Noah have?" I ask. The thought is almost laughable.

"He's better off without you," Lila says, ignoring my question. "He doesn't need you. Do you hear me?"

"Yes, ma'am," I say.

"I'm serious," Lila says. "He doesn't need you dragging him down with you when you fall." Lila slowly looks me up and down. I can feel the weight of her stare, of the ultimate truth in her words as she says, "Because people like you always fall."

It's starting to rain, and Lila doesn't want to get wet. "Come on, Megan," she snaps, and starts away. But for a split second, Megan doesn't move. For a split second it seems like Megan doesn't want to.

I think about the little girl who used to come over with her Barbies – try to reconcile her against the computer genius who just did me maybe the biggest favor of my life. And, finally, I remember the look in Megan's eyes when she told me to be careful. But whatever moments Megan and I might have shared, they are long over.

"Megan!" Lila shouts.

Megan follows.

I stand for a long time, listening to the clicking of their heels against the cobblestones. They sound like very tiny horses, disappearing into the distance.

Maybe Lila looks back. Maybe she thinks she's really gotten me, burned me with her words, and that is why I am frozen where I stand.

But she can't see what I see.

The cobblestones are ancient. Every tourist to ever visit Adria has heard about the Romans and the Mongols, the Crusaders and the Turks. They all came to Adria. They all came and saw and conquered. And fell.

Lila was right about that part. Eventually, everybody falls.

It's starting to pour, and water gushes from the gutters, filling the edges of the street. I watch it roll down the hill, presumably out to sea.

I'm still standing there, staring at the ground. But the strangest thing is happening. The water doesn't run straight. In fact, there is a place where the water doesn't run at all. It spirals. Like a tiny whirlpool in the center of the street. The stones there aren't like the others. The pattern is different. In the center stone there is an emblem. I reach down through the cold water and trace it, knowing in my gut that I've seen something like it before.

Lila is right. We all fall down.

And down.

There's laughter on the street behind me. A woman is holding an umbrella with one hand and a little girl's arm with the other. Together, they are running through the rain. "Hurry, Gracie!" she says as the little girl jumps into a puddle.

My eyes fill with tears, and I blink once. Twice.

When I see the Scarred Man from the corner of my eye I'm not entirely sure that I'm not dreaming. But no, I decide, he is very, very real. And in that moment I forget all about Lila and Megan, Alexei and his father. There is only one thing on my mind as the Scarred Man walks without an umbrella, his collar turned up, practically racing up the hill. Wherever he's going, he's in a hurry. So I do what any self-respecting mentally unbalanced teenager would do.

I follow him.

I run as fast as I dare on the wet, uneven streets. Once I actually slip but catch myself before I land face-first on the sidewalk. Shopkeepers are pulling in their displays. People huddle under the awnings of the outdoor cafés. On the hop-on-hop-off buses, everyone is rushing to hop on and nobody sits on the upper deck.

Everyone is clinging to warmth and dryness. Everyone

except the wild American teenager who is running as fast as she can down Embassy Row. My hair clings to my face. My T-shirt clings to me, cold and maybe in slightly scandalous ways. I don't care. I don't stop. I just keep running up the winding street.

The Scarred Man is moving quickly, even in the rain. I should stand out more than usual, but it's like there is a curtain of fog and water between us. He isn't worried about his tail.

He walks down a narrow alley I've never seen before, and I stay carefully back. I won't be cornered. I won't be seen. I won't be defeated.

I wait, counting, patient.

After I'm pretty sure enough time has gone by, I turn the corner and find the Scarred Man is totally gone.

It shouldn't make me happy, but it does. I laugh out loud and throw my head up to the heavens, feel the rain on my face. And then I look down at the cobblestones. Water flows out of gutters and off rooftops. There, on the hillside, it runs quickly in every place but one.

I hold my breath as I sneak toward the swirling, spinning water. A tiny tidal pool has formed in the center of the sloping street. My hand is cold but that's not why it's shaking as it sinks into the water and traces the emblem on the center stone.

My breath stops coming as I push and then watch as, slowly, the stones fall away, a narrow opening descending into darkness.

I know I'm supposed to be smart. Now is the time to be careful. For a moment, I do consider going to find a flashlight, but then he might slip away. Already, I can't see the Scarred Man in the darkness that descends below me. I will not risk losing him again.

There's a ladder on the side of the hole, and I start to climb down. I count thirty rungs before I'm standing on a floor that is hard and cold and solid. Rainwater drips from the opening overhead.

I look up in time to see the door above me closing. In the faint and disappearing light I see the system of pulleys that moves the stones. It's old, I realize. Then I correct myself. It's *ancient.*

I can't help but recall what Rosie told me my very first night here: *There are five hundred kilometers of tunnel beneath the city*. Maybe more. Probably more. And I know that is where I am. The Scarred Man's mysterious comings and goings start to make sense.

Finally, I feel like maybe the Scarred Man isn't too many steps ahead of me.

For a moment, I stand still in the silence and let my eyes adjust to the dark. There are torches on the walls, lined up like bicycles waiting for their owners. In the extreme darkness of the tunnel I can make out a distant, flickering light. The Scarred Man has already chosen a torch to guide his way, but I don't dare take one for myself. I can't risk him knowing that he's not alone. Besides, I don't have a way to light it. I've spent three years avoiding things that burn. So I start off down the tunnel, trusting, feeling my way.

The walls are rough but smooth, like they were carved out by hand but worn over time. The floor slopes slightly, and I follow a trickle of water, knowing I'm going downhill. Like the streets that run above me, the tunnels are not straight. They curve and twist, backtrack. Sometimes the entire way has been caved in. Sometimes I take out my cell phone and use it to shed a little light, but mostly I'm trusting the echoing sound of the Scarred Man's footsteps and the distant, flickering glow of his torch to guide my way...until that torch goes out.

I don't dare risk using my phone. In the blindness that follows, I creep along the tunnel until my foot kicks the torch that lies on the ground, still warm to the touch. He's coming back for it, I just know, but I don't let it scare me.

I feel the walls. The floor. And then I look up and see

a small crack of faint light coming through something like a trapdoor overhead.

The rain must have stopped because there is no more water in the tunnel. I don't know where I am. I have no idea what stands above me. But I also know that there is only one way to find out. I hold my breath.

And climb.

When I emerge into a dim space, my first thought is that I'm in a building, not on the street. There is carpet, but not the plush, soft stuff of the palace. The fabric beneath my palms is harsh, industrial. Something made to withstand a nuclear blast or a bunch of tourists with muddy feet. It's so stark and modern that it's almost like whiplash to me – like I'm literally crawling on my hands and knees from one century to the next.

The lights are off, but there is a narrow window high on the wall that probably looks out at ground level. A little ambient light filters through the glass and fills the space. I look up at the darkened fluorescent bulbs that hang overhead. The ceiling is low and there's nothing on the walls – no sign whatsoever of where I might be. I might have followed the Scarred Man into his office or his home, the basement of any house or business in the country.

There's absolutely no way of knowing where I am, so I stay perfectly still. Waiting. Listening. And then I hear the voices.

I don't even stand. I'm too afraid the floor might creak, my knees might crack. I don't dare do anything that might break the flow of that moment as I crawl on my hands and knees and peek around the corner.

At the end of the hall, there is a door that's open just a crack. A soft light burns inside, and I can make out the shape of the shoulders I have been following for days.

I recognize the voice as soon as the Scarred Man says, "There will be plenty of opportunities. More than enough."

On the other side of the door, there's mumbling. Someone speaks to him, but I can't make out the words. In the basement, water runs through pipes. Hot and cold air flows through vents. The voice on the other side of the door is lost to me. So I ease closer.

"It will be an easy job," the Scarred Man says. I see him start to turn, so I scoot backward. Faster and faster. It's like the hallway is on fire and I can't stop moving long enough to stand.

But when I reach the trapdoor I freeze, the Scarred Man's words echoing in my ear:

"There are many perfectly adequate ways to die. I just have to find one."

I'm back inside the tunnel.

I'm running – falling down. The ground is damp and I lose my footing. I crash on my side. My head spins, but I force myself to my feet, no longer caring if he hears me. I no longer want to know where he goes. What he does.

I run faster and faster down tunnels that spiral and branch. Soon I have no idea which way I came from. Without the Scarred Man's light I am shrouded in darkness. Pushing. Clawing.

When my hands land upon another ladder I have no idea where it might lead, but my options are to either climb or die, so I reach for the ancient rungs as one thought fills my head; there is one fact I cannot make myself forget. But there is no time to think about that now, so I bang my fist against the trapdoor overhead, push it harder and harder, but it doesn't want to move.

Down the tunnel, I can see a flickering light. The Scarred Man is coming closer. He's going to find me. He's going to kill me. So I throw my shoulder against the door. Over and over and—

I hear the crash as the door bursts open, but I don't stop to think as I hurl myself up and onto another unfamiliar floor, then slam the trapdoor down.

Instantly, lights flash on. My eyes, so used to the dark now, burn with the glare.

There is screaming and shouting in a language I don't know. I curl instinctively into a ball, my breath coming harder as the screaming gets louder. But the words I don't understand do not matter. There is already one thought pounding over and over in my head:

The Scarred Man killed my mother...and he is going to kill again.

Grandpa isn't happy. To be fair, I don't know that many men who would be pleased to have their granddaughter dragged home after dark, sopping wet and disheveled after turning up in the South Korean embassy totally uninvited and unannounced.

I mean, I know I'm no expert in diplomacy. But appearing on the basement floor, wet and terrified, probably isn't the best way to make an entrance. Even I know that.

But that's what I've done. And now it's time to pay the price.

The man who walked me here keeps a death grip on my arm. We stand at attention side by side in front of my grandfather's desk, as if we're here for some kind of inspection. Grandpa stares at me like an executioner might. Ms Chancellor stands over his shoulder, uncertain whether to laugh or to scream. She no longer looks at me like she wants us to be friends. I know without asking that she'll probably never again try to give me candy.

My grandfather and my captor speak to each other in rapid Korean. No one offers to translate for me, but even though I don't know the words, I know exactly what they're saying. When my grandfather lowers his voice and speaks softly, the man lets go of my arm and looks at me. The truth about what my grandfather just told him is written all over his face. I call this particular look the Dead Mom Smile. He's giving it to me now. The tilt of the head. The slightly upturned lips. *Oh, poor thing,* he's thinking. When he speaks again, I know that's what he'll say.

It's a free pass and my grandfather knows it. How am I supposed to know that it's rude to show up unannounced in the basements of foreign governments? I no longer have a mom to tell me not to.

"Gracie." Grandpa's voice pulls me back. "What do you have to say for yourself?"

It might be a trick question, so I take a moment before deciding to speak. Carefully, I look from Grandpa to the man from South Korea to Ms Chancellor, who gives a little nod to go ahead.

"Well, I was out walking, and then it started to rain," I say slowly. "And then I got lost. I didn't know where I was. The sidewalk was slick and I fell through some kind of hole and ended up in this tunnel. I couldn't get back up. So I started walking. But it was so dark down there. And I was wet and cold and afraid." I look at our visitor. "I was so afraid," I tell him. My voice breaks.

"And then I saw a ladder and a sort of trapdoor, so I started to climb and...the next thing I knew, I was in your embassy. But I didn't know it was your embassy!" I hurry to add. I'm almost shaking as I drop my gaze to the ground. "I was just trying to find a way out."

I wish I was exaggerating, but the terror I felt is still too fresh, and there is so much truth in my lie that it is maybe the most honest thing that I have ever said. But they don't know that. They just look at me for a long time. It's Ms Chancellor who finally breaks the silence.

"Mr Kim, I assure you, no one regrets this terrible accident more than Grace. I'm sure she is sincerely sorry for any shock or concern she might have caused you or your staff. Aren't you, Grace?"

"I am. I really am," I say.

Then the man turns to my grandfather and says something else I do not understand.

Grandpa laughs, pats him on the back, and shakes his hand.

"It's a deal," Grandpa says. Then he turns to me. "Gracie, what do you say to Mr Kim?"

I give a low bow and use my most reverent tone as I tell him, "*Juay song hamnida.*"

This, at last, makes the man smile. He bows back, then shakes my grandfather's hand one final time and leaves.

"That was very impressive, Grace," Ms Chancellor says before Grandpa can speak.

I shrug. "I can apologize in seven different languages. It's just something you pick up when you're me."

But Grandpa isn't pleased. "Gracie, I do not know why you were there—"

"I told you why I was there!"

"But you cannot go sneaking into places where you don't belong!"

"I didn't sneak in! I was lost! I was scared! I was…" I trail off as soon as I remember I'm not lying.

I would give anything to be lying.

"Did that boy make you do this?"

"That – Wait. What boy?"

"The Russian," Grandpa snaps, and I want to laugh, the thought of it is so absurd. That Alexei could be a bad influence on *me*…

"Well, did he?" Grandpa persists.

"I haven't talked to Alexei since…" I don't want to say *that night* or *since my attack*. I don't want to relive it in any possible way. So I simply shake my head. "I don't talk to Alexei."

"Good. The Cold War, Gracie – it was easy compared to this."

This what? I want to know but do not ask. Instead, I hang my head and nod ever so slightly.

"I was so scared."

Maybe it's the softness of my voice, the gentle quiver in the words. Maybe I look like my mother. Whatever the reason, neither my grandfather nor Ms Chancellor scold me anymore.

"I guess that does it, then," he says.

"Yes. For tonight," Ms Chancellor tells him. "We

should touch base with them in a week or so. Perhaps the Korean ambassador will—"

"He's going to kill again," I say, but the words are barely more than a whisper.

"What's that?" Grandpa says. I can't tell if he didn't hear me or he's pretending he didn't, then I decide it doesn't matter.

"Never mind." I shrug and shake my head. "You never have before."

I want to storm off, make a statement with a slamming door. But as soon as I reach the hallway I can see I'm not alone.

"Grace, are you OK?" Megan asks, tilting her head.

I don't need Megan's worry.

I do not want her pity.

I only have so much "care" inside of me and right now I can't waste an ounce of it on her.

"I hope you liked the show," I say, then storm off before she can say another word.

If the South Koreans are concerned the next morning, they don't show it. There are no extra guards. No new cameras. Probably the trapdoor in the basement will be firmly sealed after my visit, but that doesn't impact me at all. Not anymore. What I need isn't inside their embassy. It's around it. Somewhere.

I don't know where I was.

For at least an hour, I stand across the street, staring at the South Korean embassy. No one stares back, though, I'm happy to see. The guards don't even glance in my direction. I am young, small. Inconsequential. The people who do happen to notice me see someone who isn't a threat.

I don't know where I was.

The Scarred Man was meeting someone, but I don't know who. I don't know where. If I had just one piece of the puzzle then I might be able to figure out the rest. And then…what? Stop an assassination by an international hit man? Throw my body between the Scarred Man and another victim?

Keep it from happening again.

Yes. That is what I'm going to do. But I don't stop to worry about how. *How* is tomorrow's problem. Today my mission is simple.

I don't know where I was.

Today I have to fix that.

I push off the wall of the Egyptian embassy and start down the street that winds and climbs to the city center, all the time keeping my eyes glued to the stones beneath my feet, searching for any irregularities in the pattern, for the symbol that marked the entrance that I found last night.

Four hours later, I've seen three tunnel entrances, and I highly suspect I know about one more. The city is no doubt lousy with them, and they could lead anywhere. But I don't care how many there are. I only know that if I can find enough of them then maybe I can figure out where else the passageway that opened into South Korea might go.

I don't know where I was.

In the bright daylight, I'm not afraid. Not anymore. I have a purpose, a cause. A mission.

A shadow.

"What do you want, Alexei?" I ask, spinning on the sidewalk.

The sun is high and Alexei squints against the glare, staring up at me. The sidewalks are steep here, climbing toward the palace, and I'm glad for it. I like being taller than him even if it is just temporary. An illusion.

He doesn't even say hello.

"Are you OK?" he asks instead.

"I was fine until about thirty seconds ago," I tell him.

"I heard about..." he starts, then trails off, probably because I'm so fragile. He thinks I don't want to be reminded about what happened the night before. What I really want to do is push him down the hill. "Are you OK, Grace?"

"Yes! I'm fine. Do you hear me? I'm OK. Perfectly normal. Absolutely average. How do you say *hunky-dory* in Russian?"

"This isn't a joke."

I step closer, and now I can feel his chest against mine. I'm staring right into his eyes. "Do I look like I'm laughing?"

"You break into one embassy, and then you show up in the basement of another? If you're trying to start a war, you're doing a good job."

"I got lost, Alexei. I was out in the rain and I fell into one of the tunnels. It was an *accident*."

As soon as I say the word, I want to gag on it. I've heard it too frequently and for far too long. I don't want to say it now. Or ever. But I have to. So I say it again.

"It was an accident, Alexei. I'm fine."

"Are you? Are you really?" The way Alexei is looking at me makes me want to run – not to my mother's room or my grandfather's embassy. Not to any place that anyone would ever think to look. I want to disappear and never, ever come back.

Alexei inches even closer. When he inhales, his chest brushes against mine. He stares at me with eyes that are bluer than the sea and reaches for my hand. "If you need me—"

"I don't."

"But if you do—"

"I don't need you, Alexei. OK?" I can't take being so close to him. He has always been golden. Like the sun. His touch burns, so I jerk my hand away and retreat to higher ground. "Now you can go call Jamie and tell him that I'm fine. That you have done your duty and you can be released from your obligation or whatever blood oath the two of you have sworn. I'm fine. Do you hear me?"

I expect him to lash back. Or, worse, to laugh.

But he just shakes his head. "You think I care because you're Jamie's sister? Maybe I care about you, Gracie. Maybe I'm worried about *you.*"

It's the worst possible thing he could tell me. Because now I have to lose what little respect I had for him. He really should know better.

I force out a laugh. "If I wanted to start a war, we'd be in one by now."

This, at last, makes him smile. "That's true."

"I'm OK."

"You're not OK, Grace. But I want you to be."

When Alexei turns and goes back the way he came, I watch him walk away. I don't let myself think about how easily the Scarred Man could have caught me last night, how no one would have found me – maybe ever. Rosie once said that the tunnels are full of skeletons, but I don't let myself think about how easily I could have become one of them.

I woke up this morning intending to scour the streets around Embassy Row, the shops and alleys. I woke up intending to look for tunnel entrances and maybe use them to make a map and try to figure out where I'd been. To be smart. To be safe.

But Alexei has changed all that.

Smart and safe are the furthest things from my mind, and now there's only one thing left to do. There's only one place left to go.

And that place, I know, is down.

The tunnel looks different through the beam of a military-grade flashlight. I know I should be in a hurry, but I have to marvel at the walls, the ancient torches that are lined up by the entrance. This time I can shine a light up onto the clockwork gears and wheels that open and close the door that covers the shaft. It's genius, really. Hundreds of years old and still working.

It's enough to almost make me lose track of what century I'm in, so it takes a moment for me to remember to pull out the compass I've been carrying around all day. I turn the way the Scarred Man ran the night before. South, southwest. And then I start to follow.

At first it's easy – the tunnels either don't branch or else dusty cobwebs or ancient debris block the way, and there is no doubt whether or not I went that way the night before.

I go south, southwest for twenty minutes. Due east for

another ten. But when the tunnel dead-ends at a pile of old, dusty wooden crates, I start to worry. I know I've made a wrong turn somewhere along the way.

Backtracking, I pay careful attention. The floor slopes and rises. At one point I realize the tunnels don't just go left and right. They also go up and down. I may be right beneath the streets, or I could be a hundred feet deeper beneath the city – I have been walking for so long that it's impossible to know.

I'm just about to give up when I hear the drip, drip, drip of water falling into a larger pool. Suddenly, the tunnel is warmer. I pull off my favorite cardigan. Even in a T-shirt and shorts I'm starting to sweat.

And then the strangest thing happens: the tunnel ends.

Instead of an entrance in the ceiling, I reach a door and stop. The sound of the dripping water is clearer now. I'm even hotter.

According to my compass I'm pretty sure I'm on the far-north end of Embassy Row.

Gently, I push. But before the door even opens, I know exactly where I am.

"*Iran.*"

The word is a whisper I barely dare to say aloud. But there's no one around to hear me, and I make myself step slowly, cautiously inside.

The tiles around the ornate swimming pool are slick with a dampness that seems to have taken up permanent residence in the embassy's basement. My hair clings to the back of my neck as I walk toward the ornate pool and think about the story that my grandfather told me – about the hot springs that run underneath the palace and throughout the rest of the city. When I see steam rising from the water, I realize that the Iranians must have had their very own. Hot springs *and* beach access? No telling what Noah might say to the Israeli ambassador to try to convince him to arrange some kind of real estate swap now.

But Noah will never know – *can* never know – where I am. And why. It's a mission for which I don't even really trust myself.

Condensation gathers on the tile ceiling and then drops into the pool below in a steady, even beat. It's almost soothing. If the chaise lounges around the pool weren't covered with mildew, I might lie down and take a nap.

But then I hear a noise. The door starts to move. And I know that, once again, I am in the Iranian embassy.

And I am not alone.

Maybe the Scarred Man is coming. Or maybe it's the man he's been meeting. Somehow, neither option frightens me. I feel like maybe my life has been leading to this for years, and I'm grateful I no longer have to wait. To worry. To wonder. I'm ready to have it over.

The door is heavy and the hinges are rusty from the humidity and years of little use.

It catches. Stalls. And I know I should use the time to run upstairs and out through the loose piece of fence on the beach. Maybe I should hide somewhere inside the sprawling fortress.

In other words, I should save myself. It's the smart thing to do. But the downside of spending most of your life having people tell you you're acting stupid means that, eventually, you stop trying to do what is smart.

I inch toward the door.

I grab the arm that is reaching toward me.

I pull, daring whoever is on the other side to try to hurt me first.

The word that comes is loud and fast and (I'm pretty sure) dirty. It's also in Portuguese.

Noah throws his hand to his chest then doubles over, breathing hard. "You scared me!"

"*I* scared *you*?" I say, slapping at his arm. "What are you doing down here?"

"Following you," Rosie adds from behind him, entirely too cheerful. "Wow, I've never been down this way before." She pushes Noah through the doorway, then steps into the basement herself. Her eyes go up to the ornate ceiling before turning to the lavish pool.

"Cool," she says.

"Yeah. But why are you…" I trail off as my gaze settles onto Megan, who stands just on the other side of the door. Of course she's here. I'm starting to learn that Megan is always around to see too much, hear too much. Know too much. And that makes something inside of me snap.

“Go!” I shout, pointing back to the tunnels. “Rosie, Noah, go home. Now. You, too, Megan.”

“We don’t even know where we are,” Noah says.

“No.” I shake my head. “I know where we are. And you need to go.”

“How do you know?” Megan asks.

“Because I’ve been here before.”

“You’ve been here before?” Noah asks. “So that means…” He looks like he’s doing math in his head. “That means this is—”

“Iran,” I say.

“Iran!” Noah finishes at the same time. He turns and reaches for Rosie’s hand. “Come on. We’ve got to get out of here.”

But Rosie pulls away. “Cool,” she says again, walking toward the water that is part pool, part hot springs.

Amazingly, Megan doesn’t run away either. Instead, she leans down and runs her hand through the water that is surprisingly clear. “Awesome.”

“Awesome? Are you three trying to kill me?” Noah shouts.

“Ooh, we should get in,” Megan says. “Next time I’ll bring my bikini.”

Noah stumbles back like he’s been shot. “You *are* trying to kill me.”

“Noah’s right,” I say. “The three of you should go. Get out of here before you—”

“Before *we* what?” Noah says. “What’s going to happen to the three of us that won’t happen to you?”

"This isn't your fight, Noah," I snap.

"Yeah, well, it became my fight the moment I…" He trails off and, suddenly, I'd give anything to know what he was going to say.

"The moment you *what*?"

"I…"

"The moment you met me?" I guess. "The moment you heard about the man with the scar?" That still isn't it – I can tell. So I go back further. "Or was it the moment Ms Chancellor asked you to keep me out of trouble? She didn't just ask you to show me around, did she?"

Bingo.

Noah is busted, and he's actually stumbling backward, trying to find a way out of the proverbial corner.

"Great. My brother got Alexei to spy on me. Grandpa and Ms Chancellor have you. I am *covered*!"

"Grace, don't…" Noah reaches for my arm, but I push him away.

"How did you find me?" I ask.

"We followed you," Rosie says, matter-of-fact.

"No." I shake my head. "Not good enough. I've been wandering these tunnels for hours. *I* wasn't even sure where I was, so *how did you find me*?"

I look from Noah to Rosie and then, finally, I let my gaze settle on Megan.

"We might have put a tracker on you," she says.

"You might have *what*?"

Megan holds up a tiny device. "GPS location receiver. I put a transmitter in your sweater." She eyes the ratty cardigan that I've been taking with me everywhere these days. "You really should clean that sometime, you know."

"Why?" I ask.

"Well, for starters, there's a stain on the sleeve that's been there since—"

I cut Megan off. "Why were you following me?"

"Oh. That," Megan says. For a moment, the three of them are silent.

"Well, see..." Noah starts slowly. "Last night, Megan called me."

"And Noah called me," Rosie interjects.

"We were sort of..." Noah is struggling for words.

"You're freaking us out," Megan says bluntly.

"*You're* worried about *me*?" I ask.

"Well, yeah," Noah says, as if it should be the most obvious thing in the world.

"I don't need your worry," I snap. "And I don't want your pity."

I'm pushing through them, starting back toward the door and the tunnels and the answers I'm no closer to finding.

"Maybe not," Megan yells. "But you need our help."

I freeze. And then slowly – very slowly – I turn. "Well, maybe I don't want it."

There's something that comes from being the girl who is always left behind. I could only watch Jamie and Alexei disappear without me so many times before I got really good at convincing myself that I was better off alone.

But I wasn't left alone, I realize now.

I was left with Megan.

"He's going to do it again," Megan says. "That's what you said last night, isn't it? That the man who killed your mother is going to kill somebody else?"

"That's none of your business," I say, then glare at Noah so hard that he actually pulls Rosie in front of him, a human shield.

"You think you're the only one who's ever lost someone?" Megan snaps. There is ice in her voice. "Do you think you're the only one who has ever wanted to make somebody pay?"

I've never heard her talk like this, seen her look like this. She is nothing like Lila now. And she's nothing like the little girl who used to bring over her Barbies, either. It's like everything else has been camouflage. *This* is the Megan she has spent her whole life hiding. And for the first time in all the years I've known her, I realize that I have never heard Megan talk about her dad.

"Besides," she says flatly, "you do need us."

"I don't need you," I say.

"Says the girl who has wasted an entire day wandering around in circles down here," she says.

"I know these tunnels better than anyone." Rosie sounds almost hurt. "Maybe if you'd asked me, I could have saved you a day."

"I have the resources of two embassies behind me," Noah says. "You really think you're better off without me?"

I roll my eyes, look at Megan. "I'm a genius," she

says. Everyone turns to her. "Well, I am. No use trying to soft-pedal it. Plus, my mom's a spy. Any of you pick up covert-operations training in summer camp? Yeah. I didn't think so."

She has a point and, genius that she is, I'm sure she already knows it.

"So are you going to tell us now?" Rosie asks. She's looking up at me with those huge blue eyes. It's like she's asking me to tuck her into bed, tell her a story. "Grace, what happened last night?"

I'm looking at the three of them. They really are here. And they really aren't going anywhere.

I could think of a dozen reasons to send them away – a hundred. It isn't safe. It isn't their fight. Their parents could lose their jobs if someone were to catch us. The reasons are bubbling up on my tongue. But I can't bring myself to say them.

Instead I blurt, "I followed the Scarred Man."

I wait for someone to object, but no one says a thing.

"You know when he disappeared the other day?" I ask Rosie. "Well, I figured out that he must have come down here. Into the tunnels."

"Of course!" Rosie sounds so mad at herself. "I've only ever come in through the public entrances where they give tours and stuff. I never knew there were hidden entrances. I should have guessed. I'm sorry, Grace."

"Don't be," I tell her. "So…yesterday. I was following him again when he came down here. We walked for a long time and then he went up into some building."

"What building?" Megan asks.

"I don't know. That's what I've been doing all day – trying to retrace our steps. But I can't find it."

"Why do you need to find it?" Noah asks. "What did you see?"

"I followed him inside. He was meeting someone. I couldn't tell who, but they were talking about killing someone. He said – and I quote – 'There are many perfectly adequate ways to die.' *And he just has to find one.*"

For a moment there is nothing in the basement but the echo of the Scarred Man's words and the drip, drip, drip of the water into the pool. It's like sand through an hourglass, a steady, constant reminder that I'm running out of time.

"And you don't know what building you were in?" Megan asks.

"No," I snap in frustration.

"What did it look like?" she asks.

"Like a building! Carpet. Doors. Lights."

"Was it one of the embassies? Did you see any signs or books in any languages that you might have recognized?" Noah tries.

"I saw a door and a shadow and the man who killed my mother telling someone he has another assignment!"

"But if we knew—" Megan starts.

"I don't know who. I don't know when. I just know that he is going to kill again."

"No, he's not," Rosie says. She gives a wide, defiant grin.

"Yeah," Noah says. "Because we're going to stop him."

It's the right thing to say – the perfect line. They're trying so hard to sound convincing, but I'm not convinced. I know too much. I have seen too much. I have lost too much.

And now I look at the three faces that stare back at me, praying I don't have to lose anyone else.

When we leave that night, Rosie claims that she can walk on her hands all the way from Iran to Italy. Megan stays beside her, counting her steps, watching her tiny feet as they stay freakishly steady and straight in the air, but Noah and I walk up ahead. For a moment, we are alone.

"So," I say, "I hear you're a football stud."

Noah laughs. "You would be confusing me with my father," he says, then reconsiders. "Except, wait. No one has *ever* confused me with my father, so never mind."

"Are you good?" I ask.

Noah shrugs. "I'm OK."

"Lila says you're good. And Lila doesn't strike me as the type to overestimate your virtues."

"Lila wants me to be good because that would mean I could stop being…me."

"With *you* being defined as…"

"Man about town. Man of mystery. Man of many talents. Really a James Bond type with a bevy of beautiful women all eager to help me stop an international incident."

"A bevy, huh?" I ask.

"Yeah," Noah says. "I'm dangerous, is what I'm

saying, Grace." He gives me an oh-so-serious stare. "I have a license to kill."

"Good to know," I say. Noah laughs.

"Of course I usually kill through general incompetence and family disappointment."

"I know the feeling," I say, and then it hits me: the enormity of what I'm asking – of the risk we're taking. "Why are you doing this, Noah?" I ask before I even know the words are coming.

Noah looks at me, stunned. "What do you mean? I'm your friend. Friends help each other when they are... you know...going up against international hit men and stuff."

"Maybe that's a bad idea. Maybe you don't want to be my friend," I tell him, but Noah just smirks.

"Too late. Besides, I know you'd never leave me alone if I was going to do something stupid."

"Maybe I would."

"And you'd never lie to me." He runs a hand through his black hair, pushing it back, making it even spikier than usual. "That's why my parents broke up. Maybe it's because of their jobs or whatever, but they always had to keep things from each other. There were so many secrets and lies. You have no idea how much I hate it when people lie to me."

I should tell him, I think. I should tell him about what I saw the night Mom died and what came after. About the Scarred Man and the Scarred Men. I should tell him not to trust me, not to like me, not to believe a word I say because there are moments late at night when I can't even believe myself.

But I can't say any of those things. I can't bring myself to drive Noah away even though I know in my gut I probably should.

The marines are watching the street when we reach the US gates. I can see the light burning in my grandfather's office. If he knows I've been gone all day, I doubt he cares.

"Well, good night, Noah."

"Good night, Grace."

He starts toward Israel, then stops and calls, "Hey, Grace..."

"Yeah?"

His hands are in his pockets and the moonlight shines across his face. "Between you and me, I'm not as good as Lila says."

"OK."

His smirk grows into an extremely cocky grin. "I'm better."

He turns and leaves. I just smile after him, thinking, *I totally knew it.*

"You've got to be kidding me!"

Honestly, I don't know what's more worrisome: what Megan is saying or that she's saying it with Barbies. But maybe the most shocking thing is how utterly un-Megan-like Megan is being in this moment.

She's wearing a black tank top and baggy camouflage cargo pants and has a yellow highlighter stuck through her belt like a knife. Most of her glossy black hair is tucked up into a ski cap, but a few strands peek out. A decent portion of them are now a very dark shade of fuchsia.

"Is that permanent?" I ask, reaching out to touch her new pink hair before she slaps my hand away.

"I'm trying something new," she says, undaunted. She points to Barbie's Dream House and says, "We enter through the skylight in the master bedroom. Here."

Rosie points to the Barbie jeep and says, "Where are we going to get our mobile observation unit?"

"Noah's going to borrow his mom's van," Megan says.

Rosie nods, but Noah just says, "I am?"

"You are," Megan says. "Now does anyone have any questions?"

"Who are you?" I ask. "And what have you done with Megan?"

But she just cuts her eyes at me.

"Now, we can't be sure about the exact layout of Dominic's place, but judging from the plans on file with the historical preservation society, that block of row houses was reconstructed after the war, and the following changes were allowed. The skylight is our window. Pardon the pun. So—"

"I'm not sure about this," I say. I look through Barbie's skylight at the friendship bracelets that are serving as abseiling ropes, the unicorn stickers that represent cameras.

"The plan is solid," Megan says. "This is our chance and we have to take it."

"I know that, but if one of you gets hurt, I will never forgive myself."

"If one of us gets hurt?" Megan shoots back. "Have you forgotten that you overheard him saying that he is supposed to *kill somebody*? What if the Scarred Man's target is my mom? Did you think of that? Or Rosie's dad? Or one of Noah's parents? What if it's your grandfather he's after, Grace? Is it too risky then?"

She's like a little camo-clad machine gun as she talks. A little camo-clad machine gun who has a point.

"OK," I say.

"Good." Megan nods. "Let's go."

Darkness looks different in Adria than in anyplace else on earth. The flickering yellow of the streetlight mixes with the too-bright white of the moon. I look up and watch it bounce off the tile roofs of the narrow houses that stand side by side at attention. There are iron balconies and window boxes filled with white flowers. It's like something from a postcard – from a dream.

All but one house in the row.

It keeps its shutters pulled tight even on the prettiest of days. Its locks have been upgraded and the owner never, ever sits on the stoop and talks and laughs like the other people on the block. This man comes and goes at irregular hours, and no one ever gets asked inside.

It looks like a row house.

It feels like a fortress.

At 11:00 p.m., the buildings appear dark gray against an inky-blue sky. The colors are too rich, though. Almost like watching a cartoon. But it's no drawing – certainly not the dark figure that dashes across the rooftops, swooping and jumping like a low-flying bird. When it does a full twist mid-jump, I know the bird is just showing off.

"Focus, Rosie," I say, forgetting that she can hear me.

"I need to concentrate here, Grace," she replies, and I startle. There are always too many voices in my head. I really didn't need three more. But Megan insisted we wear the little earbuds that she smuggled out of the security center of the embassy. I've been back less than two weeks, and already I've turned the sweetest girl on Embassy Row into a thief and a conspiracy theorist. Even for me, it is an impressively quick act of corruption.

"OK, guys." Rosie sounds slightly out of breath but more alive than I've ever heard her. "I'm at our entry point. Waiting for your go."

And now I'm certain of two things.

1. We might actually try this ridiculous thing.
2. We all watch entirely too many movies.

Megan picks up a small tablet that shows a closed-circuit feed of the prime minister's office. Standing at attention not far from the PM's side is the Scarred Man.

"Are we clear?" Rosie asks again.

"Go. Go. Go," Megan says.

Noah and I look at each other, then both reach for the doors of the van. In a flash, we're out and crossing the street.

Megan has explained the basics. The rest I know from my dad.

Breaching a secure location isn't about speed. It's about efficiency. Going fast won't do you any good if you spend half your time turning over floor lamps and setting off alarms.

So I know what to do. I know how to do it. After all, we've gone over it a dozen times. I've seen it in my sleep a dozen more. But it feels like someone else is inside my body – like I am watching from afar – as Noah, Megan, and I walk across the street.

On the off-chance the neighbors are watching, we walk and do not run. I laugh like a normal girl would (but not too loudly) and talk to my friends (but not too excitedly) and, most of all, I watch the small window in the door of the house that is almost always dark. When the top of a tiny head appears there, I'm ready.

The door swings open.

"What took you so long?" Rosie says with a wink.

The light on the security system is blinking red. A beeping sound is counting down. But Megan already has a tiny device out and is doing something to the keypad on the wall by the door. I see numbers spiraling across the screen, running through a sequence one by one, pecking out the code.

And still the chime keeps beeping.

"Megan…" Noah warns.

"Just a—" Another beep comes, longer, louder. Then it stops. "Got it." Megan practically exhales the words, then leans against the wall and takes a deep breath. For the first time, she looks as terrified as Noah.

"Nice system." Rosie sounds impressed.

Noah turns, taking in the first floor. "Not a nice place."

He has a point. For all the security the Scarred Man has, you would think he'd be protecting art. Jewels. At the very least some high-end electronics. But the narrow room in which we stand has a fireplace and one very worn chair.

There are no books on the shelves. We walk on and find very little food in the kitchen.

"It's like a safe house," Megan says.

"But it's *his* house," Noah adds. It's easy to forget that, according to public records, the Scarred Man has lived here for ten years.

"OK," I say. "Let's split up and do this. I want us out of here fast."

No one complains. No one asks any questions. Megan goes to work on the computer, and Rosie climbs onto Noah's shoulders and starts installing cameras in the light fixtures and smoke detectors.

"What should I do?" I ask Megan.

"Don't break anything," she tells me.

I wish I had a job – something to do – but the truth is, I would be useless at it. Megan isn't just smart about computers. She knows this about me, too. I am in the Scarred Man's house, and all I can do is look at the bed, thinking, *The man who killed my mother sleeps here.* In the bathroom, I look into the mirror and imagine his face staring back at me. The face that I saw through the smoke and the fire. The face that has haunted me for years.

Carefully, I run my fingers across the top of the dresser. A little loose change lies on the table by the bed. In his walk-in closet there are five dark suits, identical in cut, and seven white shirts all fresh from the dry cleaner and still in their plastic bags. It looks more like a hotel room than a home. Like he fully expects to pack everything up and be gone at a moment's notice. Like he knows that someday the ghosts will catch up to him.

He just doesn't know today is that day.

I don't feel any pain as my fingernails dig into my palms. There is no blood, just a steady, constant throbbing to tell me that I am still alive. I am alive but my mother is dead. And I'm in the home of the man who killed her.

"Oh no."

Megan's voice isn't quite a shout, and that is why it's scary.

"What is it?" Noah asks.

"We've got to go. We've got to go *now.*"

"Where's Grace?" someone says.

I hear the question in my ear, but I can't take my eyes off of the leather jacket that hangs in the back of the closet. It's a deep, worn brown. The sleeves are so soft that I know that it used to be his favorite. The position in the closet tells me that it isn't anymore.

I step farther back into the closet, and then I'm not in the town home. *I'm standing on the street. I see the man through the window of my mother's shop, his tall frame and broad shoulders, the dark brown leather jacket that he wears.*

I reach for the sleeve, bring the soft cotton cuff to my nose. And in the confined space I swear that it still smells like smoke.

The cuff is stiff in one place and I finger it, know instantly that it's dried blood.

My mother's blood is on my hands.

"Grace," a voice says in my ear, but I don't move.

I can't. My body no longer belongs to me. It is frozen in the past.

"Grace!" Noah's hand is on my arm. "We've got to get out of here. He's coming."

"No!" Megan's voice rings out just as, downstairs, a door opens and closes.

I look at Noah. He shakes his head. "He's here."

Carefully, Noah reaches for the door and pulls it closed. He pushes me farther back into the closet. I'm pressed right up against the leather jacket, wondering how Noah can breathe so deeply in a tiny space that is so filled with smoke.

There is so much smoke.

"You OK?" Noah whispers.

I nod my head and try to slow my breathing, and yet my heart keeps pounding. I think I might throw up.

"What happened?" I whisper. "I thought he was supposed to be gone most of the night?"

Megan hears me over the mic. "He must have a secondary system. The motion detectors went off and now...hide!"

We're already hiding, but Noah doesn't say that. He's too busy looking at me.

"Grace, are you OK?"

"Fine." I force the word out. I'm grateful for the darkness and the cramped space. Noah is pressing into me. I couldn't see the door if I tried. There is absolutely no place for me to run or room for me to move. He's pressing against me so tightly that I can't even tremble.

"What do we do now?" I ask.

"I don't know," Noah whispers. "What do people usually do in these situations? I mean...we could make out?" Even in the dark, he reads the look I give him. "Or not. Yeah. I was thinking not."

I hear footsteps in the bedroom. The closet door opens and closes quickly – just a cursory glance. Noah and I stay shrouded in the shadows.

The phone rings and I hear the Scarred Man answer, but I can't make out the words.

Is it the alarm company calling to check on the disturbance? His boss calling to ask why he left his post? Wrong number?

I can't tell.

I'm not sure how long we stand in the dark. I try to focus on my breathing, the rise and fall of Noah's chest. But I can't stop thinking about the smoke.

I would do anything to stop thinking about the smoke.

"OK, guys. On our signal, head for the skylight." Megan's whisper is too loud in my ear.

"What's the signal?" Noah asks, but almost before the words are out we hear it.

There's a creak as the skylight opens. And then there are cries, screeches.

We go to the closet door, ease it open just in time to see a cat come flying through the skylight. It lands feet-first on the bed and shoots like an arrow down the stairs to where the Scarred Man will no doubt see it.

Noah and I rush out of the closet and toward the

skylight, where Rosie still dangles upside down.

"There," Rosie says. "That ought to be good for some motion."

Neither of us stop to compliment her. Noah has his hands cupped together and I'm stepping into them. He tosses me upward as if I weigh nothing at all. I grab the ledge and pull myself up just as Noah jumps and catches the ledge on the other side.

We're both on the roof in seconds. Rosie closes the skylight with a very silent push. Then, for a moment, we lie perfectly still, watching.

I see the Scarred Man come into the bedroom and look from side to side. It's like he's starting to wonder if he's hearing things. Seeing things. It's his turn to wonder if he's crazy.

Then he turns. Cradled in his arms is a very scared black cat. I watch the Scarred Man scratch its head gently, soothing it. Calming it.

I'm still holding my breath as he turns again and goes downstairs.

"I don't think we should be here," Noah says the next afternoon. He has a point, but I don't say so. "We are in *Iran*," he says again, but the three of us ignore him. "Am I the only one who is concerned about this?"

"*Yes*," Megan, Rosie, and I say in unison.

Megan sits with her feet in the water, a laptop beside her. Rosie does handstands on the other side of the pool, her bare heels resting against the tile mosaic. But me, I just sit watching the light flicker, shimmering across the ceiling, trying not to think about the smoke.

"OK," Megan tells us a moment later. "We're live."

She turns the laptop so that Noah and I can see it. Images flash across the screen, rotating between the cameras in the bedroom, living room, and kitchen. I can see the Scarred Man sitting in his solitary chair, staring off into space. He still has the cat, I notice, and it lies on his lap, sleeping. It looks as if he's finally found a friend.

"That guy creeps me out," Rosie says.

"Me, too," Megan says, turning the laptop back around.

"How long until he finds the cameras?" Noah asks.

Megan shrugs. "It depends how paranoid he is. I mean, he could do a sweep every day. Or every week. Or never. In any case, we have them while we have them. That's the best we can hope for."

"What about his phone?" I ask.

"What about it?" Rosie says, flipping herself upright.

"Someone called while we were in there last night," I say. "Who was it?"

Megan shakes her head. "The number was untraceable."

"Untraceable?" Noah asks. "I thought we were supposed to be able to trace everything."

The look in Megan's eyes says it all: *We were.*

"He's working for someone," I say. "Someone's calling the shots."

"But is this someone going to get caught by the likes of us?" Noah asks. Nobody answers. Probably because it's an answer none of us really wants to hear.

After hours of waiting, Noah goes out to get food and Rosie falls asleep on one of the lounge chairs.

Megan and I are alone, watching the Scarred Man washing his dishes by hand and putting them all away. I wonder if he is as bored as we are. But Megan doesn't complain. She sits, patiently waiting – for what, I do not know.

"Hey, Megan…" I don't know where the words come

from; I don't know how to stop them. "Did you go to my mom's funeral?"

The dripping of the water is ever present in the basement. It punctuates my every word. I wish I could turn the volume down.

"Yeah," Megan says, but she doesn't face me.

"Was it nice?" I have to ask.

Megan nods, but doesn't say anything for a moment. "I'm sorry you couldn't come." Megan swings her feet back and forth. I can see her wondering whether or not she should go on, but eventually she says, "The prime minister came. And Princess Ann, though they brought her in and out through a private entrance. I don't think the public even knew she was there."

"She and my mom grew up together. They were best friends."

"That makes sense," Megan says. "There were a lot of flowers."

"My mom loved flowers."

"Your grandpa gave the eulogy. He thanked everyone for coming and talked about how wonderful and beautiful your mother was. About how much she loved you and your brother. Everybody cried."

From the sound of her voice I think Megan is crying now. I think I might be too but I'm not going to give my tears permission to fall. Not anymore.

"Was he there?" I ask, my gaze glued to the man on the screen. "Dominic? Did he come?"

Megan shakes her head. For the first time, she faces

me. "If he was there, I didn't see him. But it was at the national cathedral and it was packed. I bet there were five hundred people there, and I don't think I saw him. Or at least I don't remember seeing him. I'm sorry."

"It's OK," I tell her, even though it isn't. Even though I'm pretty sure that nothing will ever be OK again.

A moment later, the door swings open and Noah asks, "So what did I miss?"

Rosie sits upright and stretches, catching the sandwich that Noah tosses her way.

"Nothing," I tell Noah.

He hands a sandwich to me, and I'm just about to dig in when, beside me, Megan mutters, "That's weird."

"What is it?" Rosie asks, but Megan just looks at me.

"What's wrong?" I ask.

"Nothing." Megan tries to close the laptop, but not before Noah swoops it away from her. For a second, he just stares at the screen. I can't see what he's seeing, but somehow I know what he's thinking. Maybe because I can see it in his eyes. Maybe because I've seen it so many times before.

Noah isn't angry. Not yet. He's hurt.

I don't know what it is, but I know that I've done something wrong.

"I asked you if you had ever accused any other men with scars before," Noah says.

"Noah, I—"

"I asked you, and you said this was the first time! You said—"

"I know what I said."

"Then how do you explain this?" Noah turns the laptop so that I can see it, and I look down at the four photos that I have seen before. That I'd hoped I'd never have to see again.

"What is it?" Rosie asks. "What's wrong?"

Megan exhales a guilty sigh even though she isn't the one who should feel guilty. "I was looking around the embassy's security records to see what they have on the Scarred Man, and I didn't find much on him, but…" She glances down at the computer, picks it up. "I found some other Scarred Men."

Rosie's eyes go wide as she looks through the file, the electronic equivalent of the one my grandfather threw in my face.

"I don't get it," Rosie says with a shrug, as if this subject is already boring her. But Noah isn't going to forget it anytime soon.

"You lied, Grace." He looks at me like I didn't just break my word – I broke his trust. "You lied."

"Noah" – Megan is stepping in between the two of us – "we should hear Grace out."

"You lied to me!" Even though we're in the basement of an utterly abandoned building, I'm almost afraid that someone is going to hear him shout. "I asked you if you've ever done anything like this before, and you said no."

"It's him! I swear it's really him this…" But I don't finish.

"This time?" Noah snaps. "That's what you were going

to say, isn't it? That you're sure *this time*? How many other times have there been, Grace?"

"It's him," I say.

"How many times?" he yells again.

"Well, the file says—" Megan starts, but Noah cuts her off. His gaze never strays from me.

"I'm asking Grace."

"Four. Before this there were four. I was wrong then, but I'm not now." I look around the room.

"I don't think I've ever seen that many men with facial scars," Rosie says.

Noah shakes his head coldly. "It's not hard when you're looking for them."

He never takes his gaze off of me.

"Noah, I swear I saw—"

"Listen to yourself! *You* saw him meeting someone down here. *You* followed him at the palace. *You* heard him say he was going to kill somebody else. Tell me, Grace – do you ever wonder why it's always you who hears and sees these things?" Noah shakes his head, so very disappointed in me. "If a scarred man makes a threat in a forest, ever wonder why you're always the only one around to hear it?"

The words are out and I can tell by the look on Noah's face that he doesn't regret them in the least – that a part of him has been asking that very question for days.

"But Grace heard him say that he was going to kill somebody. Didn't you, Grace?" Rosie asks. "He said that."

"Well, not in those exact words, but…he *was* talking

about killing someone. I swear! He said there are a lot of ways for a person to die and he just has to find one. He said that," I tell them. I have to make them understand. "That is exactly what he said."

I can't tell if they believe me. Or if they're afraid of me. Or both.

If they're smart, the answer will be both.

"OK." Megan steps in, the voice of reason. "It's late and we're all exhausted. So let's just go home, start fresh tomorrow."

"Yeah," Noah says, not really agreeing. "Let's go home."

"Noah–" I say.

"Megan?" Noah interrupts without looking at me and Megan stops gathering her things long enough to face him.

"Yeah?"

"Are you still spending the night with Lila?"

"Yes."

"Good. I'll walk you and Rosie home."

As he starts toward the tunnel door, I catch his arm, hold him still.

"I'm not crazy," I tell him. I don't even stop to consider that that is what crazy people almost always say.

"I'm not saying you're crazy, Grace. I'm saying you're a liar." His voice is almost a whisper, and I know my betrayal is deeper, more personal, to him than it is to Megan and Rosie. And it should be. He is my official best friend.

Or, at least, he used to be.

It's quiet as I make my way toward the embassy. Megan and Noah are far up ahead. They have already dropped Rosie off at the German gates, and now they're walking toward Israel. They don't speak to each other. They don't laugh. I expect one or both of them to look back at me, maybe wave good night, but they don't.

I feel utterly alone when a voice says, "Hello, Gracie."

"Hello, Alexei," I make myself say.

Did he see us emerge from the tunnel entrance three blocks away? How long has he been watching? I find myself wondering what exactly Alexei knows, and I tell myself that is why I'm slowing down, letting him catch up.

"And how are you today, Gracie?"

I stop cold.

"I love Jamie. That's why I let *him* call me Gracie."

"I know," Alexei says with a smile.

"*You're not Jamie.*"

I don't mean it as an insult, but it comes out like one. What a wonderful bonus. But the words slide off of Alexei. He is immune to me and whatever wimpy weapons he thinks I possess. He just shoves his hands into his pockets and falls into step beside me. "So where have you been keeping yourself?"

"I live in that one," I say, pointing to where the US embassy sits just down the street.

"What have you been doing?"

"I'm sorry," I say, spinning on him, "this concerns you *why*? And don't tell me it's because of some promise you made to Jamie. Jamie told you to keep me out of trouble. And I haven't been in any trouble."

He gives me the smirk again. "*As far as I know* you haven't been in any trouble. But there's a lot I don't know, isn't there, Gracie?"

At night, the sea air is chilly even in summer, and yet I feel myself start to sweat.

"Tell me what's going on," he says.

"Nothing to tell."

"Hey!" he snaps. "I find you lying in the street in a ball gown, and you're so sick that I have to carry you home. And then…you disappear. You're never in the embassy when I come to see you—"

"You came to see me?"

"You don't go to events with your grandfather. You haven't even broken any bones as far as I can tell. So what's going on?"

I don't know what it is that stops me – his words or his

tone. He's not playing anymore. He's not having fun. This isn't about torturing the kid sister, teasing her for being too small, too slow, too female to run with the boys.

"You scare me, Grace."

Alexei sounds like he doesn't want to admit it. But he does.

"Yeah." I take a slow step toward the embassy. "Sometimes I scare me, too."

To Alexei's credit, he doesn't follow. I can feel him watching me, though, his blue eyes tracking my every move.

"You know I'm here if you need me, don't you?" he calls out.

When I look back, there's no trace of his cocky smile.

"Be careful, Alexei. The world is a dangerous place."

When Alexei is gone, I know I should go inside. Go to bed. Rest. But I can't face the embassy's empty halls. My mother's bed and her books and her photographs still tucked into the mirror's frame. Or maybe I just can't face the mirror. So I slip back into the tunnels instead.

Noah wanted to get different colors of string and wind them through the tunnels to mark the various paths, but that reminds me of the hallways of the hospital where I went after the fire.

They took me there for the smoke. They kept me for what I saw. Or what I said I saw. They even put me in what they called a "special room." They didn't try to come up with a soft, cushy name for the restraints that bound my wrists, though – for the drugs they pumped into my system to keep me calm. As long as calm equaled quiet. No one wanted to hear what I had to say.

So I said no to Noah's string idea. Besides, we can't risk letting the Scarred Man figure out that someone else has discovered this portion of the city's tunnels. No tourists ever take tours here; the tunnels in this part of town are supposed to be abandoned, and we need whatever element of surprise we can get.

Or we did. Noah's words still echo in my ears, and I have to remind myself that there probably isn't a "we" anymore. I am alone. Again.

Small lines on the wall tell me what tunnels I've explored, so I set off down one of the branches that I haven't yet marked.

It's just like all the others. Rough walls and sloping floors. I turn the flashlight off and try imagining the space around me in the glow of the Scarred Man's torch. I try to picture myself running away from it or toward it.

I close my eyes, let them adjust to the black, and that is when I hear it. A low, steady whirling that I've heard once before.

The tunnels are so far underground in most places that the noise of the world outside disappears completely. You hear scampering vermin and dripping water, but nothing mechanical, modern, or man-made can usually permeate those old stone walls. Here, though, it's different. The sound is like a siren song, and I don't think. I just keep walking.

When the path branches again, I follow the sound until it stops. It must come and go, off and on, I realize. It's probably an air-conditioning unit, something that only runs part of the time. But I heard it. I really did. I don't think about what Noah said – I don't wonder if my mixed-up mind has imagined the whole thing. Not when I turn my flashlight on and the beam flashes across the ladder. Not when I look up and clearly see the trapdoor that lies just over my head.

I may be wrong, I tell myself. This could be the South Korean embassy all over again. I don't know for certain that I've found my way back to the place where the Scarred Man had his meeting. There's no telling what might be waiting for me on the other side of that trapdoor.

And yet, relief surges inside me, followed by an emotion I can't bring myself to name. And, as I climb, there is one thought pounding in my head: *I wish I could tell Noah.*

As soon as my fingers touch the carpet, I know that I've found the right building. There's the same stiff, scratchy feel beneath my fingers, the same dim lights overhead. I have found the Scarred Man's meeting place, but I still don't know where I am.

Slowly, I stand and close the trapdoor. The carpet is in squares, and the door drops neatly into place like a piece of a puzzle. Even in the glow of my flashlight, I can barely make out the cracks.

I turn off my flashlight and put it in my pocket, then

creep quietly down the hall. Again, there are no signs on the walls. No books. No clocks or posters or clues of any kind.

As I ease around the corner, my hands start to shake. My heart starts to pound. And that's when I realize there are footsteps on the stairs. Someone is coming. I can't be found here. I can't be dragged back to my grandfather with no good excuse for how I ended up inside another building where I'm not supposed to be.

I'm turning, starting to run, when I hear, "Grace?"

I know the voice, and that's what scares me. I'd give anything for it to be a stranger, but it's not.

"Grace, sweetheart." Ms Chancellor flips a switch, and instantly the basement is flooded with light. "What are you doing down here?"

"Exploring," I tell her as the fluorescent bulbs buzz and hum, coming to life.

"Oh, well, it's not the prettiest part of the embassy, but I suppose it does have a degree of mystery."

She makes a flourish with her hands and opens the door to the room where the Scarred Man had been. She flips on another light, and I see rows and rows of dusty shelves. There are books and old typewriters, a radio, and at least a dozen American flags, all packed neatly away and standing at attention.

It's maybe the most harmless room ever, and yet my mind is running a million miles an hour and I cannot let her see.

I cannot let her know.

"What are *you* up to?" I say, my voice light.

"Your grandfather and I are going to watch a movie later, but we only have it on – aha!"

She pulls an old projector off one of the high shelves. It's ancient, and dust cascades down onto her perfect suit. No one has used it in ages, and part of me thinks that it won't even work. But she's so proud of herself that I don't say anything.

"You should join us," Ms Chancellor tells me. "*Roman Holiday.* It's about a princess on the run in Rome, and Gregory Peck plays an American journalist who – oh, I don't want to spoil it. Please come watch it with us."

"OK," I somehow mutter. "Maybe."

"I'm going to hold you to that," she says with a wink. Then she turns and starts back toward the stairs – her high heels clicking in the distance – leaving me exactly where I am supposed to be.

I am inside the United States embassy.

And so was the man who killed my mother when he found out that he was supposed to kill again.

Technically, I'm already home. I only have to go upstairs. Close the door. Lie down on my pink canopy bed and be a normal girl. But whatever chance I had for normal disappeared three years ago. It went up in smoke.

So I creep back into the tunnels. This time I do not run away. There is no pounding in my head or in my veins. It is like I am moving in slow motion. I feel like I'm walking in a dream.

Once, I stop and lean against the rough walls and try to catch my breath. I worry I might get lost again. I worry about so many things – all the time. But I keep walking. And when I finally climb out into the street, I start to run, faster and faster down the hill.

The Scarred Man was meeting someone in the US embassy. That is where his accomplice lives – or at least works. For days I've been worrying about where the Scarred Man had been – who his accomplices might be.

Now I'm not worried.

Now I'm terrified.

So I run faster, arms pumping at my side. Is Noah spending the night in Israel or Brazil? Brazil, I think. No. Israel. I stop mid-stride. I turn in a flash.

I'm supposed to be running in the opposite direction, but my legs no longer work. My arms can't move. All I can do is stand in the deserted street. And stare.

"You," I say.

The Scarred Man smiles. "Hello, Grace."

I will not scream. I will not run. I will not lose control. Because, right now, my control might be all I have.

The man is coming closer, the slow, easy strides of someone out for an evening stroll. His hands are in his pockets. When he nears me, his smile widens.

"I'm Dominic," the man says. "Forgive me if I scared you. I know your grandfather, so I thought I'd say hello. I shouldn't have—"

"I'm not scared," I blurt.

But he looks like maybe he knows better. "I'm an old friend of your mother's."

The Scarred Man is here. The Scarred Man is looking at me, smiling at me, and talking about my mother.

The flashlight in my sweater pocket is heavy and solid, not one of those cheap plastic numbers. It's hardly a weapon, but it's better than nothing. My fingers go around it, squeezing tight. I move my feet a little, staggering my stance, balancing my weight.

"You don't know me, Grace."

There's a seriousness to his words. The pretense is gone. I know what he's really saying when I tell him, "I know enough."

He steps closer. I step back.

"And you've never been wrong about anything? Ever?"

I step farther back, into the glow of the streetlight. And when the Scarred Man joins me, for a second I cannot see his scar. It stays hidden in the shadows, and I'm looking at a man with broad shoulders and dark hair flecked with gray. He's so handsome with his strong jaw and five-o'clock shadow. And I wonder for a second if he would still look evil if he didn't have that scar.

The answer, I decide, is a definite, resounding yes.

There is something in his eyes as he tells me, "You look like her. When I first saw you – at the ball – I thought you *were* her. I can see a lot of your mother in you. And that is a very good thing."

"You don't know that," I say.

But then the strangest thing happens. The Scarred Man laughs.

"You sound like her, too," he tells me.

"You don't know anything about her!" I snap.

But this doesn't throw the Scarred Man at all. "We grew up together, Grace," he says. "I knew your mother all of her life."

Her life. Until he ended it.

"She used to love sneaking out her window when she

was your age. Tell me, is that how you got out tonight? Did you climb down the tree? Or did you use the tunnels?"

Now I really can't say anything.

The Japanese embassy is across the street. The gates for Australia are twenty yards away. There will be a guard posted. I could yell. I could run. I could–

But before I can even finish the thought, the Scarred Man steps away.

"You should go home now, Grace." His face is covered in shadow. His voice is soft but strong. "I don't want to see you get hurt."

It takes a moment for the panic to come. And when it does, it descends slowly. Like all the oxygen is being sucked out of the air. It doesn't matter that I'm outside. It makes no difference that the wind still blows off the sea. I'm running out of air.

Images are coming quickly, rapid-fire in my mind. *I see my mother in her shop. The way the light reflects off of the gun. I hear the shot and smell the smoke.*

The Scarred Man grabs her arm and I try to yell "No!" but the word is a silent sob.

My breath comes harder and harder. I can feel my heart pounding. It's like my ears want to explode. I move with cautious, careful steps because I don't want to lose my balance. I cannot bear to fall.

My fingers scrape against the wall of the embassy beside me. I double over, try to breathe. When I close my eyes I see the Scarred Man's face, his left cheek in the light.

But no. It can't be his left check because there's no scar. And for some reason that makes my breath come harder.

I'm going to suffocate in the middle of the street. I'm going to die, betrayed by my weakness. I'm not tough enough to live.

I want to go to Noah. To Megan. I want to yell for Rosie to sound every alarm in the great walled city, but I cannot go to them. Not anymore. So I force myself up the hill, past the little house where the marines are stationed. Past the gates where I live. I don't dare stop at the gates of whatever traitor the Scarred Man came to meet.

So I walk on. And when I reach the next set of gates, I start to bang. There is a guard who doesn't know how to react. He speaks to me in a language I don't know.

And I choke out the only word that I can think to say.

"Alexei! I need to see—"

"Grace."

He's in the street behind me. Worry fills his face.

I should know better – be stronger – but I rush toward him. And when his arms go around me, I don't fight them.

He isn't the boy who warned me not to climb the wall. He's the boy who gripped my hand as I lay on the courtyard, telling me not to look at the blood. Soothing me. Telling me it was going to be OK.

I still can't breathe and he sees it, takes my face in his hands, forces me to stare into his eyes.

"It's OK," he says. "You're going to be OK." Then the boy next door takes my hands and pulls me away from the staring guard. We are not American and Russian – not enemies or allies. We are just a boy and a girl in the mood to run away.

It takes me a moment to realize where we're going. I haven't been down the tiny alley in years. But it's still here, a small space between the Russian and US walls. A gap. A no-man's-land. A remnant of the Cold War that isn't even wide enough for a trash can, but Alexei and I just fit. We always have.

The stones are rougher here, jutting out from the walls on either side of us, and in such a close space they're almost like a ladder, rising to the big wall that circles the city. *I can't breathe*, I tell myself. *But I have always been able to climb.*

"You need a leg up?" he asks with a smile, taunting me just enough to make me forget my panic and my fear. For a moment we are standing so close that I can feel the pounding of his heart.

"See you at the top," I say.

It's a familiar feeling as I rise slowly to my old place on top of the wall. I sit, gripping the edge, while Alexei takes his place beside me, one leg dangling over the wall's edge, the other at my back.

I've been surrounded by boys and men my whole life, always there, making me feel smaller, weaker. Different. None of them has ever sat as close as Alexei is sitting now. None of them has ever leaned forward like he's leaning forward, like life itself might hang in the balance of my every word.

"Grace" – he leans down and finds my eyes – "breathe."

It is an order. A command. And I know that I must follow it. So I do. I close my eyes and suck the sweet sea air in through my nose and out through my mouth. I let my heart keep pounding deeply, evenly.

I am alive and strangely grateful for it. By the time Alexei says, "Just so you know, you don't have to tell me what's going on," I've almost forgotten he is here. "You don't have to say a thing. You just have to sit here. And breathe."

So I do. And, true to his word, Alexei doesn't talk again.

I listen to the ocean and feel the breeze, and soon my breath comes without thinking. Soon, it is like talking to the wind.

"My grandfather hates me. Did you know that? Is that in the Russian daily briefings? Well, he does. Really. He hates me."

"Your grandfather adores you."

"He used to. When I was little. And cute. I used to be cute once – not that you'd remember."

"He called you Snowball," Alexei adds with a laugh. It's a detail I'd almost forgotten, how it never snows here and my grandfather would watch me run around, my white hair blowing in the wind like dandelions. Like snow. He loved me then. But now…now I am something he despises.

He's a smart man.

I despise me, too.

"Grace, breathe. All you have to do is breathe."

And for a second, I let myself believe him.

I am safe, high above the city. No one can find me here. No one will get me. I can run and run and run around the wall. No one – not even my own ghosts – are fast enough to follow.

"Tell me something," Alexei says. "About you. About the past three years. Tell me what I've missed."

So I say the only thing that matters. "My mother died."

"I know." Alexei sounds like he now regrets asking the question. He looks out at the sea. "I wanted to go to the funeral, but my father said it wasn't appropriate. I should have been there. I'm sorry."

"Don't be. I wasn't there either."

He doesn't ask me why, and I am glad. I don't want to tell him that I was in a hospital, strapped to a bed, chemicals fogging my brain and making me dream terrible dreams.

I reach down and touch my wrists. I can still feel the cuffs of the restraints, the woollen lining that was probably soft once but had grown stiff from too many years of sweat and blood and terror. He doesn't know that I would jump from this wall and gladly break my other leg before I would ever let my wrists be bound again.

"Grace?" Alexei says when the weight of my silence becomes too heavy.

"I saw the man who killed my mother. He's here. I talked to him."

I wait for Alexei to tell me that I'm wrong. I wait

for his eyes to say that I'm lying. But he stays silent, watching. Listening.

So I whisper, "And he's going to do it again."

The lecture is supposed to come now, but it doesn't. Alexei shifts and leans slightly forward, hands braced between us.

"And you discussed this with your grandfather?"

I shake my head. "He doesn't believe me. But I heard it, Alexei. I swear. I saw him. And I heard him. And I—"

"I believe you."

It's like he's speaking to the sea. I'm almost certain I've misheard him. I want to lose respect for him, call him a fool. But I just keep talking. About everything. About nothing. I tell him about the tunnels and the Scarred Man's late-night trip to my embassy, about the new threat he poses and seeing him on the street. I talk like I'm not talking to Alexei at all.

"You should have told me," he says when I'm finished. But Alexei doesn't know what I know: that telling people doesn't get you help. It gets you strapped to a bed in a psych ward. It gets you three years of looks and fears and dread.

"You wouldn't have believed me." My voice cracks and I hate myself for it. I hate myself so much.

"Yes, I would have. And then you wouldn't have been on your own."

I think about Noah and Megan and Rosie. Telling Alexei about them feels more like telling a grown-up. Like maybe I might get them in trouble. But I don't want to hide anything from him either. So I tell him.

"Now" – I wipe my runny nose on my sleeve – "not even they believe me."

"Listen to me, Grace. Listen to me," he says slowly. "You don't talk to Dominic again. You don't go in the tunnels by yourself. You don't go anywhere by yourself. Do you hear me? You're going to be careful. And you're going to include me."

"I—"

"No, Grace. You don't get to be stubborn this time. This time you have to be safe. OK?"

"OK," I say, knowing it's bigger than me and my multitude of issues.

"From now on, we're a team. Right?"

When the wind blows my hair across my face Alexei reaches up and tucks a piece behind my ear.

"Right."

"Now, come on." He scoots back the way we climbed up. "I guess I should walk you home."

He doesn't mention Jamie.

There is no lecture in his tone or his eyes. We're almost to the embassy's gates, and then he's closer than he was. I feel the gate against my back. The gaslight goes dim, and there is nothing but the pounding of my heart in my chest. One more time I cannot breathe, thinking about how – right now – he doesn't look like Alexei. He doesn't feel like my brother's best friend. He is old and familiar and he is new and alive. Both. I feel it now. I feel everything.

"Hey, Megan," I say the next day.

Technically, Megan and her mom don't live in the embassy; they reside in an apartment on the grounds. Once upon a time, these rooms were servants' quarters for the large estate, but now they are reserved for the most essential personnel. I know Megan's mother's work is important. And risky. And super, super secret.

I tell myself that's why Megan doesn't bother asking me inside.

"What's up?" she says, shutting the door behind her. For a moment, I wonder if there's a boy in there. For another moment, I wonder if it's Noah.

"I wanted to tell you something. Or a couple of things, actually."

"OK." Megan doesn't look or sound as mad as she should.

"First, I'm sorry. For not telling you about…the other times."

She waves this away as if I might be wasting her time, so I take a deep breath and plow on.

"And the second thing is that I figured out where the Scarred Man went the night I followed him. I know where…if you're still interested."

"Where?" Megan asks.

"Here," I tell her. "He was meeting someone here. In the US embassy. In the basement."

It takes a long while for Megan to speak. And when she does, she just says, "Come on."

"What's going on?" I ask, but Megan keeps walking.

We're climbing up a busy street, heading toward the palace. Something big is drawing her up this hill, and I am almost afraid to follow.

"You know how we've been wondering who the Scarred Man's target might be?" Megan says to me.

"Yeah."

"Well, our list of possibilities just got a lot bigger."

We turn the corner, and I see flags – dozens of them – all standing in a row, lining the long grassy lawn that sits in front of the palace. It's royal property – a public garden on which I have never seen a member of the public set foot. Now scaffolding rises into the sky. Spotlights cover the square, and in the air there is the echo of hammers and saws – shouting men working all day as they raise a stage. Bleachers line the square.

"What is all this?" I ask.

"The G-20 summit is this week. It was supposed to be in Prague, but there was a problem with the venue, so they've moved it here. Mom told me last night." Megan glances quickly to the square then back to me. "Think about it… Presidents. Prime ministers. Kings and queens. They're all going to be in one place at one time. I wasn't that worried about it because security for the G-20 is always super tight. But if he's already gotten into our embassy…" Megan trails off. It isn't hard to figure out what comes next.

"Then he can get in anywhere," I say.

I watch the crew work, the whole time hearing the Scarred Man's words: *There are many perfectly adequate ways to die. I just have to find one.*

"Who's coming?" I say.

"Officially, the G-20 summit is a meeting of the leaders of the twenty largest economies in the world."

"And unofficially?"

"They're all people that someone might want dead."

Walking into the embassy, Megan and I can instantly feel the difference. We have to stand aside and let a parade of people carrying giant bouquets of flowers squeeze by. There are ladders against the wall, covered with workers in overalls cleaning windows. The closer we get to the kitchen, the more we can smell roasting meats and baking breads. It's like all the aromas of the café district have been pumped inside our walls. And I walk on, knowing that these are not the only intrusions.

"Whoever he was meeting had access to the US embassy," I whisper to Megan. "Whoever he's working for is *inside* the embassy."

I feel vulnerable, betrayed. All my life I've been told that the embassy was a safe place – *my* safe place. No matter what was happening, all I had to do was reach its gates and I would be OK. It's a terrible thing to realize you've been living a lie.

When a group of men in dark suits comes toward us, it's like a swarm of bees approaching.

Megan and I press ourselves to the side of the hall and wait for them to pass.

"Does it have to be an American?" Megan whispers back. "I mean...does it really? You got into the embassy through the tunnels. So did the Scarred Man. Maybe this was just a place to meet?"

The men have stopped at the end of the hall, and I can hear them talking about angles and sight lines, new cameras and barricades. But I'm looking at Megan, and I'm already shaking my head. "Pretty risky meeting place."

"But maybe it *was* just a meeting place," Megan says, hopeful.

I'm willing to let her have the point, especially since it's a point that I'm pretty sure is just supposed to make me feel better.

"Do you ever wonder why?" Megan asks after a moment.

"Why what?"

"Why would he do it? Your mom was an antiques dealer, right? A nice lady. I never heard anybody say anything against her. So why would someone travel halfway around the world and kill her?"

Honestly, it's a question I've never considered before. And I can't bear to consider it for too long now.

"They knew each other. Maybe he was her ex-boyfriend or something. Maybe it was personal."

"Yeah. I guess that could be it."

But I can tell from the tone of Megan's voice that she isn't certain. That's OK. I haven't been certain about anything in years.

"That will be *very* difficult!" I can hear Ms Chancellor's voice floating down the hall. For the first time, I notice her in the midst of the swarm of men. Her hair is up and her glasses are on. She's all business as she tells them, "This isn't the local Hilton. Our neighbors value their own privacy and security as much as we value ours."

The main man looks at her and her clipboard then chuckles like she doesn't know who she's up against. I don't have the heart to warn him that he's the one making the mistake.

Ms Chancellor takes off her glasses. She gives the men her biggest smile. "Of course you gentlemen have your protocols. And I for one am very grateful for that. Really, so impressive. But I'm afraid the fence in question is technically the property of the nation of Germany, and I can't imagine that they're going to be, shall we say, *sniper-friendly*. But if you'd like to discuss it with them, then by all means, I am happy to make a call. The ambassador is a close personal friend."

This seems to shut the men up.

"I think we can make other arrangements," the leader tells her.

Ms Chancellor gives a very sympathetic smile. "I think that might be best. Now, if you gentlemen will come with me, I'll show you to the rose garden."

They're walking away when Ms Chancellor finally sees us.

"Just a moment, gentlemen. I'll meet you outside," Ms Chancellor calls, then turns her attention fully to Megan and me. "Hello, girls. I'm so glad I ran into you. It seems there has been something of a development."

"The G-20 summit is coming to town," I say like it's totally old news. Which, by now, it totally is.

"Yes," Ms Chancellor says, impressed. "It's all very exciting. Unexpected. But exciting. And that is the nature of our business, isn't it, girls?"

In unison, Megan and I chant, "Yes, Ms Chancellor."

"And, of course, as the United States' official base of operations in Adria, it is up to us to host a very important event for our very important guests."

"Excuse me, ma'am," one of the dark suits yells to her from down the hall. "Is it possible to cut down the tree by that wall?"

"No!" Ms Chancellor snaps. "Do not touch the ambassador's magnolia!" She starts off, but Megan calls after her.

"What event?"

"A party, dear," Ms Chancellor calls back.

"What guests?" I say, though, in my gut, I'm already certain of the answer. I know who the target is even before Ms Chancellor turns and tells us, "Well, the President and First Lady, of course!"

There is a big room in the embassy. Once upon a time, I think it used to be the main entrance hall, back when the building was the home of a spice baron. The ceilings are fifty feet tall here. There are two staircases that sweep upward from the parquet floors and then turn into a second-story balcony that runs around the entire room.

This is where we hold the parties.

It only took Ms Chancellor forty-eight hours and five teams of florists to transform the space. There's a stage in the center of the room, between the two curving staircases. A string quartet plays Mozart and Ms Chancellor floats through the party in a tailored black dress and sky-high heels.

It isn't a ball. This isn't the palace. The dress Ms Chancellor forced me into this time hits me at my knees and has a wide skirt lined with crinoline – it actually bounces and makes a noise when I move. But I'm not moving.

There are lots of offices on the second-floor balcony, doors that are perpetually closed and locked. That is where I'm standing, watching, when they find me.

Megan has abandoned her camo cargo pants and is wearing a sundress with a little white sweater. She actually has flowers in her hair. Rosie is in a white dress with a full skirt and a big satin bow. She looks like she's about to be somebody's flower girl. And she hates it.

But I can't really focus on them. Not when Alexei is wearing a dark suit with a blue tie that is the exact same color as his eyes. When he looks at me, I realize that that night on the wall wasn't a dream. And now, when I look at him, I no longer think about Jamie.

"You OK?" When Alexei speaks, the words are low and almost under his breath. He's speaking only to me – looking only at me. And the intensity of it is almost too much. I'm afraid that I might burn.

"I'm fine," I say too quickly.

"No." Alexei shakes his head. "You aren't."

It makes me want to fight – to run. Not because he's wrong, but because he is right and I hate how easily he sees through me.

So I look away – anywhere but at him.

"Anything happening?" Rosie climbs onto the railing, leaning over in a way that might make anybody else tumble onto the floor below. But the difference is I know that Rosie might be secretly hoping that will happen.

"I don't know," I tell them, shaking my head and

scanning the floor. "The guests are arriving, and everything looks OK."

But things are definitely not OK. I can feel it. So I just keep leaning against the railing, watching the scene below, thinking how much easier this would be if I could just tell someone what was happening, wishing I could be the kind of girl that people would believe.

I'm still watching when Noah and Lila step through the metal detector by the door. Marines scan Lila's bag. They sweep a wand over Noah's pockets. I keep waiting for him to look up and see me, give that exaggerated curtsy, to make me laugh and feel like everything is going to be OK.

But Noah isn't looking for me, and I can't shake the feeling that nothing will ever be OK again.

"Do you want to dance, Grace?" Alexei asks me.

"No."

"Grace!" Whatever I've said, I can tell that Megan sees it as an insult, maybe to our entire gender. But I don't see what the fuss is about.

"No, thank you, Alexei," I try again. Megan and Rosie just roll their eyes as if I have totally missed the point.

I keep my own eyes on the doors and the metal detectors and the Secret Service agents that survey the perimeter of the room. Everyone who enters tonight will be scanned. The staff were all searched this morning. There are alarms on every window, guards at every door.

Well, almost every door.

"Is it secure?" I ask Alexei, who nods.

"No one is opening that passage tonight," he tells me. "We've barricaded it shut."

"Yeah," Megan chimes in. "I booby-trapped it every way I know. And I know a lot of ways. Trust me. If it budges" – she holds up her phone and shows me a blinking red dot on the screen – "I'll know it."

It should offer me a great deal of comfort, but it doesn't. I'm not exactly sure that comfortable and I will ever be on a first-name basis again.

And that is when I see him.

"There he is," I say. "There's Dominic. He's here."

The Scarred Man is down below us. I watch him walk through the metal detectors. When the machine beeps and the red lights flash, he raises his arms and steps aside so an agent can examine him more closely.

"Why are they patting him down? He's the prime minister's head of security," I say.

Megan shakes her head. "Doesn't matter. Secret Service won't allow anyone to enter with a weapon tonight."

It's supposed to soothe me. But it doesn't. I keep thinking of the Scarred Man's words, the truth in what he said:

There are many perfectly adequate ways to die. I just have to find one.

"Rosie," Alexei says. He sounds so sure of himself – of the situation. Like he's in control. I've never felt in control a day in my life, and a part of me hates him for it. The other part of me is just grateful he's on our side. "Why don't you make yourself at home in his shadow?"

Rosie smiles. She looks as if she has been waiting for this moment her whole life – like at some point fairies came into her nursery, leaned over her crib, and said that someday she would get to trail an international assassin for an entire night. It's like watching someone finally find her destiny as she says, "I'm on it."

She bolts down the stairs, skirting between couples, dodging waiters. She is a tiny blond blur as she makes her way to where the Scarred Man stands and takes up her position no more than three feet from him.

"OK, Megan," Alexei says, turning to her. "Stay with your mother. Be close to her in case we need to tip off the authorities to something."

"On it." Megan turns and starts off.

I watch her go, but I can feel Alexei staring at me.

"It's not going to come to that," he tells me.

I nod but don't dare speak.

"Grace..." Alexei's hand is on my arm, warm and comfortable.

I hear a woman's laughter. I see my mother walking across the balcony that wraps all the way around the room.

"Grace, is there something wrong?" Alexei asks, genuinely concerned. But I don't dare tell him the truth. Instead, I say, "I'm sorry."

"For what?"

"For the other night. For dragging you into this. For—"

"Hey." Alexei cups my face and finds my eyes.

"I'm sorry you promised Jamie that you'd keep me out of trouble."

"Yeah, that's why I'm here," he says in a way that sounds like he's not agreeing with me at all. "Because I promised Jamie."

"That night at the palace, where did you go?" I don't know where that question came from, but I'm not trying to take it back. Somehow it's been there, in the back of my mind, for days. "I saw you go upstairs after we danced. Why?"

"My father and I were arguing. I needed to get away and clear my head."

"What were you arguing about?" I ask.

It takes a moment, but eventually Alexei lowers his gaze. He grips the railing and says, "You."

Something in Alexei's eyes keeps me quiet as he talks on.

"Adria has always been important, you know. Strategic. It was once the main trade route between Europe and the Far and Middle East. It has always mattered."

I know what Alexei is saying, but I have no idea what he's getting at.

"The United States and Russia, we have our own complicated histories. Our countries will never be true allies, Grace. And there are those who feel that, because of that, you and I can never be friends."

Then, as if the words have conjured him, Alexei's father appears in the center of the party. There's no mistaking the look in his eyes as he sees his son standing with me.

"You should go," I tell him.

"I'm OK here," he says.

"No. Don't make your father mad just to keep me company. Go. Circulate. I'll be here." Alexei turns away. He takes two steps, then stops and turns back to me. "You should go, too," he says, and jerks his head to the bottom of the stairs.

To Noah.

I don't realize I'm running down the stairs until I hear the rustling of crinoline. This is the part where Noah is supposed to laugh, to mock me and my puffy dress. But he just turns away, starts pushing through the crowd of people.

"Noah?"

He stops and stares at me. It's like looking at a stranger.

"Noah, wait."

When I reach for his hand he pulls away and I don't try again. I just say, "The Scarred Man was meeting someone in the US embassy. That's where he was. And now all the world leaders are here and…"

"So what, Grace?" Noah raises his arms briefly then drops them to his sides. It is the universal gesture for *What do you expect me to do about it?*

He has a point. Of course he does.

"I just wanted you to know that. And that I'm sorry. For lying."

"You think I'm mad because you lied to me?"

"Well, aren't you?"

Noah rolls his eyes and then admits, "Yeah. I am. But it's not *just* that. I didn't just believe you. I believed *in* you. I told you about my parents and Lila. I let you in. But you didn't let *me* in. You didn't trust *me.*"

"I did trust you. I just..."

"What?" Noah snaps.

"I couldn't tell you."

"Why?"

Because telling him would mean changing him. Changing us. Because how could I trust Noah when I couldn't even trust myself?

Because I'm crazy.

"Because...I just couldn't, Noah. I just couldn't *say it.*"

Noah doesn't soften. His expression doesn't change.

"Goodnight, Grace." Noah gives a formal bow. "Nice party."

I watch Noah walk away, realizing that, even in this crowd of people, I am utterly, completely alone.

I'm standing at the top of the stairs an hour later when I see Rosie down below, her blond head moving back and forth, scanning the room. She walks with hurried, frantic steps. Pacing. Searching.

Panicking.

I hear the band stop. My grandfather walks onto the stage, his white hair shining in the spotlight.

"Well, hello, out there!" he says with a chuckle as he brings a hand up to shield his face against the glare. "And welcome. Welcome to the US embassy. And welcome to Adria, my home for the last forty-five years. I may still have Tennessee in my voice, but Adria is in my heart."

The crowd gives a collective *awww.* My grandfather, make no mistake about it, is a charmer. But I can't take my eyes off of Rosie.

My grandfather keeps talking, but I don't hear a single word. Soon the string quartet begins to play again. Not the boring music they've been playing all night. This is a song I know. A song that makes everyone in the room stand a little straighter. And, in unison, we all turn toward the door as "Hail to the Chief" fills the room.

The spotlights shift and soon the president enters, smiling and waving through their glare. He shakes hands and pats backs as he makes his way toward the stage.

"Rosie, what happened?" I say when I see her climbing the stairs toward me.

"I don't know," she says. "I lost him. I was following him and then he was just…gone."

The quartet is still playing. The president is still walking – waving through the parting crowd. And, suddenly, I feel like a fool.

What if Megan was right? What if he wasn't meeting someone *from* the US embassy when I followed him? What if he was meeting someone *in* the US embassy? What if – instead of smuggling in a weapon tonight – he brought one in days ago?

It's hot in the ballroom, with the lights and the crowd of bodies, and yet I feel my blood turn cold.

"It's tonight," I say, not caring whether or not anyone can hear me. "It's right now!"

Down below, I see the president walking up the steps

to the stage.

And then I hear Rosie gasp. "Grace, I found him."

"Where?" I practically shout.

"Down there," Rosie says.

He's so close to the balcony that I actually have to lean against the rail to see him. He is almost beneath me, but I realize he is actually moving *away* from the president.

I see Alexei's father waiting in the wings, and when he spots me, a disappointed look crosses his face. But I don't have time to worry about him and why he hates me, about all the ways I'm not good enough to be friends with the boy next door.

The US president is on the stage. I hear his voice echoing in the ballroom. "It is so good to be here tonight, with our friends and our neighbors." He raises a glass in the direction of the Russian president, who nods solemnly in agreement.

The tension between the two men is palpable. I can almost feel the tightrope that our two nations have to walk in this moment. And I think of the look on the Russian ambassador's face as I stood in his office, a teenage girl apologizing for accidentally hitting him in a garden.

What kind of chaos would rain down if something worse were to happen – if something worse were to happen to the president of Russia? If that something were to happen *here*? Now?

It would mean bloodshed.

It might mean war.

I think about my first day here, about the sight of the

embassies all standing in a row like dominoes, and I know that something – or someone – is getting ready to knock them down.

The Russian president is standing with Alexei's father, and the Scarred Man is approaching them quickly. As he walks, I notice something in his hand. Something black and shiny and…

He's almost there.

It's almost too late.

"No!" someone yells, and it takes me a moment to realize that it's me.

I don't take the time to think about anything else. Not the number of people in the room or the height of the balcony. I'm not thinking about my pretty party dress or the look on my grandfather's face as the whole room seems to freeze.

The president is shaking my grandfather's hand. But everyone turns at the sound of my voice. Everyone is watching as I hurl myself over the railing. Even the US Secret Service can do nothing but watch as I fly through the air and crash onto the Scarred Man's back.

It was a cell phone in the Scarred Man's hand, they tell me. My grandfather is meeting with the prime minister now, apologizing and explaining the situation. Telling him about me and all of my issues.

The US president made some kind of joke from the stage – always good on his feet – even as the Secret Service swarmed around me. The Russian president and Alexei's father were quietly ushered aside and offered some kind of explanation.

No harm done, everyone keeps saying, but I know that's not true. At the very least, it's an embarrassment. *I* am an embarrassment. Some things never do change.

"Grace," a familiar voice breaks through the darkness, but I don't dare open my eyes. "Grace, I know you're awake."

Ms Chancellor won't let me go to my room. She insists I stay in her office, sitting in her least comfortable chair, an utterly polite kind of torture. One of the Secret Service agents sits behind me. I can feel the man's eyes boring into the back of my head. I wonder if anyone can ever drill deep enough to cut all the crazy out.

Probably not, the tone of Ms Chancellor's voice tells me.

"What time is it?" I ask as, groggily, I open my eyes.

There's an ice pack on my knees. I have bandages on both elbows. I'm not a pretty sight, I know. But I can't bring myself to care.

"After midnight." Ms Chancellor brings both of her hands together, gripping them gently as she leans back against her desk. It's her diplomacy stance. I can tell she's trying to muster all of her kindness. It's hard, though.

"Agent Gregory" – Ms Chancellor looks back at the man in the dark suit – "I believe we will no longer be requiring your assistance."

The man rises and buttons his dark suit coat. "Ma'am," he tells her, then disappears out the door without another word.

For a second, I am glad to be out of his glare. Then I realize I'm now alone with Ms Chancellor and I'd give anything for him to come back.

"He's going to kill again," I start right in.

"Grace—" Ms Chancellor tries, but I talk on.

"He was here!" I shout. "He was in the US embassy last week – meeting someone. I followed him, and I heard him say that he is going to kill again."

"You followed him?" Ms Chancellor asks, but it's not

a question. It's a threat. "I thought your grandfather and I were very clear that you were to stay away from him!"

"You and my grandfather were wrong."

"Oh, Grace." Ms Chancellor shakes her head slowly. "What have you done?"

When she starts around her desk, I bolt out of the uncomfortable chair.

"What have *I* done? He's the one going around the city meeting with shady men and planning assassinations!"

"He is the prime minister's head of security, Grace. Do you know what that means?"

"Yeah. It means people like you will always believe him over people like me."

I hold my breath, waiting for Ms Chancellor's witty retort, but she only looks sadder. When she speaks again, her voice is soft and kind and tender.

"Grace, we have no reason to believe that he would ever do anything like that."

"He killed my mother!" I'm shaking now, yelling so loudly that I know people can hear, and I don't care. I want the world to hear – to know. I am tired of secrets. "He killed her!"

Ms Chancellor gently pulls a file from her desk – almost like she's afraid of what it holds. It isn't just a file, I can tell. It is her weapon of last resort.

"Dominic did not kill your mother, Grace."

"You don't know that," I say.

"Yes." She opens the file and drops it on the desk. "I do."

For a second, I'm not sure what I'm seeing. It's just a newspaper. I pick it up and read the headline in Adrian, something about a labor strike with the national train service. There's a photo of the prime minister shaking hands with a man I've never seen before. It's the kind of picture that's in every paper in the world every day.

"It's an old newspaper. So what?"

"Look closely, Grace. Look closely."

Then Ms Chancellor places a black-and-white photograph over the newspaper. The picture is glossy and new, but it's the same image as the one in the paper. Identical. Almost. It's a slightly wider shot and, in it, you can see the people in the background, aids and guards and…

"Look," Ms Chancellor says, pointing to the Scarred Man. Only his arm had been visible in the paper, but in this picture you can see Dominic clearly as he stands at the prime minister's side.

I recognize the handsome features, the salt-and-pepper hair. But the face, I know, is different.

"Is that—" I start slowly.

"It's Dominic."

But there's no scar on his left cheek. His skin is smooth, his face handsome. He is spectacularly handsome.

"So? What's an old picture supposed to prove?" I toss the file at her.

"It's not that old, Grace."

"I'm telling you," I start again. "I know what I saw."

"Yes." Ms Chancellor comes closer, sounds almost desperate as she says, "And you're saying that three years ago, you saw a man with a scar murder your mother. Is that right?"

"No." I shake my head and point at Dominic. "I'm saying that I saw *that* man – with *that* scar – murder my mother."

Pity fills Ms Chancellor's face, and I don't know why. I only know that I hate it.

"Look at the date, Grace," she says softly as she picks up the newspaper and holds it out to me. "Look at the date."

I do as I'm told, but something is wrong. Something doesn't make sense.

"It took me a while to track it down," Ms Chancellor says. "I had hoped that maybe you wouldn't have to see this – that you'd believe us. Move on. But now..."

"Now what?" I say, my throat too dry – my voice too scratchy.

"This photo was taken three days before your mother died, Grace," she tells me.

"No." I'm shaking my head and backing away. I have to get out of this room – this moment. I have to get out before it kills me. "No. That's not possible."

"He had no scar, Grace. Even you must realize that there's no way a scar could form in three days. At the time your mother died, *Dominic had no scar.*"

"I saw him. He was there."

I don't realize I'm sitting until my fingernails start

digging into the upholstery of the uncomfortable chair.

"I know what it must feel like, wanting someone to blame." Ms Chancellor crouches on the floor in front of me. Her hands are very warm as they rest on top of mine. "But all this blame, Grace. This anger. It's time to let it go."

"I know what I saw," I tell her, but my voice is too frail. I can't stop thinking about Noah's words: *If a scarred man makes a threat in a forest, ever wonder why you're the only one around to hear it?*

"I saw him. I saw..."

Ms Chancellor shakes her head and squeezes my hands. "He's just a man with a scar, Grace. He's just a man."

I want to tell her that she's wrong – that he's been having meetings in Iran and running around in secret tunnels.

But then again, I realize, so have I.

I sit in the darkness, the pink canopy hanging overhead. There's a tap at the window. I walk to the glass and see a tuft of white-blond hair peeking over the sill as Rosie stands, perfectly balanced, on the limb of the tree outside.

"Grace!" she calls softly through the glass. "Let me in."

She smiles. Her eyes shine in the moonlight, and in the darkness, my reflection blends into her image. I'm twelve years old again, climbing trees and chasing after the big kids.

I am about to get hurt.

"Grace." Rosie taps against the glass again. "Come on."

I reach for the window and smile down at her.

"Be careful out there, Rosie," I say and draw the blinds.

"Good morning, Grace," Dr Rainier says two days later. She's French and very thin. She wears black cigarette pants and a white linen tunic, and she's so pretty it almost hurts to look at her. It's like getting your head shrunk by Audrey Hepburn.

"How are you today?" she asks.

I don't answer.

I'm not staging a rebellion here. This isn't a silent protest. I stay quiet because I don't want to break down, and I learned a long time ago that, sometimes, the only way to silence the cries is by making no sound at all. So I shrug and bite my lip. I do not utter a single word.

"Do you know why you're here?" she asks. I nod because I do know. I'm here because thirty-six hours ago I humiliated my grandfather and jumped from a balcony. I'm here because, for once, I don't want to see anyone get hurt.

Not even me.

"Good," she goes on. "I've had an opportunity to talk to some of the physicians you saw in the States. They all told me to tell you hello. Everyone likes you, Grace. Everyone wants you to get well."

I shrug, but still I don't say a thing. Even if she's not lying, I know she can't possibly be right.

R U OK?

I look down at the text from Jamie. I haven't taken any of his calls. He's no doubt talked to Alexei by now. And Grandpa. He'll be worried, but I don't want to lie to him, and I don't want to tell him the truth, so I don't say anything at all. At least Dad is on a mission and out of reach. I don't think I could handle him storming the embassy and taking me home. Wherever that is.

I turn my phone off and place it on the table by the bed. For once, the embassy is silent. It's the last day of the G-20 summit and everyone is too busy to worry about me.

Well, almost everyone.

When Noah appears in my room it is with a great deal of fanfare. He doesn't just walk in. He has to grab the door frame and practically whip himself inside – like some kind of self-contained slingshot.

"Hello, stranger. How have you been?" he asks, but he doesn't hold my gaze when he says it. It's not like he's actually looking for an answer. He's the one person smart enough to know that I'm not going to give one.

"So…the G-20 is wrapping up tonight, and Lila is

throwing a shindig on the cliffs to watch the fireworks, so I thought that *we* could—"

"What are you doing here, Noah?"

"I came to see my best friend. I came to tell her that I'm sorry for being a…whatever I was being. I'm here because we miss you."

"We?"

"Hi," Megan says from the doorway. She doesn't have Noah's natural bravado, his swagger, or his charm. She also isn't as good at pretending that I'm OK. Maybe that's because she isn't even trying. "How are you?"

"Crazy. Haven't you heard?"

"Grace…" Megan's voice is low. "I'm serious."

"So am I," I tell her.

"Grace," Noah says, desperate. "Talk to us."

"I think you'd better leave."

"You look different," Megan says.

"The medicine." I shake my head too quickly, blink my eyes too hard. When I rock back and forth, I no longer feel it. I can only see it in the reflection in my mother's mirror, my body like a pendulum that can never quite stop moving. "I don't eat much when I take it. It makes me…"

My hands shake. The light is too bright. Their voices are too loud. I want to turn everything down, dim the world until it is barely there at all. But I can't because they won't get out of my room.

"Maybe you should stop taking it." Megan's voice is harder. She's challenging authority, and I instantly regret letting her become my friend. It's maybe the worst thing I could have done to her.

"I can't," I say. "I have to get better."

"This is what better looks like?" Noah doesn't even try to hide the shock in his voice, and I can't blame him. I've gotten good at hiding the truth. Even from myself. It's not his fault he got to know the lie first.

"I didn't mean to lie to you," I say too quickly. "I just didn't like the idea of one more person knowing the truth." Noah doesn't say anything, so I lower my gaze. I'm pretty sure I rock harder. "I'm sorry I'm crazy."

"Grace—"

"I'm sorry," I tell them. "I'm sorry you got sucked into this. I'm sorry. I won't bother you anymore."

"You weren't bothering us!" Noah sounds offended.

"You should go," I tell them again.

"Yes, I am going to go. I'm going to get my best friend to leave her tower for the night. We're going to watch the fireworks and get something to eat – not necessarily in that order. I was thinking crepes." Noah gives a dramatic nod. "I mean we can do whatever you want, but there's this place I know that makes Nutella crepes and, let's just say, world peace has frequently depended upon them."

It's a beautiful day and he glances outside. "Come on, let's go sit on the wall and make fun of Lila. Let's go to the carousel. You've got to get out of here."

I have to get better.

I have to move on.

I have to make amends for my mistakes.

I have to keep Megan, Noah, Rosie, and Alexei from doing anything else that's stupid.

I have to keep my friends away from me.

"Come on," he tells me. "You have to eat."

"No!" I think I might be shouting. I think I might be crying. But the tears don't actually fall. I don't know what's real and what is fake anymore. I can't even trust my own eyes. "I don't have to do anything!"

"Yes." Noah grips my arms, holding me still. "You do. You've got to get out of this room. You've got to live."

"Don't you get it, Noah? You were right. There's a reason why I'm the only one who ever hears the Scarred Man make a threat in the forest. Or am I the Girl Who Cried Scarred Man?" I let out a nervous laugh. "I can't decide which cliché suits me better. Which one do you like? I can't decide which one I like."

I watch Megan look at Noah. There is something between them that wasn't there a moment before, an unspoken question. But I can't think about that.

"I was wrong," I say. My voice breaks. "My mother's death was an accident."

I turn to the window and look out at the big tree, but for once I don't have the urge to climb it – to run away. If anything, I wish the Secret Service would come and cut it down.

"Grace," Megan starts slowly, "you know how we still have cameras and stuff in the Scarred Man's house?"

I repeat Ms Chancellor's words. "His name is Dominic. He's just a man with a scar."

"Yeah, Dominic's house," Megan talks on, waving my words away. "Well, I called up the feeds last night just because."

For the first time, I notice that she's carrying her laptop. She opens it and pulls up an image from Dominic's town house. We look down at the same sparse furniture. The same dismal, empty shell of a life. For the first time, I feel sorry for the Scarred Man.

"He's looking at a bunch of pictures," Megan says. "I thought it was kind of strange. He doesn't seem like the sentimental type. And when you zoom in, you can make them out. See."

Megan works as she talks, and soon we are looking at the same images as Dominic.

"That's my mother," I tell them, but my gaze is frozen on the screen. I see the old storefront and quaint windows. "That's her shop. She was an antiques dealer, but we moved too much for her to ever open her own store. Then when we got to Fort Sill…it was supposed to be my dad's last post. We were going to make a life there. She really loved that store."

"Isn't that where—" Megan stops, then regains her courage. "Isn't that where she died?"

I'm already shaking my head. "It doesn't mean anything."

No one speaks. The silence is worse than anything either of them can say.

"What?" I ask, my eyes darting around the room. "*What?*" I almost shout.

"He looked at those pictures for four hours last night," Megan says. "He was obsessed with her. And now…"

Megan fast-forwards the recording, but Dominic barely moves. Eventually, though, the images change. I recognize the streets and the light, but it's like looking at a stranger. I barely know the girl with the blond hair blowing all around her as she strolls down Embassy Row.

"And now he's obsessed with *you*," Megan says, studying me, expecting this to change things. She doesn't know what I know: that the Scarred Man didn't have that scar the night my mother died.

Nothing Megan says can change that fact.

"I didn't see him that night." I shake my head and push away. "I didn't see anyone. It was an *accident*," I say again very, very slowly, trying the party line on for size.

But it doesn't quite fit, so I rock harder.

"OK." Noah eases closer. He places a firm, strong hand over mine. For the first time, I am still. "Then let's—"

"You should go," I tell them, hopefully for the last time.

"But—"

"Really." I walk toward the door. "It's time for you to leave."

Megan looks like she wants to argue but she can't find the words. Noah just looks at me – for the first time, ironically – as if I am a stranger.

"This isn't you, Grace," Noah tells me.

"No. This is exactly me," I say, and push him out of my room.

"Come on!" Noah bangs on the door once I've closed it behind them. "At least come watch the fireworks! It'll be fun." When I don't answer he bangs again. "I thought you were a fighter! I thought you were tougher than I look!"

Noah's voice is too loud – too close. I put my hands over my ears, but that can't keep the words out of my mind. It doesn't silence the screaming.

"*Grace, no!*" *my mother yells.*

"*Grace, stop!*"

When the cry rises in my throat, I don't try to hold it in. There is too much bile rising up within me. I grab the closest thing I can find – one of the old paperback books on my mother's dresser. It hasn't moved in years, and when I pick it up, it leaves a perfect outline of dust behind.

I can't help myself. I hurl the book at the wall. It lands with a smack, pages splayed and bent. And, instantly, I hate my carelessness. My rage.

The book crashes to the floor as a photograph flutters to the ground, landing at my feet. It's just a snapshot, really. Something taken quickly to capture a moment. Something tucked inside my mother's favorite novel and left there for twenty years.

I look down at the image of my mother standing on the wall, her arms thrown out. The sea is blue and beautiful behind her. Her hair blows across her face, but I can tell that she is smiling, laughing. She's my age and there is a boy holding her hand. He's smiling and laughing, too.

Now that I know what he looked like before the scar, I recognize him instantly.

"Dominic," I say, then I reach for another book and hurl it against the wall as well. And then another.

And another.

And another.

My mother's paperbacks lay scattered around me. The contents of her medicine cabinet are strewn across the bathroom floor. Hurricane Grace has swept through my mother's room, and I'm not finished.

The rocking comes faster now. My blood is pumping too hard, and I know I should get out of the room, go for a walk or a run. There are too many live nerve endings in my skin. I am about to catch fire.

But in this moment, I don't want to stop it. I just want everything else to burn with me if I have to go.

I think about the file in Ms Chancellor's office – the one where she kept the Scarred Man's picture and the newspaper clipping. I want to know what else she might have under lock and key. So I allow myself one more foolish act. I don't even look back.

It's easy enough to get there. I just put on clean clothes and brush my hair and my teeth. No one is going to bother the ambassador's granddaughter on the last day of the G-20 summit. There are way too many other things to do.

When I reach Ms Chancellor's office, I pick the lock. The filing cabinet is easy to get open. Inside, I find lots and lots of diplomatic documents, staff forms, and personnel information. The embassy has entire rooms for filing. These are the things Ms Chancellor holds most valuable or maybe needs most often. But it's not just that. These are the things she doesn't want anyone else to keep.

Quickly, I thumb through her personal notes and records. I'm not sure what I'm looking for, but I know it the moment that I see it.

Caroline.

My mother's name makes me stop. I'm perfectly still, not shaking or trembling. Even my breath slows down as I look at the carefully written word and pull the file from the drawer.

As always, Ms Chancellor is thorough. She has a copy of my mother's obituaries – the ones that ran in the States and here. There are cards of condolence from the president and the prime minister – even the king and queen.

I know what this immense file is supposed to say – supposed to mean. I am supposed to walk away from this knowing that my mother was adored and treasured and loved. I am supposed to feel like I am not alone in my grief, that my mother left me with dozens or hundreds of powerful people who want to make sure her only daughter will be fine.

But I am anything but fine, and everybody knows it.

Especially me.

When I reach the final piece of paper in the file, I almost miss it. It's just plain copy paper, white on one side, and it sticks to the back of the file. I pull it away, stare down at the words *Certificate of Death*.

It is only a copy, but I'm not surprised that Ms Chancellor has one – not in her incredibly thorough files in her incredibly tidy office. She would want all the information, the facts. She would keep this for my grandfather – proof that his daughter is really gone.

I know my mother is gone.

I don't need to see proof.

And yet I cannot tear my eyes away from it.

I see my mother's name. The date. The coroner's signature scrawled across the bottom of the page.

And, finally, the words—

Cause of death: Gunshot wound to the chest.

The door must open and close. Time must pass, but I don't sense it. I am frozen, not shaking, barely breathing. I close my eyes and hear the report of the shot, shake with the sound. Three years have passed, and still I can't stop shaking. I'm thousands of miles away and the blowback has finally reached me.

"Grace." I hear Ms Chancellor's voice, turn to see her standing in the doorway. "You weren't supposed to see that."

My breath is coming too hard. I want to cry. To scream. To die.

I honestly think I'm going to die.

"She was shot," I say between ragged breaths. "She didn't die in the fire. She was shot!" Now I'm shouting.

Three years' worth of lies are swirling around inside me. *I see the darkened shop more clearly. My mother's face. I actually hear the sound of the gun and I startle, eyes squeezed tightly shut, recoiling from the sound.*

"Grace."

I can feel something cold in my hand.

"Grace!" Ms Chancellor shouts, shaking me. I can see that she has given me a glass of water. Condensation seeps between my fingers.

"Drink, Grace. And breathe. Deep breaths."

I do as she says, sucking the cold liquid down in one long gulp.

"Good," Ms Chancellor tells me.

"You lied," I say. "She *was* shot. It wasn't an accident. It was—"

"It was an accident, Grace." Ms Chancellor grips my arms tightly.

"She was shot! It says so." I hold up the death certificate. "She was shot," I say again.

"Have a seat, Grace. Take another drink," Ms Chancellor orders, and I do as I'm told, suddenly docile and meek.

"I was right," I mumble to myself. And then I settle on the one thought that calms me. "I'm not crazy."

"No, Grace." Slowly, very slowly, Ms Chancellor shakes her head. "I'm afraid you aren't."

The words are wrong. The tone. The feeling in the

room has shifted. I look at Ms Chancellor, who is backing away from me. I glance down at the glass that is blurry now. Spinning. I try to call it into focus but the room is spinning, too. My arms feel heavier than they should, and I know that, even for me, this feeling is not normal.

"What happened?" I say. "Why do I feel so… What did you do to me?"

"I'm very sorry it has to be this way," Ms Chancellor says, but she sounds very far away. The words echo. "It's for your own good, dear. I hope you will believe me. It has always been for your own good."

I want to argue and demand answers, but it is all I can do to focus on the glass that is falling, shattering on the floor.

Two seconds later, I follow.

The floor is cold and hard, and the first thing I realize when I wake up is that I can't stop shaking. Did I hit my head? Am I hurt? Is this some sort of shock like I've never known before?

Then a new fear washes over me: *maybe I'm in the hospital again.*

Or worse. Maybe I never left.

Instantly, I am certain that the last few months – or even years – have simply been a dream, a very sad illusion. I miss Rosie and Megan and Noah. Alexei. I wish my friends were real and not some figment of my messed-up mind.

I might lie here forever, wallowing in that fear, except the smell is wrong. There is no strong scent of antiseptic. The air that fills the room is not so clean that it almost hurts to breathe. No. The air around me is salty and clear, and that is why I open my eyes. That is when I know that everything has been real.

Everything.

Slowly, I try to sit upright, and I notice the heavy packing tape that binds my hands, pressing my wrists together so that my pulse beats in stereo at the place where skin meets skin.

Suddenly, I'm back in the hospital. Rocking. My hands shake no matter how desperately I try to hold them still. Even though I'm free to stand, to walk, to roam, I am bound. A cry rises in my throat, and I cannot hold it back. I wouldn't even if I could.

I am thirteen years old again. Cold and confused, knowing that the world is over. There is no place safe for me to go.

I bite at the tape now, teeth gnawing against flesh until blood runs down my wrists, but I only feel its warmth. Finally, my teeth pierce the tape and I rip at it, tearing it from my skin, but I don't feel the pain, only the sense of being alive as my wrists break free and I start to think again.

I am still alive.

Terror fades and, slowly, I push myself upright and crawl toward one of the four windows that look out, due north, south, east, and west. The windows are long and narrow, made for archers and lookouts, perfect for a city under siege. But as I look down at the city below me, there are no rival armies. Whatever enemies await us are now inside the walls.

The Scarred Man. Ms Chancellor. They didn't kill me,

and I should be grateful for that, but I can't help but wonder why. Perhaps they didn't have time. Maybe I'm locked away in this ancient tower as some kind of bargaining chip, a hostage. I can think of a dozen reasons why they've left me alive, and none of them are good.

There's no glass in the windows. A few candles burn in sconces, their light flickering and dancing in the gentle breeze and fading sun. In so many ways, I am no longer in the twenty-first century. There's no phone in my pocket. Megan and her nifty earbuds are far, far away. I have spent the past two days trying to get my friends to let me stay locked up in my tower, and now I want to cry at the irony – the knowledge that absolutely no one will miss me.

I stand on my tiptoes and look out the window as far as I can. The sun is almost down. Only a thin ray of light bounces off the sea, and soon the sky will be a dark, inky blue. Already the crowds are gathering outside. I can see them from my place in the sky. There atop the highest hill in the city, inside the highest tower, I can see everything. I can even see the future.

The G-20 summit is going to conclude tonight, and the Scarred Man will have access to even the most secure parts of the gathering. All the world leaders will assemble there. The prime ministers of England and Adria, the monarchs of the Middle East. The presidents of the United States and Russia.

This conspiracy is far from over, and it's almost time for all the players to take the stage.

And I won't be there to stop him. Not this time. I will

be stuck in a tower like Rapunzel, cursing my choice of really short hair.

"Help!" I yell out the narrow window to the east. Down below, people are filing out into the streets. They carry brightly colored banners and balloons. Adria has always liked a show. They adore their ceremonies and traditions, and tonight all the world will be watching. They will want to make the moment last.

"Up here!" I yell again. "Help! Help! Look up here!"

But no one does. Mine is just another voice in the city, another set of cries. Already the darkness is descending. I see the streetlights growing brighter, and I doubt that anyone will even be able to see this far up in the dark.

So no one will see me. No one will hear me. I will die in this tower alone, never being able to tell the world that I'm not crazy.

I sink to the ground. Broken. Defeated. And then I do what I always do. I lash out, kicking and screaming. I'm almost glad that no one can hear me. No one is going to tell me I'm behaving like a child. I kick so hard that my feet hurt. I stand and hurl myself at the window, banging against the stones.

But then the strangest thing happens:

One of the stones moves.

There is an upside, evidently, to being locked in a thousand-year-old tower, I realize as I examine the wall, the small sliver of fleeting sunlight that shines through the place where the mortar is cracked and split. The stone actually shifts when I touch it, so I push harder and harder until it falls free of the wall and tumbles into the sky, but I never hear the crash. There is nothing below to catch it – to catch me – but I push again and again. Stone by stone the hole in the side of the tower grows larger until, finally, I can stick my head out to see the stretch of grass beneath me. I'm in one of the touristy parts of the palace, but there are no tourists now. Everyone is on their way to the celebration. There is absolutely no one to see me, hear me, catch me if I fall.

Down below, there are no stairs, no landing. There's nothing but a sheer wall. And me.

I want to yell again, but my voice fails me. In the distance, the music has started. In an hour, there will be speeches and photo ops and fireworks. And at some point during it all, I know, someone is going to die.

I spot a cable embedded in the stone above me and slightly to the right. I run my gaze along it until the cable disappears into the twilight. Maybe it goes all the way to the ground? Perhaps it runs between the tower and the other buildings of the palace? I'm not sure. I only know that it is barely within my reach and it is my only way out.

I take off my sweater, place my hands into the arms, and roll the sleeves over and over until my hands look like very puffy paws.

Carefully, I climb onto the ledge of the small hole that I've made in the side of the tower.

I don't look down.

I don't think about what will happen if I miss.

I focus instead on all the reasons I have to make it.

"I'm not crazy," I say aloud, and then I leap as high as I can, stretching, reaching.

My hands latch onto the cable.

And I begin to slide.

My first thought as I hit the ground is that I'm free. My second is that I am anything but safe. And I know the worst thing that Ms Chancellor and the Scarred Man have taken from me. It wasn't my freedom. It was my confidence. They made me doubt myself. And now the whole world doubts me, too.

I am the Girl Who Cried Wolf. And now I am the only one who can save the lambs.

My feet ache as I run down the hill toward the park. One lands between the cobblestones and my ankle turns. But I don't fall. I just keep running.

The crowd is growing thicker now, the closer that I get to the bleachers and the grassy lawn. I can hear the music stop. The speeches are starting. Soon, the president and all the other world leaders will take the stage. The Secret Service will be there, yes, but they won't be looking to protect the president from their counterparts from Adria.

After what happened at the embassy, they probably won't dare challenge the Scarred Man in any way, lest they risk another international incident.

So I run faster.

There are barricades. People fill the street. I push and claw, but I can't get closer.

"Let me through!" I try. "I have to get through!"

But it's no use. Even if I could fight the crowds, there would be no getting behind the barriers, no pleading with the Secret Service. I have to reach my grandfather. I have to warn him about Ms Chancellor and the Scarred Man. I have to make him see. Somehow.

I know exactly where the nearest tunnel entrance is. I'm not afraid as I slip inside the darkness and feel my way along the tunnel, to a place that will probably be behind the barricades. There is an opening overhead. I have no idea what lies above me, but I know it's my only way. So I climb and open it, peek slowly out, take a deep breath and try to get my bearings.

Even with the setting sun, it's too dark here. I must be underneath the bleachers because there are rafters above me. I can hear the muffled sound of the prime minister's amplified voice. To my right, there is something of a staging area in the distance. I can see cars coming and going, lots of big guys in dark suits. Everyone in that area either moves with incredible efficiency and purpose or stands perfectly still. No loitering. No lingering. This is where the Important People gather, and now I am among them.

There is some applause from the masses. When it dies down, I can hear the flags that line the promenade cracking in the breeze.

There is only one thing to do – one thing that matters. I will find the Scarred Man. I will find him and then…

I don't let myself think about that.

"You shouldn't be here, Grace."

I feel the Scarred Man's breath on my neck, hear his voice in my ear. And I know I haven't found him; he's found *me.*

I know it is far too late to run.

But somehow I'm not terrified. I don't tremble with fear but with rage.

"You can't kill me, can you?" I ask, proud that I have figured out that much.

"No." I can feel him shake his head slowly. "I can't kill you."

"Because, if you could, I'd be dead already."

"Yes. I'm afraid you would be."

The words should sound menacing. Terrifying. They should make me want to run, but I just stand there, demanding answers. I feel that I have earned them.

But the Scarred Man doesn't give me answers. Instead, he picks me up. Faster than Jamie, stronger than my father when he tries to teach me to punch and kick. The Scarred Man isn't playing, and before I can stop him, I'm over his shoulder and he is carrying me away from the people who fill the staging area, from the Secret Service and the guards.

When I push up on his shoulder, I can see the stage

getting smaller. I can hear the speeches getting softer. The Scarred Man is carrying me farther and farther from help.

But to me, there is only one fact that matters.

My grandfather is on that stage. The Russian president will be nearby. Whoever the Scarred Man's target is, we are getting farther and farther away from them as well. And I am grateful for the distance. It might be the only way that I can keep them safe.

"Where are you taking me?"

His voice is cold. "Away."

When we turn a corner, he drops me then points toward one of the tunnel entrances, and says, "In there. Hurry."

"I'm not going anywhere with you!"

"Grace," he snaps, holding me still, making me look him in the eye. "Stop fighting. Please. Just listen. Look. See?" He reaches into his pocket and pulls out a handful of papers. There's a US passport with my picture, but somebody else's name. Someone else's address. A birth certificate. And a second passport, this one with his picture.

"Why do you have these?" I shout. "What are you doing?"

"Take them. Go! Head back to the embassy and wait for—"

"No! I'm not going to leave and let you kill someone. I'm not... Why do you have a passport with my picture on it?" I can feel my anger fading, confusion rising in its wake.

"We don't have time for this, Grace." When he reaches for me again, his jacket gapes open, revealing the gun in his holster. I'm not thinking now. I'm acting on instinct, driven by fear as I pull the gun from his holster and hold it toward him.

"Back off. Get away from me. I'll do it!" I shout. My hands don't shake. The gun feels light as air. My nerves are steady, even. "I will pull this trigger."

The Scarred Man's eyes are wide. It's almost like he's confused, but then his gaze falls to the ground and he whispers, "I know."

It's the way he says it – the look on his face. There is no rage, no guilt. Just pity and…love. He is remembering someone he loved.

"*What aren't you telling me?*" I scream.

"You really don't remember, do you?"

"Remember what?" I say.

The Scarred Man brings a finger to the jagged line that runs from his eye to his jaw. "The night that I got this."

I struggle for words. "*The night that you…*"

I flash back to the photograph Ms Chancellor showed me – the man who had no scar three days before my mother died. It doesn't make sense, and yet something catches in my mind, like a sweater caught on a nail. I can feel my whole world beginning to unravel.

"Think, Grace," he tells me, easing closer. "Think! They've spent years filling your head with lies. And maybe they were right to try to make you forget what happened that night. I know I wish I could. I wish that every day. But you can't forget it, can you, Grace? And you can't quite remember. Now the truth is like a tightrope that you can't walk forever. *Think!* Think before it gets you killed."

"Get back!" I tell him. "You can't hurt me. *I* have the gun."

"No, Grace." He shakes his head slowly and reaches

for my hands. My *empty* hands. He holds them up for me to see. "You don't."

I look down at my hands and then stupidly glance around at the ground. Where did the gun go? When did I lose it? I don't know. So I cling to the only thing I know for certain – the only fact that will ever really matter.

"You killed my mother. You killed her. You—"

"I came to save her!" The Scarred Man's voice cuts through the cool night air. "I was there. You're right. You did see me. People did want her dead, but I would never kill your mother, Grace. She was the last person…I would have never killed her. So I came to get her, to take her away, to hide her. We were going to stage her death, and then–"

"You're lying."

"Your mother's death was an accident," he says softly, but he doesn't know that they are the exact wrong words. Before I know it, my fists are pounding against his shoulders, glancing blows that do nothing to shake him. I can't stop trembling.

"No!" I shout. "It was no accident. I saw her death certificate. She was shot!"

"Grace" – he grabs my arms and pulls me to his chest, holds me still and shakes his head very slowly – "it doesn't have to be one or the other."

And then his arms let go, and I'm stepping away, suddenly numb. Even the tears on my cheeks seem to freeze.

"I don't know what you're talking about," I say.

"You do know, Grace." He sounds so sad. "They tried to make you forget – to tell you you were seeing things, misremembering things. But you have always known."

It's too much. I can't think. I can't feel. I can't do anything but tremble.

The Scarred Man is so close to me. Right here. Staring into my eyes. So I kick him as hard as I can. My shoe makes sharp contact with his shin. He doubles over in pain and I strike him in the eye with an elbow.

And then I start to run.

Fire streaks across the sky. There's a sound like cannons booming as the night becomes a kaleidoscope of color and sound and fire.

There is so much fire.

I have to outrun the smoke. I have to get help. I have to—

I stop too quickly – realize too late – that I've run into something. Someone. Arms are around me. But the face that is staring into mine does not belong to the Scarred Man.

"Well, hello, Grace," the man says. "Do you remember me? We met at the palace. I'm—"

"The prime minister," I say. Or I think I say. How am I supposed to know what's real? "Have you seen my grandfather?" I ask, then think about Ms Chancellor, the person closest to him, and I know that he's not safe. "I have to see my grandfather!"

"Grace, dear." The prime minister looks at me, concern in his eyes. "Are you OK?"

"Yes!" I yell, even though I honestly feel like I am breaking.

I am breaking free.

There are barricades up ahead. Signs shout *Caution! Explosives!* in three different languages. I have no idea how far I've run, but there is no one around. Long lines of cables stretch across the cobblestones. I see stacks of equipment. Scaffolding reaches toward the sky. The yells of the crowd still echo in the distance, but I am a far cry from safety.

"You shouldn't be here," the prime minister says, and suddenly I know he's not talking about the restricted area filled with pyrotechnics, not the closing ceremonies. Not even Adria. He means here. Alive.

I shouldn't be alive.

Slowly, I start to back away. When he reaches for me, I recoil.

"You don't trust me?" The prime minister actually laughs.

"I don't trust *anyone.*"

"Smart girl," the prime minister says. There's a fence at my back. I can't move any farther, and that is when the prime minister lunges for me, grabbing my arms in his massive hands, squeezing like a tourniquet.

I can't think anymore, so I just start kicking, screaming. My training is gone, instinct and raw emotion are taking over, pounding through me. Finally there is something I can hit. There is someone I can make bleed. When my elbow makes contact with his nose, I hear a sickening snap and feel the warm gush of blood on the back of my neck. I feel somehow vindicated.

I want to do it again.

"Let her go." The Scarred Man's voice is cold and hard and even, and that is the only thing that stops me.

"It was supposed to be done by now!" the prime minister shouts at him. Then recognition seems to dawn. "Why isn't it done, Dominic?"

But the Scarred Man doesn't answer. He just stands, unwavering, holding his gun with a remarkably steady hand. For the first time, I realize it isn't pointed at me.

"Come here, Grace," the Scarred Man says. "Now!"

"No. I'm not going anywhere with you!" I shout.

The prime minister laughs. "It seems the lady has spoken. She's right not to trust you, you know."

But nothing can make the Scarred Man flinch.

"Step away from him, Grace. He can't hurt you. He isn't the type to get his own hands dirty. Never was."

"Why should I?" The prime minister laughs. "That was always your specialty." Then he's whispering in my ear, saying, "He killed your mother, Grace," but the words are too far away. When the fireworks sound, I shudder. The smoke is all around me. I hear someone calling my name.

"*Grace! Grace, sweetheart, no!*"

"Let her go, sir," the Scarred Man shouts, ever the respectful servant.

"No."

And then my mother is on the ground in front of me. She lies at the bottom of the stairs, her body mangled, broken. I see Dominic standing on the balcony overhead. He's actually taking a picture of her, like she is some kind of prize.

"*Grace, no!*" the voice comes again.

There is a bag at my feet. I see knives and gloves and gasoline. A gun. I reach down and get it.

"Get away from her," I tell him.

"Grace, it's OK," the Scarred Man says. I feel his hand on my arm but I see him at the top of the stairs. Both.

"You killed my mother!" I scream.

"Grace—" the Scarred Man starts.

I feel a push, and suddenly I'm falling, landing too hard on the ground. My head swims. My eyes blur. And breath comes harder than it should.

The smoke is growing heavier. I see the fire whipping up the stairs. The crowded shelves of my mother's shop are igniting, item by dusty item. The dominoes are falling now, sweeping through the room.

"I can't breathe," I say beneath the sounds of struggling and cursing and fighting.

I close my eyes and see my mother move. I watch her sit up and look at me, her face morphing from confusion to terror. Dominic is starting down the stairs toward my mother.

"Get away from her!" I yell, struggling to my feet.

"*Grace, no!*" *the woman screams again.*

I don't know what is real and what's remembered, what is true and what is imagined. All I know is that air is precious and fleeting. I know the all-consuming rush as it leaves my lungs and sends me crashing to the ground, clawing for oxygen and space and sanity.

I see the gun. I can feel it in my hand.

There are cries and pleas and panic. And smoke. There is so much smoke.

"Grace, run!" the woman yells, but my mother doesn't sound like herself.

I fire the gun once. Twice. I keep shooting until the gun won't fire anymore.

But the man doesn't fall because my mother is standing, running toward him until she can't run anymore. And I'm just standing there, watching my mother fall, bloody and broken, into Dominic's arms.

The smoke is heavier now.

I see the balcony shift, fall.

Dominic should raise his hands to protect himself, but he holds my mother's body instead, hunched over her while the balcony crashes down upon him. His right cheek presses against the top of her head – one last embrace – as fire and debris rain down on his left.

"No." I can feel myself backing away. "No. No. No."

I see the prime minister stumble backward, but for a moment I don't recognize the blurry figure who stands behind him as he falls, bloody, to the ground. I just stand there, waiting for the smoke to clear.

"Grace, are you OK?" Ms Chancellor holds the gun at the ready in case she has to fire again, but she doesn't.

In my head I keep hearing the shots, over and over and over. In my mind, it's another figure on the ground. And in my heart, I know I've always been the one to blame.

I look at where the prime minister lies, and then I see the Scarred Man. I see him as if from a very great distance. I watch him rise like a phoenix. I see him in two places at once.

There is a man in a suit in front of me, crouching in the shadows.

And there's a man in a brown leather jacket slowly standing in a swell of smoke. Blood rains down his face. His left eye is swollen shut. And the skin on this left cheek is almost black with blood, singed skin, and a rugged cut that runs from brow to jaw.

That is going to leave a scar.

"Are you getting any sleep, Grace?" Dr Rainier asks me. I nod. It's not a lie. I *am* sleeping. I sleep all the time. It's waking up I have a hard time bringing myself to do. Because as long as I can sleep, I can dream. And as long as I can dream, I can live in a place where that night might have a different ending.

But it never, ever does.

"How do you feel?" the doctor asks.

My clothes feel too big. I can't remember the last time I washed my hair. My friends try to come see me, but I can't face them. Not yet. Ms Chancellor brings me food, and I think I eat it. But maybe not. I don't remember, and even if I could, I wouldn't trust my memories anyway. I don't trust anything – anyone. Least of all myself.

Mostly I lie in my bed, smelling smoke.

Mostly I try to go back in time.

"I shot my mother." I say the words that have been haunting me for days. But longer than that, really. Years. They have been haunting me for years. The weeks in the hospital come back to me slowly. I remember in bits and pieces why Dad put in for a transfer when he'd sworn just months before that we would never have to move again. I know why my grandfather can't look at me, his granddaughter – the selfish, reckless teenager who shot and killed his only child.

And I know the Scarred Man was right – the truth was like a tightrope and eventually I had to fall. Part of me just wishes the fall had killed me. Part of me rejoices that I am achingly alive.

"I'm the reason she's dead."

"No."

I've never heard Dr Rainier sound so firm before, so resolute. Almost like I've made her angry.

"*It was an accident.*" I can't believe the words until they are out of my mouth, spilling forth in painful, sloppy sobs. The very words I have spent the last three years despising. But they were right, weren't they? My family didn't lie to me. They just never actually told me the truth.

"Does Jamie know?" I finally ask the question that I fear the most. "Does he...does he hate me, too?"

"Your brother does not hate you, Grace." The doctor smiles sadly, nods slowly. "And yes, he has always known you fired the gun."

"I killed his mother," I say.

"It was an accident," the doctor tells me, and then I

really start to cry.

Dr Rainer hands me a tissue and continues. "The human mind is a miraculous thing. Somehow, it knows what it can take. It self-limits in that way. And three years ago you knew that you weren't ready to process this information. You let yourself forget. And the people in your life couldn't bring themselves to remind you. They thought it was best."

Was it? I'm still not sure. I want to go back to before I knew. Anger is a far easier emotion than guilt.

"The grief and guilt were simply too much for you, and so your mind chose simply to forget. But it couldn't forget everything."

"The Scarred Man," I say.

Dr Rainer nods slowly. "You have a condition known as acute stress disorder. You have a condition, Grace. And we are going to help you get better."

She smiles when she says it. I try to smile back, knowing you can't possibly put a name on who I am and what I've done.

"Come on," the doctor says, rising. "There's something we think it's time for you to see."

"We?" I ask.

When the door opens, Ms Chancellor is standing there, smiling at me. "Come now, Grace. It's time."

I'm quiet as I follow Ms Chancellor down the street. I don't ask where we're going. Somehow, I already know she won't tell me.

"Your friends have been asking to see you, Grace. Noah and Megan and Rosie come over nearly every day."

"I know," I say, then realize someone is missing. "Alexei?"

"Well, I'm afraid Alexei has returned to Moscow. There are some...*changes* going on next door."

Alexei's leaving? I wonder. Then I realize, no, Alexei left. And I have a brief moment of relief. I'm glad he's gone. He's safe. And far, far away from me.

Ms Chancellor turns onto a narrow street that runs behind the Costa Rican embassy. I realize that I have never been this way before, but I just follow, listening to the sound of Ms Chancellor's high heels on the cobblestones as a heavy mist begins to fall. But still, she doesn't hurry.

"You killed the prime minister," I say.

"Actually, he is in a coma at the moment. But I did shoot him, yes." She stops and studies me. There is a strength in her brown eyes. "And I would gladly do it again, if that's what I had to do to save you. I would do anything to save you."

I'm just starting to say something when Ms Chancellor turns and examines the alley around us. "Here we go!" she says as she finds the odd symbol in the stone and presses.

I don't say a thing as the stones begin to move, revealing an entrance into one of the ancient tunnels. It's funny watching her navigate the old ladder in her skirt and heels, but she does it with a great deal of class, of course. It's almost like she does it every day.

"Why do I get the feeling there is a lot that you aren't

telling me?" I ask after a moment. "Will you tell me now?"

"Yes, Grace. Now I tell you everything."

Outside, the rain grows harder, and I hear water dripping in the tunnels. The air is hot and humid. It's like walking through a very warm fog.

"For starters," Ms Chancellor begins, "I suppose you have figured out by now that three years ago the prime minister ordered Dominic to kill your mother. But Dominic was loyal to her."

I read the truth in her eyes, the fact she can't quite say. "He was in love with her, wasn't he?"

Ms Chancellor nods gently. "They were childhood sweethearts. Your mother grew up and married your father, but I believe Dominic loved Caroline all of his life. Then he was ordered to kill her. Of course, he didn't dare refuse the prime minister's order, because he couldn't risk someone else being hired to do the job. That was when Dominic formed another plan."

"He staged her death. I saw her through the window and it looked like she was dead," I say, half explaining myself. As if there is any explanation. My body is numb. "I saw my mother dead."

"Yes, sweetheart. You did. Or, you *thought* you did. He was going to take a picture to prove it was over, and then he was going to burn her shop to the ground and take her into hiding. He'd already secured another body. They'd faked her dental records. Really, he had thought of everything except..."

"Me."

"Yes," Ms Chancellor says softly. "When your mother did pass away, Dominic returned here and resumed his old job. The prime minister assumed that he had killed your mother, and Dominic was able to get closer to his boss. And closer. But when you returned to Embassy Row and began talking about how you had seen the 'Scarred Man' kill your mother, the prime minister panicked. And he ordered Dominic to kill again."

"Me." The word is barely more than a whisper. "He was supposed to kill me, wasn't he?"

"Yes, Grace." Ms Chancellor tilts her head. "If you had never identified Dominic as your mother's murderer, then you would have never been seen as a threat. But you did. And so you were."

"He was meeting you, wasn't he?" I ask her. "That night in the US embassy."

Ms Chancellor smiles. It's like I've finally given her a reason to be proud of me. "He was indeed. That night Dominic came to tell me about his new mission, and together we tried to form a plan to keep you safe. Or safer. I'm sorry to say we weren't as successful as either of us would have liked. He was going to leave the country and take you with him, but now...well, now our plans change once again."

And then I think about Megan's question – the one neither of us could ever start to answer.

"Why?" I stop, force Ms Chancellor to turn back and study me. "Why did the prime minister want my mother dead?"

"That, my dear, is an excellent question. And one that – even after three years – we aren't quite sure how to answer." Ms Chancellor takes a step toward a pair of double doors, but stops, her hands resting there. As if this threshold matters – this question matters. As if neither of us will ever be able to turn back.

"The one thing we do know," Ms Chancellor says, "is that it probably had something to do with her job."

"Her job?" I have to laugh. "She was an army wife – an antiques dealer."

Then it is Ms Chancellor's turn to smile.

"No, Grace. Your mother was those things, of course. But she wasn't *just* those things. There were aspects of her life that she could never tell anyone. Not even you."

When Ms Chancellor pushes open the doors, I expect another room – perhaps another stretch of tunnel. What I see doesn't make sense. There are more doors beyond the threshold. And more than doors. I recognize the gears and wheels – the same type of mechanisms that open and close the entrances to the tunnels that lay scattered throughout the city.

And there, in the center of all the wheels and gears, I see the same emblem that I have never really stopped to study before.

Ms Chancellor places her hand on that emblem and pushes. Instantly, the gears spring to life. Turning, spiraling, shifting like a well-oiled machine. Sections of the wall begin to move, tumbling together one after another, until there is a great, round hole where the wall used to be.

I've been running around these passageways for days now. I know the low ceilings and musty-smelling corridors like I know the back of my own hand. But I don't know anything, really, I'm coming to realize as I follow Ms Chancellor through the great round hole.

The room that greets us isn't even a room, really. It's more like a cathedral, stretching out beneath the city. A high arched ceiling stands above a marble floor. And with one glance I can tell that it is old. No, not old. *Ancient.* I'm half afraid to follow Ms Chancellor out onto the landing that sweeps around the massive room, overlooking rows and rows of books. One long stone wall is lined with weapons – swords and shields and spears. I look at Ms Chancellor.

"You're going to be OK, Grace," Ms Chancellor says, the words almost knocking me off balance.

"I'm going to be OK," I repeat, then grip the ancient railing in front of me, looking down into the past.

Ms Chancellor holds out her hand, gestures for me to follow. "Come, Grace. There is so much for you to learn."

HAVE YOU READ
ALLY CARTER'S BESTSELLING
GALLAGHER GIRLS
SERIES?

FIND OUT HOW CAMMIE'S
ADVENTURES BEGAN IN
BOOK ONE,

*I'd tell you I love you,
but then I'd have to kill you*

Chapter 1

I suppose a lot of teenage girls feel invisible sometimes, like they just disappear. Well, that's me – Cammie the Chameleon. But I'm luckier than most because, at my school, that's considered cool.

I go to a school for spies.

Of course, technically, the Gallagher Academy for Exceptional Young Women is a school for *geniuses* – not *spies* – and we're free to pursue any career that befits our exceptional educations. But when a school tells you that, and then teaches you things like advanced encryption and fourteen different languages, it's kind of like big tobacco telling kids not to smoke; so all of us Gallagher Girls know lip service when we hear it. Even my mom rolls her eyes but doesn't correct me when I call it spy school, and *she's* the headmistress. Of course, she's also a retired CIA operative, and it was her idea for me to write this, my first Covert Operations Report, to summarise what happened last semester. She's always telling us that the worst part of the spy life isn't the danger – it's the paperwork. After all, when you're on a plane home from Istanbul with a nuclear warhead in a hatbox, the last thing you want to do is write a report about it. So that's why I'm writing this – for the practice.

If you've got a Level Four clearance or higher, you probably know all about us Gallagher Girls, since we've been around for more than a hundred years (the school, not me – I'll turn sixteen next month!). But if you don't have that kind of clearance, then you probably think we're just an urban spy myth – like jet packs and invisibility suits – and you drive by our ivy-covered walls, look at our gorgeous mansion and manicured grounds, and assume, like everyone else, that the Gallagher Academy for Exceptional Young Women is just a snooty boarding school for bored heiresses with no place else to go.

Well, to tell you the truth, we're totally fine with that – it's one of the reasons no one in the town of Roseville, Virginia, thought twice about the long line of limousines that brought my classmates back to school last September. I watched from a window seat on the third floor of the mansion as the cars materialised out of the blankets of green foliage and turned through the towering wrought-iron gates. The half-mile-long driveway curved through the hills, looking as harmless as Dorothy's yellow brick road, not giving a clue that it's equipped with laser beams that read tire treads and sensors that check for explosives, and one entire section that can open up and swallow a truck whole. (If you think that's dangerous, don't even get me started about the pond!)

I wrapped my arms around my knees and stared through the window's wavy glass. The red velvet curtains were drawn around the tiny alcove, and I was enveloped by an odd sense of peace, knowing that in twenty minutes, the corridors were going to be crowded; music was going to be blaring; and I was going to go from being an only child to one of a hundred sisters, so I knew to savour the silence while it lasted. Then, as if to prove my point, a loud blast and the smell of burning hair came floating up the main stairs from the second-floor Hall of History, followed by Professor Buckingham's distinguished voice crying, "Girls! I told you not to touch that!" The smell got worse, and one of the seventh graders was probably still on fire, because Professor Buckingham yelled, "Stand still. Stand still, I say!"

Then Professor Buckingham said some French swear words that the seventh graders probably wouldn't understand for three semesters, and I remembered how every year during new student orientation one of the newbies will get cocky and try to show off by grabbing the sword Gillian Gallagher used to slay the guy who was going to kill Abraham Lincoln – the first guy, that is. The one you never hear about.

But what the newbies aren't told on their tour of the school grounds is that Gilly's sword is charged with enough electricity to…well…light your hair on fire.

I just love the start of school.

READ

I'd tell you I love you, but then I'd have to kill you

TO FIND OUT WHAT HAPPENS NEXT!